D1502307

He was wanted for questioning in a hate crime, but it looked like someone got to him first...

Jake knocked on the door. "Are you here, Crockett Wood?"

"Sheesh," Mev said. "Smells like death!"

Jake knocked again. He tried to open the door, but it had been bolted. Then he peered through the crescent moon cut-out.

"Christ! There's a dead man sitting on the john!"

With a screwdriver Jake pried the wood door open. A thin man with unkempt white hair and grizzled beard, his jeans around his knees and his white T-shirt stained with blood, tumbled out.

"Oh, my god! He was shot!"

"Could be suicide. But who'd kill himself in an outhouse?" Jake looked inside. "I don't see a gun."

"He may have been shot through the moon."

"Must have been."

"There are no tracks."

"So he was shot before the storm."

"Rigor mortis hasn't left his body," Mev said. "He died within the last thirty hours."

"From the looks of it I'd guess yesterday morning, maybe twenty-four hours ago, or around that."

"If this is Crockett Wood, he looks older than sixty-five."

In this tale of two intertwined crimes, the consequences of a 1968 Ku Klux Klan murder and rape in Witherston, Georgia, come back to haunt the town some fifty years later. The body of Crockett Wood, a member of a radical white supremacist group called Saxxons for America, is found in his dilapidated outhouse, shot in the heart. Then a local candidate for mayor turns up missing in the midst of rumors of a scandal in his youth. As Detective Mev Arroyo and her teenage twins, Jorge and Jaime, dig for the truth, they uncover a past filled with bigotry, betrayal, and deceit, revolving around the 1968 murder of a black man and the rape and disappearance of his pregnant white fiancée. Is Crockett Wood responsible for the murder and rape so long ago, or did he perhaps identify the guilty party and was shot to ensure his silence? After all, it's an election year in Witherston, and some people will do a lot more than commit murder to keep their dirty little secrets safe...

KUDOS for *Saxxons in Witherston*

In *Saxxons in Witherston* by Betty Jean Craige, Mev Arroyo and her two teenage twin sons, Jorge and Jaime, are involved in another murder investigation—Mev officially as a detective for the town of Witherston, and Jorge and Jaime unofficially as intrepid teenagers. What they uncover is bigotry and betrayal stemming from a 1968 murder and rape of a black teenager and his pregnant white fiancée. Then another man goes missing and they don't know if he is a guilty party or another victim, but white supremacy seems to be alive and well in Witherston…unless the good people of Witherston can stop it. Well written, fast paced, and intriguing, this one will keep you guessing until the very end. ~ *Taylor Jones, The Review Team of Taylor Jones & Regan Murphy*

Saxxons in Witherston by Betty Jean Craige is the fourth book in her clever and thought-provoking Witherston Murder Mysteries series. This time the town is peppered with white-supremacist flyers from a group called Saxxons for America. Then one of the group's leaders is murdered and a mayoral candidate turns up missing. The murder and disappearance seem to be linked to a cold case murder from 1968, when a local black teenager was murdered and his pregnant white girlfriend raped. The consequences of those crimes are now coming back to haunt the quiet little Southern town some fifty years later. Craige's character development is superb and her plots well thought out and intriguing, and *Saxxons in Witherston* is no exception—a first-class whodunit you won't be able to put down. ~ *Regan Murphy, The Review Team of Taylor Jones & Regan Murphy*

ACKNOWLEDGMENTS

It is a generous act indeed for a friend to read a writer's manuscript when it needs help. I am very fortunate that Margaret Anderson critiqued my manuscript before I sent it to Black Opal Books and gave me invaluable advice. Thank you, Margaret, for reading my books, over many years, when they were still in the process of being created.

I thank Susan Tate for showing me the glorious mountains of north Georgia and inspiring me to set the Witherston Murder Mystery series there. Susan told me the story of an ancestor who, according to one family member, skirted prohibition laws by burying bottles of moonshine in the pasture and selling maps to the bottles. That story got me started writing *Saxxons in Witherston*.

I thank Sue Moore Manning for her cartoon *Good Guys whoosh Saxxons*. I have admired Sue's drawing skills and her sense of humor since we were classmates in first grade.

As always, I thank Terry Kay for urging me to write fiction.

And finally I thank my friends at Black Opal Books: acquisitions editor Lauri Wellington, for her confidence in me; artist Jack Jackson, for his imaginative book covers; and copyeditor Faith C., for her superb editing skills.

I learned late in life, after I had retired from the University of Georgia, that I loved writing fiction. So I thank my readers for encouraging me to keep telling stories.

SAXXONS IN WITHERSTON

BETTY JEAN CRAIGE

A Black Opal Books Publication

Black Opal Books

BECAUSE SOME STORIES JUST HAVE TO BE TOLD

GENRE: COZY MYSTERY/WOMEN SLEUTHS

This is a work of fiction. Names, places, characters and incidents are either the product of the author's imagination or are used fictitiously, and any resemblance to any actual persons, living or dead, businesses, organizations, events or locales is entirely coincidental. All trademarks, service marks, registered trademarks, and registered service marks are the property of their respective owners and are used herein for identification purposes only. The publisher does not have any control over or assume any responsibility for author or third-party websites or their contents.

Everyone leaves tracks.

~ Charlotte Byrd

WITHERSTON, GEORGIA

LOCATION: Lumpkin County, Georgia, USA. The town of Witherston, founded in 1860, is located in the southern Appalachian mountains twenty miles north of Dahlonega in Saloli Valley. The incorporated area includes Tayanita Village, a community of fifteen to twenty young men and women whose Cherokee ancestors occupied north Georgia, southern Tennessee, and western North Carolina for a thousand years.

POPULATION: 3,857 (2016)

AREA: 39.9 square miles

WITHERSTON CITY OFFICIALS as of July 1, 2018: Rich Rather, Mayor; Atsadi Moon, Chair of the Town Council; Alvin Autry, Dr. Charlotte (Lottie) Byrd, Jonathan Finley, Lydia Gray, Ruth Griggs, and Blanca Zamora, Members of the Town Council

TAYANITA VILLAGE OFFICIALS as of July 1, 2018: John Hicks, Chief; Amadahy Henderson, Treasurer; Atsadi Moon, Historian

WITHERSTON POLICE: Jake McCoy, Chief; Mev Arroyo, Detective; Ricky Hefner, Pete Senior Koslowsky, Pete Junior Koslowsky, Officers; John Hicks, IT specialist.

ONLINE NEW SOURCE: *Witherston on the Web*, sometimes called "Webby Witherston." Publisher: Smithfield ("Smitty") Green. Staff: Catherine Perry-Soto, editor; Amadahy Henderson, photographer and reporter; Dr. Charlotte Byrd, columnist; Jorge Arroyo, columnist and cartoonist; Tony Lima, Weatherman.

SCHOOLS: Witherston Elementary School; Witherston Middle School; Witherston High School

CHURCHES: Witherston Baptist Church; Witherston Methodist Church; Frederick Douglass Baptist Church

ANNUAL FESTIVAL: Labor Day Moonshine Festival

POINTS OF PRIDE: In the early twentieth century during Georgia's twenty-seven years of statewide Prohibition Witherston became famous all over Georgia for the quality of its moonshine.

CITY HISTORY: Witherston, once a Cherokee village, took its name from the line of Hearty Withers, who made a fortune in the 1828 Dahlonega Gold Rush and then won forty acres in the 1832 Georgia Land Lottery. Hearty Withers was killed by a Cherokee in 1838. Hearty Withers was the great-great-grandfather of centenarian billionaire Francis Hearty Withers, who resided in the family mansion at the top of Withers Hill Road until his murder by Dr. George Folsom on Memorial Day weekend of 2015. Withers bequeathed $1 billion to be divided evenly among the residents of Witherston—approximately $250,000 to every man, woman, and child.

PROLOGUE

*F*riday, August 30, 1968:
Dear Diary:
Tonight I told Tyrone I was pregnant, two months pregnant. I cried. I told Tyrone my father would throw me out of the house if he found out I was pregnant, and that he might even kill him. I told Tyrone that I had to get an abortion and asked him if he knew of anybody who could do it. Tyrone said he didn't want me to have an abortion because abortions are so dangerous that some women die from them. He said he loves me and wants to marry me and have a family. I told him I love him too. And I do. He said it's no longer illegal for Negroes and white people to get married, not since last year. He said we could go to Atlanta and get married next week. He said he has almost $2,000 saved up from working summers at the chicken plant and that since he has a scholarship to Morehouse College we would be okay financially if I worked till the baby came. He already has an apartment near Grant Park.

I love Tyrone. I want to marry him. I am not afraid of what people will say. I want to be his wife, and I want to

*have his baby. Tyrone will be a lawyer like Donald Hol-
lowell, and nobody will look down on him. I will be a
writer like Lillian Smith, and nobody will look down on
me. And nobody will look down on our baby.*

*I told Tyrone I would marry him. Tyrone was so
happy he got tears in his eyes. We decided to elope on
Monday. But we'll have to keep our marriage a secret
from Father—for Tyrone's sake and for our baby's sake.*

*I am so scared of Father. He preaches against inte-
gration. He says that integration will lead to miscegenation and to an inferior race of brown people with kinky
black hair. He keeps a gun on his bedside table in case
"some Negro breaks into the house." No telling what he
will do to Tyrone if he finds us. But he won't.*

*Tomorrow I won't get to see Tyrone. He's going to
move out of his mother's house and take his things to his
apartment in Atlanta. He'll return here Sunday morning.
He wants to tell his sweet mamma so she can come to our
wedding. I said that's fine since she won't tell.*

*I still miss my mother. She would have loved Tyrone.
She would have come to my wedding..*

ɛɔɛɔ

Saturday, August 31, 1968:
Dear Diary:
*I wish I could be totally happy. I love Tyrone. He
loves me. We're going to get married. We're going to
have a baby. We're going to be a family. What experience
could be more wonderful than that? Yet we have to get
married in secret as if we were committing an unspeaka-
ble crime. I wish we could celebrate our love the way
other couples do, with friends sharing our joy on our
wedding day, watching us cut a cake, drinking our cham-
pagne, and dancing late into the night in honor of us.*

Well, I won't think of what cannot be. I will think of what can be, a life with Tyrone and our child.

This morning at breakfast I told Father I was going to postpone college for a year to work in Savannah. I mentioned Savannah because he knows I like the beach. He got furious, like he always does when he can't control me, but I said I'd been earning my own money as a waitress and I'd bought my own car so I didn't need him anymore. And I don't! I slammed the door and left the house. I went to the bank and emptied my savings account. I took the $2,140.39 in cash, put it in my blue clutch bag, and locked the bag in my glove compartment.

Then I drove over to Mary Lou's house. I told Mary Lou that I was going to elope with Tyrone, and I swore her to secrecy. I trust her.

Tomorrow morning I'll go to church at 9:00 as usual. It will be the last time I'll ever hear Father preach!! I'll pack my suitcase while Father is at the second service and take it with me to Mary Lou's house. Tyrone will pick me up there to go to his mother's house. We'll finalize our plans with his mother. Then he'll bring me back to Mary Lou's house and I'll spend the night with Mary Lou. I'll leave Father a note.

On Monday, which is Labor Day, we'll go to Atlanta. I will follow Tyrone to his apartment. On Friday afternoon a probate judge will marry us. Tyrone will ask his father to be his best man. I met Mr. Lewis once. Lincoln Lewis. He is a bus driver in Atlanta and a friend of Hosea Williams. I can't ask anybody to be maid of honor. I wish I could ask Mary Lou, but I can't involve her.

∽∾∽

Sunday, September 1, 1968:
Dear Mamma,

I write you this letter to tell you what I've never said to you out loud. Thank you for your blessing on my marriage, which is legal now. And thank you for your willingness to attend my wedding. On Friday morning I will pick you up at 10:00 and bring you to my apartment.

More importantly, thank you for all the sacrifices you have made for me, from the time you dropped out of high school to marry my father and give me his name, through all the years of cleaning other people's homes to give us a home of our own, to sitting alone at my graduation as the only Negro mother in the bleachers. I will never understand why my white friends' parents wouldn't sit with you. You looked beautiful in your pink dress and hat, and I was so proud—and grateful—you were there.

Thank you for loving me, no matter what mistakes I made, and for teaching me to forgive others, no matter what mistakes they made.

Someday, I will buy a house for you near mine, so that you can be with your grandchildren.

Your devoted son,
Tyrone

CHAPTER 1

WWW. ONLINEWITHERSTON.COM

WITHERSTON ON THE WEB
Sunday, September 2, 2018

NEWS

Witherston Celebrates Labor Day Tomorrow

*T*omorrow's Moonshine Festival marks Witherston's ninety-fourth Labor Day celebration. Spon-
sored by the Witherston Roundtable, the events
will begin with a parade led by Mayor Rich Rather de-
parting from Emmett and Lydia Gray's farm at 4:00 p.m.
and following the route of the first Witherston Labor Day
parade on September 1, 1924. The parade will go down
Possum Road through town, turn west onto Black Fox
Road, and stop at Slater Ball Park.

At the ball park Mayor Rich Rather will read a Labor Day Proclamation, and Witherstonians will enjoy a
traditional Witherston picnic.

Tony Lima's Mountain Band, composed of Dan Soto on the harmonica, Jaime Arroyo on the guitar, Pete Koslowsky III ("Pete Three") on the snare drum, and Tony Lima on the banjo, with Annie Jerden singing, will play music popular in 1924. Songs will include the old favorite "Does the Spearmint Lose Its Flavor on the Bedpost Overnight?"

Red Wilker will bring legal moonshine. Ernesto and Blanca Zamora, of Zamora Wines, will bring wine for those not caring to drink the moonshine. Gretchen Green, of Gretchen Green's Green Grocery, will provide apple juice, kombucha, and lemon ginger iced tea. Atsadi Moon and Paco Arroyo will grill hot dogs, tofu burgers, and corn on the cob, all courtesy of Witherston Inn.

Catherine Perry-Soto, Editor

Rich Rather and Red Wilker Launch Campaigns

At tomorrow's Labor Day picnic Mayor Rich Rather will launch his campaign for representative to the Georgia General Assembly. Mayor Rather, owner of Rather Pre-Owned Vehicles in Dahlonega, is stepping down as Witherston's mayor in the middle of his second term to run in the November election. His Democratic opponent in the General Assembly election is Juanita Madrugada-Reyes, a thirty-year old accountant in Dahlonega.

At the picnic Red Wilker, owner of Wilker's Gun Shop, will launch his campaign for mayor. As of today, Wilker has no opposition.

Amadahy Henderson, Reporter

Witherston Gets Senator's Attention as a Sanctuary City

Last Wednesday the Witherston Town Council approved Dr. Charlotte Byrd's proposal to designate Witherston a "sanctuary city." The vote was four to three, with Atsadi Moon, chair, and Dr. Byrd, Jonathan Finley, and Blanca Zamora saying Aye, and Alvin Autry, Lydia Gray, and Ruth Griggs saying Nay. Mayor Rich Rather, who showed little enthusiasm for the project, did not oppose the action.

As a sanctuary city, Witherston will not cooperate with ICE (Immigration and Customs Enforcement) in enforcing federal immigration laws.

On Friday state legislator Comer Clydesdale called Witherston "an outlaw city" for defiance of Georgia's 2009 law prohibiting sanctuary cities.

In response, Dr. Byrd said, "Witherston will provide refuge for individuals less fortunate than the politicians who want to deport them."

On Friday night Council chair Atsadi Moon, in an interview on Channel 2, announced that the designation ceremony would take place on Sunday, September 9, at 4:00 p.m. in front of the courthouse.

Amadahy Henderson, Reporter

ANNOUNCEMENT

Labor Day floats will be assembled this afternoon, beginning at 2:00 p.m., at Emmett and Lydia Gray's farm on Possum Road.

Photographs will be taken at 3:30 p.m.

Amadahy Henderson, Reporter

NORTH GEORGIA IN HISTORY
By Charlotte Byrd

Ninety-four years ago, on the afternoon of Sunday, August 31, 1924, twenty-five-year-old Obadiah Wilker was making moonshine on Tayanita Creek in a heavily forested area a mile south of Witherston when Sheriff Caleb McCoy rode into his camp. "Obie," the sheriff said, "you gotta get outta here tonight. Load up your mule with your whiskey and anything else valuable to you. Your corn, your sugar, whatever you can grab. My boys and I are fixin' to raid your still tomorrow morning about ten o'clock. I can't arrest you if you ain't here. So be gone."

I imagined Sheriff McCoy's visit to Obadiah's still after reading the diary of Gertrude Harper Wilker which I found in the University of Georgia Library. I photocopied it. On that Sunday night Gertrude Wilker had written:

Our friend Caleb rescued us today from certin ruin. He warned my dear husband that him and his deputies would have to raid our still tomorrow morning. There being a full moon Obie and Pappy went out at midnight and loaded Azalea with all the shine, mash, corn, and sugar she could carry. Enough to get us back in business before winter. Thank the Lord. We would have no way to feed baby Buehler if we couldnt sell our whiskey. Caleb is a fine and de-

cent man. *Last May he saved our neighbors*
Fred and Mamie from the revenuers.

To understand life in 1924, you need to know that
since the War Between the States, when Congress established the Internal Revenue Service to collect taxes on
"luxuries" like liquor and tobacco, poor north Georgia
farmers had been forced to make their whiskey where the
revenuers couldn't easily find them. They could make a
living if they converted part of their cash crop of corn,
apples, or peaches into alcohol, but only if they avoided
taxes. So the "moonshiners" set up their copper stills
alongside creeks deep in the woods and worked under the
light of the moon.

They thrived during Prohibition, which lasted na-
tionally from 1920 to 1933 and statewide, in Georgia,
from 1915 to 1935.

By the way: Obadiah and Gertrude Wilker were the
parents of Buehler Wilker, nicknamed "Bullet" at the age
of four, who served as mayor of Witherston from 1984 to
1988 and bequeathed his gun shop to his son Red Wilker
upon his death in 1999.

Caleb McCoy was the grandfather of Witherston's
police chief Jake McCoy.

This week, at the request of my great nephews Jaime
and Jorge Arroyo, I will dedicate my column to north
Georgia's moonshiners.

WHAT'S NATURAL
By Jorge Arroyo

Did you know that African Grey Parrots in the wild
spend the whole first year of their lives with their imme-

diate families learning how to chirp from their parrot parents?

And they learn to chirp just exactly like their parents, and not exactly like their friends. They hatch in need of chirp instruction.

They are home-schooled.

So when African Grey chicks are taken away from their parents and sent to human homes before their intense learning period is up, the chicks turn to their human for instruction. Thus, they learn to chirp—I mean, talk—like their human.

My great aunt Lottie, whom you all know as Dr. Charlotte Byrd, has a young African Grey named Doolittle.

Doolittle speaks in Lottie's voice, and he speaks intelligently. Doolittle declares, "Doolittle wanna go to kitchen," "Doolittle wanna cuddle," "Telephone for Lottie," and "Doolittle saw a squirrel," when he's seen a squirrel. And Doolittle asks, "Lottie gonna go in a car?" and "We're gonna have company?"

Aunt Lottie is Doolittle's significant other.

My twin brother Jaime and I are Doolittle's extended family, even though we don't look like him. Jaime and I don't have feathers and a beak, and Doolittle doesn't have hairy skin and ears that stick out. Doolittle is six inches tall, and Jaime and I are six feet tall, almost. Doolittle can fly, Jaime and I can't.

Doolittle is different from us, but we communicate, and we love each other.

Doolittle can teach us a lesson on how to get along with folks who don't look like us or act like us. He did not come into this world able to love only his own kind. And neither did we humans.

LETTERS TO THE EDITOR

To the Editor:

Yesterday I saw a black truck parked at that ram-shackle log cabin on Saloli Stream about a mile north of Withers Fork. I thought the cabin was deserted.

The cabin is an eyesore. You can see it if you're fishing near there. It should be torn down. And so should its prehistoric outhouse.

Could you please tell me who owns that property? The man could be making bombs up there. Somebody needs to check.

The door of the outhouse has a cut-out crescent moon. Could you also please tell me why outhouses have cut-out crescent moons on the door?

Alvin Autry
Witherston

From the Editor:

Mr. Autry, you are probably referring to a fifteen-acre wooded property at 4200 West Bank Road that is owned by Harper B. Wood of Heron Brook, Georgia. Mr. Wood inherited it from his uncle, Edward Harper, in 1968.

A cut-out crescent moon on an outhouse door lets in light and air, necessary to the comfort of anybody inside. The cut-out also allows people to peek in to determine whether the outhouse is occupied. In times past the crescent moon signified the women's outhouse, and the sun signified the men's. In the absence of separate outhouses, the crescent-moon outhouse became uni-sex.

By the way, evidence from waste pits has shown that the men's outhouses were frequently used for drinking and smoking.

Let me know, Mr. Autry, if you would like more information.

Catherine Perry-Soto, Editor

To the Editor:

This weekend is the fiftieth anniversary of an unsolved racial murder. On the evening of Sunday, September 1, 1968, in Witherston, Tyrone Lincoln Lewis was stabbed to death on Orchard Road. Allie Marie Camhurst was with him. Tyrone was eighteen and black, and Allie was eighteen and white. Later that night the Ku Klux Klan burned a cross on the lawn of Tyrone's mother's house. Allie Camhurst was never seen again. The crime was never solved.

I got interested in the KKK in my Georgia history class last spring, and now I want to write my senior thesis on the Tyrone Lincoln Lewis murder. I am working with Dr. Charlotte Byrd, who is an historian, to solve the mystery. I ask anybody with information to contact me (beaulodge2001@gmail.com, 419 South Pine Cone Road) or Dr. Byrd (lottiebyrdwitherston@gmail.com, 301 North Witherston Highway).

By the way, my father is black and my mother is white. They got married in 1998. I go out with a girl who is white. We are lucky to be living in 2018, when nobody cares.

Beau Lodge
Witherston

From the Editor:

Beau, you and Dr. Byrd may look through the archives of "The Witherston Weekly" in the courthouse

basement. *There is an article about the murder in the September 6, 1968, issue, on page 2.*
   Catherine Perry-Soto, Editor

WEATHER

Today's high will be in the upper eighties. Today's low will be in the upper sixties.
   Skies will be clear. Creeks will be high. Grass will be green. Trees will be tall. Squirrels will be squirrelly.

   Tony Lima, Weatherman and Director of Tony Lima's Mountain Band

   ◌◌◌

   Sitting on the porch of an old hunting cabin on Saloli Stream, Crockett Boone Wood finished reading the morning's news on *Witherston on the Web*. He put out his cigarette, sent a text message, read the reply, and made a phone call. Then he launched a Phantom Four Pro hobby drone equipped with a video camera.

   ◌◌◌

   Lottie Byrd spotted the small black drone, a quad-copter, while she washed her lunch dishes. It first appeared over the tall red maples on the banks of Founding Father's Creek. Now it hovered fifty feet above the two-story house next door to hers where her niece Mev Arroyo lived with her husband Paco and their seventeen-year-old identical twin sons Jaime and Jorge.

Nobody was home. Paco and the boys had gone to Emmett and Lydia Gray's farm to transform Gregory Bozeman's pick-up truck into a "Moonshiners" float. They had taken with them the ninety-year-old moonshine still Lottie had uncovered in the thicket along creek. Mev had gone to the grocery store.

Lottie grabbed her binoculars and went outside. This was the first time she had seen a hobby drone, which differed significantly in size from the combat drones that had been used by the United States for three decades. She was well acquainted with combat drones, unfortunately. She suspected that collateral damage from a US drone strike was responsible for Brian's death in Iraq in 2009. But what did it matter how he had died? He was gone, her only son. Like her husband Rem, one minute alive and healthy, the next minute dead.

Lottie had moved to Witherston to be close to her niece's family after her retirement from Hickory Mountain College. She had grown to love the small mountain community twenty miles north of Dahlonega and sixty miles northeast of Atlanta.

Here she quickly established herself as a local historian, a wine connoisseur, a gourmet cook, a social activist, an aficionada of folk music, the companion of Doolittle, a talkative African Grey parrot she had bought in an auction, and a writer of public letters to the president of the United States.

Lottie had a coterie of friends who loved her for her wit and wisdom, and she had innumerable fans who followed her column in *Witherston on the Web*.

Lottie scrutinized the drone through her binoculars as it drifted over her house. She could see its camera. Why would someone be photographing our houses, she wondered. The drone flew off to the southeast.

Lottie put away the dishes, got into her lavender Smart Car, and drove to the Grays' farm.

ᏟᎳᏟᎳ

"Come here, Lauren!" Jim Lodge called to his wife. He was sweeping the driveway of their contemporary cedar home on South Pine Cone Road. "Is that a toy helicopter?" He pointed to a small object floating forty feet above the house.

Lauren came out on the deck. "That's a drone," she said. "It's got a camera, and it's recording us. The red light is on. Come inside, Jim. Now!"

Lauren and Jim had made their home in Witherston for the past twenty years, and they had earned the respect and affection of Witherston's diverse community. Yet Lauren never forgot the anonymous letter they had received when their wedding picture had appeared in the *Augusta Chronicle*: "You are violating God's order, and you will be punished for it."

They had hoped to shield their son Beau from such cruel bigotry, but they could not. As a first-grader at Witherston Elementary School, Beau had asked them one evening at dinner, "What's a pickaninny? Billy called me a pickaninny."

From that day forward, they educated their young son about the ideologies of race.

A decade later, when he was studying Reconstruction for Atsadi Moon's history class, Beau found an 1867 pamphlet arguing that the Negro had entered Noah's Ark as a beast. He wrote his term paper on it. At the end of the semester he read his paper aloud to his white classmates without embarrassment and provoked what he told his parents was a "heavy discussion" about prejudice.

"Why would a drone be recording us, Lauren?"

"I hope it's because somebody wants a video of our tin roof, Jim, but I think it's because somebody wants a video of us. I'm glad Beau is not here."

e⁄ɔe⁄ɔ

When the drone descended over Tayanita Village, the chickens scattered, the goats Grass and Weed ran to the far side of the pasture, and Franny the mule bucked. Amadahy Henderson was trying to hitch Franny to the Village's antique delivery wagon.

"Franny, hold still!" Amadahy said. Then she too heard the drone.

"Atsadi, come here!" Amadahy shouted to Atsadi Moon, her husband.

Atsadi came out of the large green canvas yurt that served as the Tayanita Village Council House.

"Look! What's that?" Amadahy said, pointing to the approaching drone.

"That's a miniature drone," Atsadi said. "It has a camera. See that little red light? It's taking our picture."

"I'm taking its picture," Amadahy said. She pulled her smart phone out of her pocket and aimed it at the drone. "Gotcha."

The drone flew off to the north and disappeared.

"Why would somebody send a drone to spy on us?" Atsadi asked. "The drone is invading our privacy. We need to respond."

"Bring it up on Wednesday for villagers to decide what to do."

Tayanita Village, situated on Tayanita Creek off Possum Road, was the home of sixteen young people between the ages of twenty and thirty who honored their Cherokee ancestry by their lifestyle. They had built their commune in 2015 with their inheritance from Francis

Hearty Withers. Witherston's reclusive billionaire had left a quarter of a million dollars to every resident of the town named by his great-grandfather Harry Withers.

The villagers took Cherokee names, slept in small green yurts, grew vegetables, fished in the creek, and kept chickens, goats, cats, and a mule. They wove baskets using traditional Cherokee techniques, and sold them online. They cooked in a log-sided kitchen, bathed in a log-sided bathhouse, and warmed themselves in the winter by the wood stove in the large yurt that served as their council house.

But they also had running water and electricity produced by solar panels. They had smart phones, computers, cars, bank accounts, and day jobs. And like Atsadi and Amadahy, most of them had graduated from college.

Atsadi was the village historian. On Wednesday nights in the council house he instructed villagers in Cherokee language and culture. He also taught history at Witherston High School and chaired the Witherston Town Council.

Amadahy was photographer and reporter for *Witherston on the Web*, the town's online source of news. She and Atsadi had gotten married in June and had moved to an A-frame log house on Tayanita Creek adjacent to the village. They still considered themselves villagers.

She was two-months pregnant.

"Time to go, Franny," Amadahy said, as she adjusted Franny's harness. "Look pretty for your picture!"

Atsadi mounted the wagon. "I'll see you at the Grays' farm," he said.

Amadahy climbed into their red pickup.

ᎥᏍᎥᏏ

The Labor Day paraders had just gotten into place

for picture taking when dozens of four-by-six-inch flyers floated out of the sky.

"Look!" shouted John Hicks, grabbing one. "A fiery cross!"

John Hicks, always called by his full name, leaned his *TAYANITA VILLAGE* flag against the fire engine and grabbed a flyer.

"Gracious," Lottie exclaimed, grabbing another one. "I've seen this image too many times."

Chief Jake McCoy picked another one up off the ground. "It's white supremacist garbage! From 'Saxxons for America.' Never heard of them."

"I have," John Hicks said. "They're Ku Klux Klan wannabes. We must have caught their attention. Yea, us!"

Lottie saw Red Wilker stand up in the 1933 Packard convertible that displayed a *BOOTLEGGERS* banner. Red pointed his shotgun thirty feet above the Grays' farmhouse and pulled the trigger.

"Jeepers! What was that?" Jaime Arroyo exclaimed.

Mighty jumped out of the MOONSHINERS parade float.

"Mr. Wilker shot something," Jorge said.

"Mr. Wilker hit a hawk," Jaime said, jumping out after Mighty. Mighty raced toward the farmhouse.

Beau Lodge's dog Sequoyah leaped out of the KEEP NATURE NATURAL float and followed Mighty. John Hicks's dog Bear joined them.

So did Jorge and Beau.

"Wait, you all! Please. Amadahy hasn't finishing taking pictures," Catherine Perry-Soto shouted.

Catherine was editor and manager of *Witherston on the Web*. She had grown up in Dahlonega, graduated with a journalism degree from Brenau College in nearby Gainesville, Georgia, and obtained her first full-time job with Webby Witherston. In December of 2015, she had met Dan Soto when his eighteen-wheeler stalled in a blizzard and she interviewed him about his work hauling chickens to the poultry plant. Dan quit the job he hated, they moved out to a farm that Rhonda bought as a sanctuary for barnyard animals, and they married the following May. Catherine gave birth to Alex two years later.

"Not a hawk," Lottie called out. "A drone. The drone that dropped these flyers."

"That's the drone that flew over Tayanita Village this morning," Atsadi said.

Mayor Rich Rather seized a flyer that floated over his red Cadillac convertible.

"Must be the Ku Klux Klan," Mayor Rather said. "The Klan left a load of them in Centerville a couple of years ago on Martin Luther King Day. The fiery cross is their signature."

"If this flyer came from the KKK, it would say so," Lottie said. "The Saxxons for America must be another organization using the fiery cross to intimidate Muslims, Jews, gays, and people of color. And so-called foreigners," Lottie said.

"What's the fiery cross mean?" Atsadi Moon asked.

"War, basically," Lottie said. "War against non-Christians. The Scots used the fiery cross as a declaration of war in the eighteenth and nineteenth centuries, long before the KKK adopted the image to symbolize white supremacy.

The KKK got the idea of burning a cross in 1915 from the movie *Birth of a Nation*.

Jake read aloud:

"'When immigrants invade the USA
And foreigners steal your jobs
When blacks marry whites and whites marry blacks

When men marry men and women marry women
When white Christians are a minority
You have lost your country to cultural genocide.'"

"Whose country?" Gregory Bozeman said. "Who do they think the country belongs to?"

"The straight, white, and uneducated," Jonathan Finley said.

"Clearly not us," Gregory said.

"Not us because you're Cherokee," Jonathan said. "And educated."

Gregory Bozeman, PhD, was a retired Environmental Protection Agency ecologist. Jonathan Finley, with a BA in English, was a hair-dresser. The two of them owned Scissors Hair Salon.

"Half-Cherokee," Gregory said.

"Why would anyone drop these flyers on Witherston?" the mayor said. "We don't have any problems."

"Dear husband, the Saxxons, whoever they are, think we do," Rhonda said. "Jonathan is married to Gregory. Jim Lodge, who is black, is married to Lauren, who is not. Paco Arroyo, who is brown, is married to Mev. We think that's fine. The Saxxons don't."

"Lots of us are brown," Yolanda said. "I'm brown, and so are Jorge and Jaime, who look like their father."

"I'm brown too," said Tony Lima, weatherman and musician. "And I'm an immigrant. I was born in Mexico."

"Dan is brown," Catherine Perry-Soto said. "And our baby Alex is brown." She carried four-month-old Alex in a baby sling.

"Brownish," Jonathan said.

"Beau is black," Sally said. "And he dates me."

"Blackish," Jonathan said. "Beau's mother Lauren is white. More accurately, pink."

"I'm half-Cherokee," Atsadi Moon said. "So is Amadahy. And we're going to have a half-Cherokee baby."

"Do two half-Cherokee parents make a whole Cherokee baby?" Jonathan asked.

"The dogs found the drone!" Jaime shouted from Lydia Gray's vegetable garden. "It looks like a toy helicopter."

"It's a quadcopter," Beau said, taking the drone from Sequoyah's mouth. "Sally's father has one just like it. It's fancy."

"Mr. Wilker is a good shot," Jaime said. "This phantom is full of holes."

Beau carried the drone back to the parade.

Red Wilker approached them. "I'll take that, boys," he said.

Jorge, Jaime, and Beau were actually no longer boys. They were entering their senior year at Witherston High and preparing their college applications. Jorge was editor of the student newspaper *The Bobcats' Purr* and contributor of cartoons and essays to *Witherston on the Web*. He already had a weekly column titled "What's Natural" and a weekly fifteen-minute local radio program. He intended to study journalism at the University of Georgia. Jaime was president of the environmentalist club Keep Nature Natural and a guitarist in Tony Lima's Mountain Band.

He intended to study ecology at UGA. Beau, KNN's ex-president, intended to study history at UGA and get a PhD in African American studies.

Jorge, Jaime, and Beau were well known and well liked in the community, as were their parents. Mev Arroyo was a detective on Witherston's police force, and Paco Arroyo, whom Mev had met in Madrid on her junior year abroad, was a biology teacher at Witherston

High. Lauren Lodge was a probate judge in Dahlonega, and Jim Lodge was a gynecologist in Witherston.

Beau looked at Chief McCoy.

"Shouldn't the police have it?" Beau asked.

"Give it to the police if you like," Red said. "But you might want to turn off the drone's camera. No telling who is surveilling us."

"*¡Huy!* The recording light is on!" Jorge exclaimed. "You're on TV, Beau."

Beau found the switch and flipped it. He handed the drone to Jake.

"Now we're no longer under surveillance," Jorge said. "The GBI will have to investigate us by other means."

"You'll look into this, Chief. Right?" Catherine asked. "And you'll let me know what you find?"

"I'll call the Georgia Bureau of Investigation this evening, Catherine."

"Could we please finish getting pictures?" Amadahy implored.

The participants returned to the parade line-up. After five minutes of posing, they abandoned their floats and vehicles and gathered around Lottie.

"The Saxxons didn't just now notice Witherston's diversity," Lottie said. "There's a logic to their timing. Next Sunday Witherston becomes a sanctuary city."

"Thanks to you, Dr. Byrd," Amadahy said. "Your proposal convinced the council."

"Well, four out of the seven members of the council."

Rhonda Rather came over holding Coco Chanel. The blond Pomeranian wore a red ribbon. Rhonda wore a red silk shirt with a *RHONDA RATHER, SANCTUARY COORDINATOR* name tag.

"I've confirmed that the Ortegas will be staying with your family, Beau. They'll arrive on Monday with our other guests. And Diego Amado will arrive at the Arroyos' house on Saturday."

"Woohoo," Jorge cheered.

"I'll ask Diego to take part in the Sanctuary City dedication on Sunday afternoon," Atsadi Moon said.

"What are these white supremacists so afraid of?" Lottie said, reading the flyer.

"They must think that people who don't look like them will get their stuff and they'll lose out," Jorge said, "as if whoever has the most stuff wins."

"They must think that people who don't look like them are inferior," Jaime said. "They're afraid we'll procreate with their children."

৶৶৶

Crockett Wood watched the video his drone had fed to his monitor before the drone stopped recording. He sent an email. Then he fed Bedford, took a pill, and lay down on the cot for a nap.

CHAPTER 2

Sunday Evening:

I can't imagine Red Wilker as Witherston's mayor, Aunt Lottie," Mev said. "He thinks that because his father was mayor he deserves it. That's why he's already announced that he's running."

"The Wilker dynasty," Paco said.

"Red announced early to scare off competition," Lottie said.

Mev was putting anchovies and croutons on the Caesar salad she had brought to Lottie's house for Lottie's regular Sunday night dinner party. Paco arranged the mussels on the seafood paella he had brought. Lottie got out the wine.

"Red Wilker will make us all carry guns," Paco said as he uncorked one of Lottie's Riojas.

"Maybe I should oppose Red for mayor," Lottie said. "There's still time."

"Excellent idea," Paco said. "You'd get my vote."

"You'd get the vote of anybody who ever came to one of your parties, Aunt Lottie," Mev said.

"That's probably fifty votes, right off," Lottie said. "And Jorge and Jaime could manage my campaign!"

"Good idea, Aunt Lottie!" Jaime exclaimed as he came through the kitchen door followed by his girlfriend Annie Jerden, Jorge, Jorge's girlfriend Yolanda Gallo, and Mighty. Jaime, Jorge, and Annie wore black T-shirts with *KEEP NATURE NATURAL* on the back and *I BRAKE FOR TREES* on the front. Yolanda wore a red *WITHERSTON BOB-CAT* T-shirt.

"I'll make your signs. One will say 'Drop your gun. Vote for Charlotte Byrd,'" Jaime said.

"And the other will say 'Do no harm. Elect Dr. Byrd,'" Jorge said.

"You're sure to win, Aunt Lottie!"

Lottie was sure not to win, despite the popularity of her column. She had encountered resistance to her proposal to make Witherston a sanctuary city, as well as to her long-time advocacy for social justice, which for her included the rights of humans, animals, and trees. Nor would she want to win. She much preferred writing history to making it.

She expressed her views in her Smart Car's bumper stickers: *THE EARTH DOES NOT BELONG TO US— WE BELONG TO THE EARTH* and *SUPPORT THE RIGHT TO ARM BEARS*. "I have a better idea. How about getting Mayor Rather's wife to run? She'd actually enjoy it," Lottie said.

"Rhonda would have no more chance of winning than you would, Aunt Lottie," Mev said. "She would advocate outlawing guns, allowing dogs in restaurants, and requiring every house to have solar panels," Mev said.

"And she wants to help undocumented aliens," Paco said.

"Like Yolanda," Jorge said.

"I'm undocumented," Yolanda said, "but I've lived

in the United States since I was nine months old. I'm a Dreamer, at least in President Obama's eyes."

"Would Rhonda have any chance of winning?"

"No, Jaime, but she could make Red Wilker spend his precious money to win," Lottie said.

"Mom, Dad. Look at this flyer," Jaime said, pulling it out of his back pocket and handing it to his father.

"*¡Caramba, hijos!*" Paco exclaimed.

"A drone dropped a bunch of them on the Grays' farm this afternoon," Jorge said. "It's from a group that calls itself 'Saxxons for America.'"

"The distributor could be someone who doesn't like sanctuary cities," Lottie said.

"Or someone who doesn't like *us*," Jaime said.

"By the way, a drone—probably that same drone— hovered over our houses today about noon," Lottie said. "I saw it through my binoculars. It had a camera, and the red light was on."

"Why would a Saxxon want a video of our houses?" Paco said.

"The Saxxon probably wanted a video of you, sweet Paco," Lottie said. "You're a Spaniard who has an American job."

"And you're brown, *querido*," Mev said. "*¡Y muy guapo!*"

"So that's why you fell in love with me!" Paco said. "I fell in love with you because of your beautiful American accent. And your beautiful brain, of course, and your sweet smile."

Lottie cared for Paco as much as she cared for Mev. She and her son had traveled to Spain to meet Paco when Paco and Mev were students at the Universidad Complutense de Madrid, and the four of them had spent a week in Barcelona together. Lottie was matron of honor at their wedding in Gainesville in 1997.

"I just visited the Saxxons' website," Yolanda said. "It's very scary. The Saxxons want to send undocumented aliens back to Mexico. Look." She handed her phone to Jorge.

"The Saxxons are afraid that undocumented aliens will take their jobs," Jaime said.

"Undocumented aliens who aren't white," Annie said.

"They're afraid that documented aliens like me will become their bosses," Paco said.

"Documented aliens who aren't white," Annie said.

"It's a power thing," Jorge said. "White supremacists don't want to lose power to people they consider inferior. So they don't want brown or black bosses."

"White supremacists believe in a divinely ordained hierarchy of humans in which whites rank higher than browns and blacks, and white Christians rank higher than Jews and Muslims. To them, working for a black or brown boss is unnatural," Lottie said. "They think that whites are more intelligent and more virtuous than non-whites and that miscegenation weakens the white race."

"White supremacists must spend a lot of time being afraid of us," Paco said.

"They think we have genetic cooties," Jorge said, giggling.

Jaime poked Annie, who giggled. Annie was blonde and blue eyed. Annie had been Jaime's girlfriend all through high school.

"Gotcha!"

Paco poked Mev.

"The Saxxons must think Jonathan and Gregory have genetic cooties too," Yolanda said.

"The fear of contamination motivates hate crimes," Mev said.

"There's no membership list on the Saxxons' website, but there is an application form," Jorge said after a moment. "Maybe I'll join them undercover to find out who they are. Then I can write about them in Webby Witherston."

"You're brown, bro," Jaime said. "They won't let you join."

"I'll shave my head. Then I won't look brown."

"You'd better change your name."

"I'll be George Gully."

"You won't pass the DNA pedigree test," Jaime said, reading the application form over Jorge's shoulder. "And you're not eighteen."

"I'm eighteen," Annie said. "I'll apply."

"You're not getting close to those guys," Paco said. "They could kill you."

"I'm here!" Doolittle called out from his T-perch in the dining room. "Doolittle wanna kiss feathers."

"Okay, Doolittle. I'm coming. Jaime wanna kiss feathers," Jaime said to the parrot. Jaime picked him up and kissed his back, Doolittle's preferred place to be kissed.

"Doolittle wanna cuddle," Doolittle said. Jaime sat down on a kitchen stool, put the bird on his lap, and gently stroked his neck.

The front door opened.

"Hey, there! Anybody home?"

"Hey, Jim! Come in," Mev called out.

"Welcome, welcome!" Lottie greeted Jim and Lauren Lodge, their son Beau, Beau's girlfriend Sally, and his dog Sequoyah.

Sequoyah barked.

"Woof," Doolittle said. "That's doggy bark."

Mighty and Sequoyah began their wrestling ritual.

"Here's enough green beans to feed a baseball team," Lauren said, handing Mev a casserole dish.

"I have something to read to you all," Beau said. He pulled his phone out of his pocket. "After Jorge and Jaime left the Grays' farm this afternoon, I got an email from a person named Crockett Wood. This is the message." He showed it to them.

From: Crockett Wood crockettbwood@gmail.com

To: Beau Lodge <beaulodge2001@gmail.com>

BEQUEST
Sun 09/02/2018 4:36 p.m.

> *Dear Beau Lodge:*
> *I am sixty-five years old and I would like to leave land to your environmentalist club Keep Nature Natural. I invite you to visit me tomorrow night at 8:30 after the Labor Day picnic. Come to 4200 West Bank Road.*
> *Crockett Wood*

> *Sent from my phone*

"Who is Crockett Wood?" Jaime asked, coming into the living room with Doolittle perched on his hand.

"I don't know," Beau said. "Sally and I read this email to everybody, and nobody said they'd heard of him."

"We wondered how Mr. Wood knew Beau," Sally said. "And how he got Beau's email address."

"Beau put it in his letter to the editor this morning," Paco said.

"Crockett Wood may be the son of Harper B. Wood, who owns that piece of land on Saloli Stream," Mev said.

"Mr. Autry complained about the outhouse in Webby Witherston today."

"Old Mr. Autry is always complaining."

"He's adamantly opposed to immigration," Lottie said. "He voted against the sanctuary city motion."

"Why did Mr. Wood contact you, Beau?" Jorge asked. "Jaime is president of KNN now."

"Beau was president until July," Jaime said.

"I don't think you should go there alone, honey," Lauren said. "We don't know anything about him."

"Except that he doesn't flush," Jorge said. "And he's old."

"He is not old, Jorge," Lottie said. "He's sixty-five, three years younger than I am."

"Jorge and I will go with Beau, Mrs. Lodge," Jaime said. "We can go in our car."

"And we'll take the dogs," Jorge said. "They'll be with us at the picnic anyway."

"We'll leave the ball park tomorrow night at eight fifteen," Jaime said.

"You can reply to Mr. Wood and just say, 'Okay, thanks,'" Jorge said.

❧❧❧

By eight thirty the Lodges had departed with Beau, Sally, and Sequoyah, and Paco had gone home with Jorge, Jaime, Yolanda, Annie, and Mighty. Lottie and Mev cleaned up the kitchen.

"Doolittle wanna peanut."

Lottie handed Doolittle a pistachio nut and handed Mev a cup of chamomile tea. They moved into the living room.

"You've seen my column this morning," Lottie said. "I promised to give a history of moonshine in Witherston starting in 1924, the year of our first Labor Day Parade. I got hold of Gertrude Wilker's diary of that year. It's a treasure trove of true stories. You could call it 'the life and times of Gertrude Wilker.' I tell you, a diary like Gertrude's makes an historian high."

"Will it make Red Wilker high?"

"Not likely. Wait till you see tomorrow's column. Miss Gertrude records for posterity the fact that her husband Obie and her brother-in-law Boone Wood were joining the Ku Klux Klan. I sent the week's columns to Catherine last Friday before I knew that Boone Wood's grandson Crockett had moved up here."

"So Red Wilker and Crockett Wood are related."

"They're second cousins."

"I wonder whether Crockett moved to Witherston to be close to Red. Strange that Red has never mentioned him."

"Here's an ethical dilemma, Mev. Do I publish the rest of my columns, for which I used Gertrude Wilker's diary as the basis of my history of Witherston's moonshiners in 1924? Or do I cancel their publication and keep what I have learned to myself because Red wants to get elected mayor?"

"Like his father."

"If I don't publish them, I'll be suppressing information and, in effect, colluding with Red to hide his background."

"Is an historian dishonest when she refrains from disclosing something that might cause unhappiness?"

"Mev, I've always believed that the historian should tell the whole truth and nothing but the truth, insofar as she can figure it out."

"So should a detective. A detective should disclose whatever she, or he, can figure out, so long as it's rele-

vant to the case, though not during the investigation. Is
Gertrude Wilker's diary relevant to today?"

"If I hadn't discovered the diary, it wouldn't be relevant. But I did discover it, so it's suddenly become relevant."

"Publish what you have learned, Aunt Lottie."

"I will."

"Time to go to bed," Doolittle said. "Goodbye."

Mev's cell phone rang.

"Hi, Jake."

"I just heard back from the Georgia Bureau of Investigation. The GBI has had no reports of other Saxxon flyer drops in Georgia. Looks like the flyers were meant to
be a special treat for Witherston, Mev."

"So now we have to find a connection between the
Saxxons and Witherston. After all these years, someone
has decided that Witherston needs to change."

"See you tomorrow, Mev."

"Good-bye, Jake."

"Good-bye," Doolittle said.

Mev updated Lottie.

"I think that my sanctuary city project provoked the
drop," Lottie said.

"I'll ask Jake for police presence at the opening ceremony Sunday."

"Good night, dear."

"Good night, Aunt Lottie."

"Good night," Doolittle said.

Mev left.

ᔕᔕᔕ

Jaime, Jorge, Yolanda, and Annie sat on the floor in
the boys' bedroom. Jaime strummed his guitar softly
while Jorge, Yolanda, and Annie stared at Annie's phone.

"I'm going to fill out this Saxxons application," Annie said, "just to see what happens."

"Go, Annie! We'll help you," Jorge said.

"How much truth will you tell them, Annie?" Jaime asked, putting down his guitar.

"Enough truth to make them think I'm for real."

"But not too much," Jaime said.

"What if they discover Annie's a spy?" Yolanda asked. "They could hurt her."

"We'll be her bodyguards," Jorge said.

Within thirty minutes they had completed the form.

NAME: Ann Josephine Jerden
EMAIL ADDRESS: anniejerden@gmail.com
CHURCH: Witherston Baptist Church
AGE: 18
DATE OF BIRTH: August 30, 2000
HEIGHT AND WEIGHT: 5'8" and 125 lbs
HAIR COLOR: Blond
EYE COLOR: Blue
POLITICAL PARTY: Republican
ANCESTRY: British, Scottish, Irish
ADDRESS: 2019 Daksi Circle, Witherston, Georgia 30533
SPOUSE: Not applicable
CHILDREN: Not applicable
RELATIVES:
FATHER AND PATERNAL GRANDPARENTS:
James Dodd Jerden, father
Reverend Harold Dodd Jerden, grandfather
Mrs. Emily Peters Jerden, grandmother
CHURCH(ES):
St. Gregory's Episcopal Church, Augusta, Georgia
Witherston Baptist Church, Witherston, Georgia
POLITICAL PARTY: Republican

MOTHER AND MATERNAL GRANDPARENTS:
Mrs. Josephine Quinn Jerden, mother
Arthur Laurence Quinn, grandfather
Mrs. Ann Josephine Quinn, grandmother
CHURCH(ES):
St. Gregory's Episcopal Church, Augusta, Georgia
POLITICAL PARTY: Republican
REASON FOR JOINING THE SAXXONS FOR AMERICA:

I take pride in my ancestry, which includes Captain William Quinn and Colonel Bartholomew Bates of the Confederate Army who fought and died in the War Between the States, Major Archibald Bates who fought and died in World War I, and Nathaniel Peters, who fought and was wounded in World War II. I ask myself, What did they sacrifice themselves for? They thought they were fighting for a country of God-fearing white Christians like themselves who obeyed the Ten Commandments and believed in the truth of the Holy Bible. But the country they fought for has disappeared into a stew of brown people—Muslims, Jews, and dark immigrants who can't speak English—and others who hate American values. I am proud to be white. I want to carry on my family's tradition of fighting for the America of our forefathers, not this sordid assortment of people from elsewhere.

I am applying to join the Saxxons today because my home town of Witherston is about to let in caravans of illegal immigrants. I want to help stop them.

AFFIRM (by initialing):

"I am at least eighteen years old, native-born, white, and Christian; I believe in the literal truth of the Bible; I support the right to bear arms as guaranteed by Second Amendment of the Constitution; I acknowledge the supremacy of the white race: I oppose interracial marriage and same-sex marriage." INITIAL: AJJ

ATTACH RECENT PHOTOGRAPH.

"Wow, you guys, this is good!" Yolanda exclaimed. "Jorge, you wrote a great reason for Annie to join the Saxxons!"

"Thank you, thank you!" Jorge said. "Now do you all think I'm good enough to write fiction?"

"You'll write the great American novel, Jorge," Yolanda said. "You can write about the new American civil war, between the alt-right and everybody else."

"Why did they want my height and weight?"

"So that nobody can come in your place, Annie," Jorge said.

"That's why they want your picture," Yolanda said.

"If you send them a picture of yourself they can come get you," Jaime said.

"I say you just forget to attach the photograph," Jaime said.

"Yes. And see what the Saxxons say," Yolanda said.

"Do you think you should have given your real address?" Jaime asked Annie.

"Sure. No problem. Anyway, I had to give my parents' real names. They can always find out where I live."

"Okay. Should I press SEND?"

"Go ahead, Jorge," Annie said. "I'm in."

"We can't tell anybody," Jorge said.

"And especially not my parents," Annie said. "Let's investigate the Saxxons on our own."

CHAPTER 3

WWW. ONLINEWITHERSTON.COM

WITHERSTON ON THE WEB
Monday, September 3, 2018

NEWS

Hate Flyers Land on Grays' Farm

A hobby drone (a small "unmanned aerial vehicle" for individual use) dropped dozens of four-by-six-inch flyers yesterday afternoon on Labor Day parade participants who were preparing their floats at Emmett and Lydia Gray's farm. The flyers, depicting a burning cross, urged "white Christians" to "take back your country" and join the "Saxxons for America," an organization opposed to "cultural genocide."

Police Chief Jake McCoy took possession of the drone.

The Saxxons for America website includes an application form requiring applicants to declare that they are at least eighteen years old, native-born, white, and Chris-

tian, that they believe in the literal truth of the Bible, that they support the right to bear arms, that they acknowledge the supremacy of the white race, and that they oppose interracial marriage and same-sex marriage. Applicants must agree to be interviewed and, if accepted as members, must swear loyalty to the Saxxons and must not disclose their membership in the organization. Apparently, Saxxons for America is a secret organization. The term "Saxxons" probably alludes to the "Saxons," a Germanic people who invaded and populated England in the fifth and sixth centuries. The "Angles" already inhabiting the island and the "Saxons" became the Anglo-Saxons. The website gives no geographical address.

If you have any information regarding the Saxxons for America, please contact the police immediately.

Catherine Perry-Soto, Editor

TAKE BACK YOUR COUNTRY!

When immigrants invade the USA
And foreigners steal your jobs
When blacks marry whites and whites marry blacks
When men marry men and women marry women
When white Christians are a minority
You have lost your country to cultural genocide

Say <u>NO</u> to cultural genocide!
Fight back!

Saxxons for America
www.saxxonsforamerica.com

Join now!

Drone Spies on Tayanita Village

The same miniature drone that dropped Saxxons leaflets on Emmett and Lydia Gray's farm yesterday at 3:30 p.m. had flown over Witherston earlier in the afternoon. It was spotted over Tayanita Village at 1:15 p.m. with its red recording light was on.

Amadahy Henderson, Reporter

ANNOUNCEMENT

Labor Day paraders will line up at Emmett and Lydia Gray's farm at 3:30 p.m. today. Departure time is 4:00 p.m. Festivities at Slater Ball Park will begin upon the parade's arrival there. Dogs, cats, and children are welcome.

Amadahy Henderson, Reporter

NORTH GEORGIA IN HISTORY
By Charlotte Byrd

Sheriff Caleb McCoy was appreciated in Lumpkin County. On Friday, September 5, 1924, the Witherston Weekly carried the following front-page story:

Moonshine Still Destroyed

On Monday, September 1, at 10:00 a.m. Sheriff Caleb McCoy and deputies Benjie Par-

son and Archie Statham destroyed a still on the bank of Tayanita Creek. Although they failed to catch the moonshiner, they received praise from Witherston's chapter of the Anti-Saloon League at the league's monthly luncheon at the Withers mansion. President Maud Olive Withers said, "The Anti-Saloon League gives gracious thanks to Sheriff McCoy. Every still he destroys means a hundred families he restores."

Obie Wilker's brother-in-law, Boone Wood, was not so lucky. On Saturday, September 6, Gertrude Wilker wrote the following:

Sister Geraldine came to visit today with her and Boone's three-week old baby, Harper B Wood. She said that revenuers found Boone's still on Tuesday, destroyed the still, took his mule, and confascated his whiskey. She said the Lord watched over Boone when Boone hid in the woods. She said Boone wants to leave Dawson County and could they move here near us and Boone go into business with Obie. I said why not. Obie said that was fine. Our son Buehler and his cousin Harper B could grow up together. Obie said that he would help Boone build a house right next to ours. After Buehler and Harper B went to sleep tonight Obie and Geraldine and I played canasta.

The next day, September 7, Gertrude Wilker wrote:

Boone came and told us he joined the Nights of the Ku Klux Klan. Boone said he wants to protect our race from misegenation with Ne-

groes and foreigners. He said he found out about the Klan from Hiram Wesley Evans who is a wizard from Alabama. Boone wants Obie to join. Obie said the Klan don't like moonshiners but since Governer Walker is in the Klan he would join anyway. Boone said the Klan don't need to know what him and Obie do for a living.

Note: William Joseph Simmons founded the second Ku Klux Klan in Georgia in 1915, when he and some sixteen like-minded men burned a cross on Stone Mountain on Thanksgiving night. Simmons declared himself the Klan's Imperial Wizard. He was succeeded in 1922 by Hiram Wesley Evans. In the 1920s KKK membership increased significantly in reaction to the immigration of Jews and Catholics from southern Europe. Clifford Mitchell Walker was aligned with the KKK when he ran for governor of Georgia in 1922. The Klan spread quickly across the country and by 1924 numbered six million Americans.

WEATHER

Today's high will be in the mid-eighties, but dropping quickly in the afternoon. Today's low will be in the low sixties.

The record-setting storm system that has drenched Arkansas, spawned three tornados, and left 100,000 homes and businesses without electricity will reach our valley this evening.

Lord willing and the creek don't rise, Witherston will stay lit. But likely the creeks will rise. If you live alongside Saloli Stream or Founding Father's Creek or

Tayanita Creek, get out your boat. If you don't have a boat make reservations with Noah.

Tony Lima, Prophet

LETTERS TO THE EDITOR

To the Editor:
Don't I get veto power over Dr. Byrd's publication of the contents of my grandmother's diary?
How did my grandmother's diary get into the University of Georgia Library anyway?
Red Wilker
Witherston

From the Editor:
Mr. Wilker: According to the librarian of UGA's Rare Book Room, your grandmother, Gertrude Wilker, specified in her will that her diary and a bound manuscript of her poetry go to the University of Georgia upon her death in 1954. The unpublished manuscript, which included only 11 poems, was titled "Widowed."
As you know, your grandfather, Obadiah Wilker, was shot to death on August 15, 1930, supposedly by agents of the Internal Revenue Service.
You do not have veto power over the publication of the diary's contents, Mr. Wilker, because you do not own it. The diary belongs to the public now. It is part of history and as such it is available for scrutiny to anyone interested in it.
Catherine Perry-Soto, Editor

৩৩৩

At eight thirty on Labor Day morning Crockett
Wood sat in the outhouse reading Witherston's online
news on his smartphone. He made a call.

Crockett heard Bedford bark suddenly. Then he
heard a shot.

Crockett leaned up and bolted the door. Moments
later he saw a gun barrel enter the crescent moon.

A bullet penetrated his heart.

ᏣᎳᏣ

Witherston's ninety-fourth Labor Day parade went
as scheduled. Dozens of Witherstonians, many of them
accompanied by their dogs, swelled the procession as it
made its way down Possum Road onto Black Fox Road
to Slater Ball Park.

By five o'clock the parade had disbanded, and the
paraders had joined the several hundred Witherstonians
already enjoying the refreshments.

"Hey, folks," Lottie called out, making her way
through the crowd to Mev and Chief Jake McCoy by the
Slater Ball Park bandstand. She carried a plastic glass of
red wine.

"Hi, Aunt Lottie. Come join us," Mev called out.

On the bandstand Annie Jerden was singing "John
Henry," accompanied by Jaime on the guitar, Tony Lima
on the banjo, Dan Soto on the harmonica, and Pete Three
on the snare drum.

"'Hammer's gonna be the death of me, Lord, Lord.
Hammer's gonna be the death of me.'"

"Hey, there, Lottie," Jake said, giving her a hug.
"You look beautiful as always."

Lottie was wearing white jeans with a purple cotton tunic and a purple cross-over purse that matched her purple cane.

Jake wore his uniform, as did Mev. Jake and Mev were on duty to make sure all went well for the Labor Day partiers. They had found no more flyers. The parade had gone without incident.

"Have you all seen what Grace Wilker is handing out?" Lottie put the crook of her cane on her wrist and pulled a red squirt gun out of her purse. "Guns! Look! 'Red Wilker for Mayor' is stamped on the barrel and 'Wilker's Gun Shop' is stamped on the handle. Good God!"

"This is a squirt gun, Lottie," Jake said.

"But squirt guns are symbolic, Chief. They are symbolic of Red Wilker's values. Mayor Rather Rotund is no intellectual leader for Witherston, but at least he doesn't sell guns."

Annie began singing "It Ain't Gonna Rain No More." Fifty rowdy Witherstonians, many of them waving half-empty plastic cups of moonshine, joined the chorus.

> "'Oh, it ain't gonna rain no more, no more
> It ain't gonna rain no more
> How in the heck can I wash my neck
> if it ain't gonna rain no more'"

Rhonda Rather, wearing a red silk blouse, black silk pants, and a floppy straw hat, ascended the steps to the platform. She handed Coco Chanel to Annie, and Annie handed her the microphone. Rhonda belted out the last verse.

> "'We had a cat down on our farm

It had a ball of yarn
When her kittens were born
They all had sweaters on

"'Oh, it ain't gonna rain no more, no more
It ain't gonna rain no more—'"

"Enough, Rhonda! Enough, enough!" Mayor Rich Rather, huffing and puffing, climbed up the steps and took the mic. "It's time for my proclamation. These folks are waiting for my Labor Day proclamation."

"Oh, that must be why everyone's here," Rhonda said.

"Keep on singing!" Jorge yelled from the foot of the steps.

"Don't stop singing!" Tony Lima shouted.

"Go, Rhonda," someone else yelled.

Rhonda gave the mic to her husband and retrieved Coco Chanel from Annie.

Rich Rather, proud owner of Rather Pre-owned Vehicles in Dahlonega and now the outgoing mayor of Witherston, placed his plastic tumbler of clear liquid on the podium. Although he had been reelected for a second term in November of 2016, Rich was an object of fun. His constituents called him "Rather Rotund" and his dealership "Rather Used Cars."

"Thank you, thank you," the mayor said after the light applause. "Today, the first Monday in September, Witherston follows our country's longstanding tradition of honoring our fellow workers with a parade and a picnic. Although the government made Labor Day a federal holiday in 1894, Witherston did not celebrate the holiday until 1924, when Mayor Jethro Sullivan on his horse led a convoy of automobiles and mule-drawn wagons down

Possum Road to Black Fox Road turning right toward Founding Father's Creek."

"To Rosa's Cantina?"

"May I continue, Rhonda?" Rich asked. "Rosa's Cantina was established in 1964, long after the first Labor Day parade. Now let me read my proclamation."

"Speed it up, Rich," Rhonda said.

Rich did. "Whereas in Witherston we all have a right to work, and whereas in Witherston, we all have a right to enjoy spirits after work, and whereas in Witherston we traditionally observe our national holiday of Labor Day, and whereas in Witherston we remember our history with moonshine, I, Rich Rather, your mayor and soon to be your representative to the Georgia General Assembly, hereby proclaim Labor Day of 2018 to be a celebration of the hardworking moonshiners who toiled in these mountains to earn a living and bring pleasure to others. Now let our Labor Day moonshine party begin! Let it begin!"

"It's already begun!"

The crowd cheered.

"Hic, hic, hooray!"

"Is everybody happy?" Rich roared. "Is everybody happy?"

"Hic, hic hooray!"

"Your moonshine's good, Red," the mayor said, after taking a long sip. "But not as good as Old Forester."

Red Wilker waved his straw hat. "I'd like to speak, Rich," he called out from the front of the crowd.

"After me, Red," the mayor said.

Rich held up a white cardboard fan with red lettering under his picture: *YOU'D RATHER HAVE RATHER FOR STATE REPRESENTATIVE.*

"As you all know, I am running for representative from our district to the Georgia General Assembly. My opponent is a woman from Dahlonega nobody's ever heard of. So vote for me in November!"

He pulled out of his back pocket a white baseball cap with similar red lettering across the front: *RATHER FOR REPRESENTATIVE*. His picture was stamped on the back. He put it on his balding head.

"Will you all support me?" he yelled through the microphone.

"Yes, yes!" Some of the crowd roared.

"Go, Rather!"

"No go, Rather!"

"Thank you, thank you, those who told me to go. I'll remember you all. Now, folks, Mr. Red Wilker, who has brought us our moonshine, wants to speak."

"So do I," Rhonda said.

"Let Red speak, dear wife," Rich said.

Red ascended the stairs with his German Shepherds Smith and Wesson eagerly following him. He took the mic.

"First, I want you all to know that Wilker's Mountain Moonshine is concocted from a recipe my grandfather Obadiah Wilker developed not far from this very spot where I'm standing. My esteemed friend Dr. Charlotte Byrd wrote about him in Webby Witherston this morning."

"Did Obie go to jail, Red?"

"He did not, Rhonda! He went to heaven."

"Is this stuff legal, Red?"

"Wilker's Mountain Moonshine is legal. I pay my taxes."

"Sure, sure."

"Second, I announced a month ago that I'm running for mayor of our historical town. I promise to continue Mayor Rather's policies. I seek your vote, even though I have no opposition."

"Oh but you do, Red," Rhonda said from behind him. "I am running too!"

"What?" Red exclaimed, turning to face her.

"What?" Rich echoed. "Are you kidding, Rhonda? You? You for mayor?"

"Not kidding, dear husband. Now it's my turn." She took the mic from Red and spoke to the crowd. "And I promise not to continue Mayor Rather's policies."

"Jesus, Rhonda! Now I'll have to support Red," Rich groaned.

"I'll seek everybody else's vote."

"What's your platform, Rhonda?"

"I will make all of Witherston's municipal services available to all of the undocumented immigrants seeking sanctuary in our lovely town."

"I will help you win," Yolanda Gallo shouted.

"So will I," Jorge shouted.

"Then we have a contest," Red said, "because I say Witherston must obey federal law. Sanctuary cities violate federal law. Who is with me?"

A few applauded.

"So everybody who breaks the law goes to jail?" Rhonda asked Red.

"Everybody who breaks the law gets punished, that's what I say."

"Have you never broken the law, Red?"

The mayor reclaimed the microphone. "I say we'll have plenty of time later for campaigning. We need to party now before the storm comes."

Rhonda took the microphone. "You all are invited to next Sunday's ceremony to designate Witherston a sanctuary city. Four o'clock in front of the courthouse. My esteemed husband will preside."

Mayor Rather grimaced.

Rhonda continued. "The ceremony is getting publicity. CNN interviewed John Hicks last Friday."

John Hicks jumped up on stage. "And you know
what I told them," he shouted. "I told them that Witherstonians were too kind to perpetuate the racist policies of
our federal government."

"Wait, where does that leave me?" Mayor Rather
asked.

"You're about to climb aboard the kindness train,
dear," Rhonda said. "Anyway, folks, we Witherstonians
will welcome undocumented immigrants from Latin
America who need work and shelter. Some of us have
already opened our homes to them. The Lodges, the Arroyos, Jonathan and Gregory, and Tayanita Village will
all take in immigrants seeking sanctuary. So will Rich
and I. We'll be taking in a single mother and her three
young children."

"We will? Why didn't I know that?" the mayor exclaimed.

"You didn't ask, sweetie," Rhonda replied to her
husband. "And Pastor Paul Clement will provide sanctuary in the Witherston Baptist Church for the few who
have yet to find homes."

"So what do you say about undocumented immigrants, Mayor Rather?"

"Time to party, folks!"

"Mr. Mayor," Lottie called out. "What are you going
to do about the Saxxons for America?" She reached up
and handed him a flyer.

"The police will handle this," Rich said. "Witherstonians don't need to worry. Now it's moonshine time!"

Annie went up on stage and took the mic from Rich.
Tony Lima's Mountain Band struck up another century-
old tune, to which Annie sang:

"'Does the spearmint lose its flavor
on the bedpost overnight?
If you pull it out like rubber
Will it snap right back and bite?
If you paste it on the left side
Will you find it on the right?
Does your chewing gum lose its flavor
on the bedpost overnight?'"

❧❦❧

Annie showed Jaime and Jorge the email she had just read. It had been sent to her at four o'clock.

From: Ace Barnett pacebarnett@gmail.com

To: Ann Jerden <anniejerden@gmail.com>

APPLICATION TO JOIN SAXXONS
Mon 09/03/2018 4:00 p.m.

Dear Miss Ann Jerden:

Thank you for your application to join the Saxxons. You forgot to include a picture of yourself, but never mind. Just meet me on Sunday at 3:15 p.m. in front of Kroger. Wear white. I will find you. Come alone. Tell nobody.
Ace Barnett, Saxxon

Sent from my phone

"And here I am telling you all," Annie said.
"We won't tell anybody," Jaime said.
"We'll tell nobody," Jorge said.

"Should I reply to this email?" Annie asked.

"Sure. Just say, 'Will do.' And then we'll figure out what to do between now and Sunday," Jorge said.

"Will do," Annie said. She typed in the message and sent it.

CHAPTER 4

Monday Evening:

The storm was in full force when Jorge, Jaime, Beau, Mighty, and Sequoyah turned onto the long muddy driveway at 4200 West Bank Road. Half-way down, the driveway forked.

"Go right," Jaime said.

Jorge pulled up to the dilapidated cabin's front door.

"I don't think Mr. Wood is home," Jorge said. "The cabin is dark."

"Totally," Beau said.

"We have a couple of flashlights," Jaime said, extracting them from the glove compartment.

"I have a hood on my jacket, so I'll go," Beau said. "You all stay in the car. Give me a flashlight."

Beau ran up the front steps onto the decaying porch and knocked on the door. He waited a moment and knocked again. He turned the knob. The door swung open. Beau looked back at Jorge and Jaime.

"Nobody's here," he hollered. Lightning struck nearby. Thunder obliterated the rest of his words.

"Turn on some lights," Jaime hollered back.

Beau flipped a switch. "No electricity."

"Look inside."

Beau stepped inside and scanned the interior with the flashlight.

"Yikes!" he exclaimed. He returned to the porch and signaled for his friends to join him.

"Dogs stay here," Jaime commanded Mighty and Sequoyah as he closed the car doors.

The twins ran through the rain into the cabin. In the beam of Jaime's flashlight they saw an assault rifle, a hunting rifle, and a stack of Saxxon flyers on the table in the center of the room.

"That's a semi-automatic assault rifle." Jorge picked it up. "I've seen it in movies. Look. It's loaded." He carefully set it back down on the table.

Jaime picked up the hunting rifle. "This is a fancy rifle," he said. "A Winchester. It's loaded too."

"Does he keep all his guns loaded?"

"Was Mr. Wood going to shoot me?" Beau said. "I thought he wanted to talk about giving his land to KNN."

"Maybe he didn't plan to invite you in, Beau," Jaime said.

"Let's see what other stuff he has," Jorge said.

Beau panned the room with his flashlight.

"He doesn't have much stuff," Jaime said. "Cot, wood-burning stove, basin, and bathtub."

"The bathtub looks about a hundred years old," Jorge said. "It has feet. Creepy."

"No privacy," Beau said.

"The man lives alone, Beau! This is his living room, bedroom, kitchen, and bathroom," Jaime said.

"And foyer, parlor, dining room, and dance hall," Jorge said.

"He eats a lot of rice," Beau said, pointing his flashlight into the pantry. "And he smokes."

"What's under his bed?" Jaime squatted down and yanked open the storage drawer. "Mostly blankets and old clothes. Here are a couple of LED lanterns. Holy moly! And three tear gas grenades. What does Mr. Wood need grenades for?"

"For tear gassing crowds of people, bro. This is one crazy dude."

Jorge took a picture with his iPhone.

"Let's get out of here," Jaime said. "If Mr. Wood finds us here, he might shoot us."

"Yeah. He might have a gun on him," Beau said. "I wonder if he went to the picnic."

"I'm taking more pictures," Jorge said. "Point the flashlight beam on the table, Beau."

"Come on, Jorge! This is dangerous!"

"Got it. Okay, Jaime. One more picture. Come here, Beau."

Beau aimed the flashlight at the grenades, and Jorge clicked.

Mighty and Sequoyah began barking inside the Jetta.

"Somebody is coming!" Jaime yelled. "Turn off the flashlights!"

The boys heard a vehicle come the driveway from West Bank Road and turn into the woods. They glimpsed the taillights through the trees. The vehicle disappeared.

"Sounds like a truck!"

"Maybe it's Crockett Wood!"

"Why didn't he stop?"

"He's gone now."

"Let's go."

Jorge grabbed a flyer.

As Jaime opened the back door of the Jetta, Mighty and Sequoyah pushed past him and escaped into the rain.

With Jaime chasing them the dogs ran around the cabin to the back where they started barking. A bolt of lightning illuminated a big truck parked under the trees.

"Mighty! Sequoyah! Come," Jaime shouted.

Jorge and Beau helped Jaime catch them.

"Now let's get out of here," Jaime said. "No telling where Crockett Wood could be."

ೂಀೲ

Mev and Paco were sitting on Lottie's screened porch listening to the rain when the three boys arrived with the dogs.

All were soaked.

Mev called Jake as soon as she heard their story.

"Jorge is emailing us the pictures he took," she told the chief. "They found a stack of Saxxons flyers, Jake. Now we know who dropped them on the parade. Mr. Crockett Boone Wood."

"Crockett Boone Wood may be a white supremacist, but he didn't do anything illegal."

"They also found a loaded hunting rifle, a loaded semi-automatic rifle, and three tear gas grenades. Crockett must have expected to use them."

"Jesus! Wood could have shot the boys as burglars. Where the hell was he?"

"Can we pay him a visit, Jake? We'd say we're checking on him since he wasn't home to meet Beau."

"Sure. Let's leave the station at nine in the morning. We go armed. And we take Tracker." Tracker was Jake's hundred-pound bloodhound.

"See you then." Mev disconnected. "Time to go to bed, Paco. We have to get up early tomorrow. Boys, will one of you take Beau home?"

"Okay, Mom."

"In ten minutes, Mom."

Mev and Paco left.

"Why do people join white supremacist organizations?" Beau asked.

"To protect our race from miscegenation, Beau," Jaime replied. "Didn't you read Aunt Lottie's column this morning?"

"To protect our race from folks like your parents, Beau, who miscegenated and made you," Jorge said.

"Whoopee," Beau said.

"They're stuck in the past. The Civil War was over a hundred and fifty years ago."

"Racism got stuck in Western mentality from the time the concept of race was invented," Lottie said. "And in a percentage of our population it never got unstuck."

"The concept of race was invented?"

"Yes, Beau. Invented. The modern concept of race was invented in Europe in the sixteenth century, when European explorers discovered humans in other parts of the world with astonishingly different appearances, and European scholars classified these strange humans by their skin color, hair texture, and the like. The scholars used the term 'race' to refer to the strange humans' physical appearance. The concept stuck."

"And the Europeans decided that blacks were the worst?"

"The Europeans understood nature in terms of a hierarchy—as in God, humans, gorillas, monkeys, dogs, fish, and roaches—so they ranked the races. Naturally, they ranked whites the highest because they themselves were white and they considered Europeans the most civilized, and they ranked blacks the lowest because they considered Africans the least civilized."

"Christians didn't feel guilty about importing Africans as slaves?"

"I suspect most did not, Beau. The American slave traders and slave owners considered the African slaves sub-human, so they treated them as animals. Even otherwise enlightened people in the South thought of their slaves as incapable of learning. Of course, on the plantation the slave owners deprived the slaves of education to keep them subordinate and then viewed them as their intellectual inferiors because they couldn't read."

"Not fair."

"Nothing in the history of race is fair. Many slave owners assumed that God made black people to serve white people."

"And that God made women to serve men," Jorge added.

"My father did some research and found the name Lodge in the records of the Calhoun gold mine slaves. Tom Lodge and Zeke Lodge," Beau said. "And he found his mother's name, Hogg, in the records of a plantation near Charleston. May Hogg, Tom Hogg, John Hogg, and Monday Hogg, probably all Gullah. Their ancestors must have come over from West Africa. Lots of Hoggs still live in Charleston."

"Maybe May and Tom and John and Monday got their name from tending hogs," Jaime said.

"Or their parents did," Beau said. "Somebody tended the hogs, and that somebody would not have been the white plantation owner."

"The plantation owner made the Hoggs tend hogs and then said they smelled bad," Jaime said. "He made the Hoggs tend hogs and then called them stupid."

"Hogs are not stupid," Jorge said.

"He made the Hoggs tend hogs and then considered them inferior."

"You asked why people join white supremacist organizations, Beau," Lottie said. "After President Lincoln freed the slaves and the slave-owners lost the source of their wealth, the poor white Southerners still considered themselves superior to the uneducated blacks, such as the Hoggs, who were probably illiterate. The white Southerners viewed egalitarianism as an affront to God's order. The Ku Klux Klan sought to re-impose white supremacy, which they believed was God's plan for mankind."

"The Klansmen and the Saxxons must still believe this."

"Obviously. Racism did not disappear with the end of slavery. The concept of divinely ordered racial relations has lived on in the mentality of the uninformed and uneducated, passed down from one generation of bigots to another."

"If the concept of races was invented, then racism is unnatural," Beau said.

"It's complicated, Beau. It may be natural for people to fear others who are different. That's an aspect of tribalism. Education overcomes tribalism. But racism is embedded in prejudice against poor people, and the blacks were poor for a century after they were freed from slavery."

"They were kept poor, because of prejudice," Beau said.

"The blacks were caught in a vicious cycle," Lottie said. "Whites considered them inferior, so they didn't provide them the same opportunities for education they established for whites. Since the blacks were less educated, whites gave them low-paying jobs. Since the blacks had low-paying jobs, the blacks couldn't give their children good education, and their children got low-paying jobs."

"And the whites became white supremacists."

"A few whites, Jaime," Lottie said.

"A few whites joined the Klan to enforce white supremacy."

"I'm going to write about this in my column," Jorge said. "I'll do some research."

CHAPTER 5

WWW. ONLINEWITHERSTON.COM

WITHERSTON ON THE WEB
Tuesday, September 4, 2018

NEWS

Rhonda Rather Will Oppose Red Wilker for Mayor

*R*honda Rather surprised attendees at yesterday's Labor Day picnic by announcing her candidacy for mayor of Witherston. Rhonda Rather is the spouse of outgoing mayor Rich Rather. She will oppose Red Wilker in the November election.

Redford Arnold Wilker, age sixty-five, is the son of Buehler ("Bullet") Wilker, who served as Witherston's mayor from 1984 to 1988, and Nelly Redford Wilker. He is the grandson of legendary moonshiner Obadiah ("Obie") Wilker and Gertrude Harper Wilker of Wither-ston. He graduated from Witherston High School in 1971, served two years in the Air Force, graduated from

*North Georgia College in 1977, married Grace Egging-
ton, and went into the firearms business with his father.
He owns and operates Wilker's Gun Shop.*

*Rhonda Rather, age sixty, is the daughter of Sha-
nahan and Betsy Barnes O'Leary, founders of the Sha-
nahan's Restaurant chain, and wife of Mayor Rich Rather. She graduated from the University of Georgia in
1980 with a major in journalism. She is currently president of the Witherston Humane Society.*

*Rhonda Rather supports the proposal adopted by the
Town Council to make Witherston "a sanctuary city for
undocumented immigrants." On this issue she is aligned
with her husband's opponent for representative to the
Georgia General Assembly, Juanita Madrugada-Reyes of
Dahlonega, who advocates amnesty for undocumented
immigrants. Red Wilker promises to uphold federal law.*

*The issue of undocumented immigrants may divide
our community this fall.*

Catherine Perry-Soto, Editor

NORTH GEORGIA IN HISTORY
By Charlotte Byrd

*Gertrude Harper Wilker's diary ought to be
published for the stories it tells of life among the rural
poor before electricity and indoor plumbing came to
Witherston.*

*She did not complete high school, having to drop out
in the tenth grade after her mother died to take care of
her younger brother and her three younger sisters, but
she was a remarkably good writer.*

On September 10, 1924, Gertrude wrote about her

brother Eddie Harper who lived not far north of here in Saloli Valley.

> *Eddie has devised a plan to not go back to jail for distributing our whiskey. He buries jars all over his land and then sells maps with an X on the spot where his customer can dig one up. Eddie says it's not illegal to sell maps. Eddie told Obie that in August he sold 2 maps to Mister HaHa Withers, the snooty millionaire in the mansion on the hill. Mister Withers does his drinking in his fancy outhouse to keep his snooty wife Maud Olive from finding out. Mister and Missus Snooty I call them. Missus Snooty is president of the snooty Anti-Saloon League. She says drinking is a sin against God. I say Missus Snooty is guilty of the sin of Pride, and I look forward to seeing her in Hell.*

Lumpkin County records show that in 1924 Edward Harper owned fifteen acres of land that included a 464-square foot hunting shack on the west bank of Saloli Stream that had been in the Harper family since 1881.

Upon his death in 1968 Edward Harper bequeathed the property to his nephews Harper B. Wood and Bullet Wilker. In 1971 Bullet Wilker sold his half to Harper B. Wood for $3,000.

ANNOUNCEMENT

Jorge Arroyo will interview mayoral candidates Rhonda Rich and Red Wilker on his radio show "Fifteen Minutes of Fame" on WITH-AM at 12:00 noon today.

Amadahy Henderson, Reporter

WEATHER

Sunshine on my shoulders makes me happy. After last night's storm the sun will be out today. High will be in the high seventies. Low will be in the high sixties.

But watch out! There's a full moon rising at 3:04 a.m. tomorrow.

Tony Lima, Weather Bard

കൗകൗ

Jake and Mev, with Tracker in the patrol car's back seat, stopped at 4200 West Bank Road where a *PRIVATE PROPERTY ~ KEEP OUT* sign had been nailed to the mailbox post. They turned right onto the steep driveway that took them down to the cabin.

Jake got out of the car.

"Stay here till I signal you, Mev," Jake said. "Tracker, come with me."

Tracker accompanied Jake up the porch steps to the front door, which swung open when Jake touched the knob.

"Anybody home?" Mev heard Jake called out. "This is Chief McCoy."

Jake and Tracker disappeared into the cabin.

Then Jake reappeared and beckoned to Mev. "Nobody's here. Let's look around back."

Tracker, with his nose to the ground, led them past a battered black Dodge Ram with a Confederate flag bumper sticker, past the bloodied body of a large male puppy, to the outhouse, where he pawed the door and commenced to howl.

Jake knocked on the door. "Are you here, Crockett Wood?"

"Sheesh," Mev said. "Smells like death!"

Jake knocked again. He tried to open the door, but it had been bolted. Then he peered through the crescent moon cut-out.

"Christ! There's a dead man sitting on the john!"

With a screwdriver, Jake pried the wood door open. A thin man with unkempt white hair and grizzled beard, his jeans around his knees and his white T-shirt stained with blood, tumbled out.

"Oh, my god! He was shot!"

"Could be suicide. But who'd kill himself in an out-house?" Jake looked inside. "I don't see a gun."

"He may have been shot through the moon."

"Must have been."

"There are no tracks."

"So he was shot before the storm."

"Rigor mortis hasn't left his body," Mev said. "He died within the last thirty hours."

"From the looks of it I'd guess yesterday morning, maybe twenty-four hours ago, or around that."

"If this is Crockett Wood, he looks older than sixty-five."

"Could have had a hard life."

Mev took pictures of the deceased from several different angles.

"See if he's got ID on him," Mev said.

Jake removed a wallet from his jeans and flipped it open.

"Driver's license issued to Crockett Boone Wood, date of birth August eighth, 1953, male, blue eyes, height six feet one, weight one seventy, address Ten Split Road, Heron Brook, Dawson County, Georgia."

He showed the license to Mev. "He's a veteran."

"The picture looks like him but without long hair and beard."

"He's got no credit cards in his wallet," Jake said. "He carries cash. A couple hundred dollars here."

"So he wasn't robbed. He was murdered for another reason."

"Here are three keys. One must be for this place and another for his Heron Brook place. The third could be for a desk." Jake pocketed the keys.

"How about a phone?"

Jake checked the dead man's jeans. "None on him. He might have been holding it. There it is. On the floor." Jake picked it up. "I'll give it to John Hicks. He may be able to tell what secrets this phone holds."

"There must be a shell casing around here, Jake" Mev looked at the ground. "Here it is. Crockett Wood was shot with a nine millimeter NATO bullet."

"I've got the bullet," Jake said. "It was lodged in the wood behind the hole."

Mev walked over to the body of the puppy. She took a picture with her phone.

"Poor puppy. Shot through the head. Let's see what his tags say. Oh, his name must be 'Bedford.' Poor Bedford."

"Rigor mortis?"

"Yes. Here's the casing. Also nine millimeter."

"He would have been killed at the same time Wood was killed," Jake said. "Someone sure wanted Crockett Wood dead. I'll call the Petes." Jake phoned his deputies Pete Koslowsky Senior and Pete Koslowsky Junior, known to all as Pete Senior and Pete Junior, or "the Petes."

"I'll call Dirk." Mev phoned Dirk Wales, the Lumpkin County coroner in Dahlonega.

While Jake secured the area with yellow *CRIME SCE-*

NE ~ DO NOT CROSS tape and Tracker explored the woods, Mev put on latex gloves and looked inside the log cabin. The century-old building was basically a wooden box, with pine plank floors, walls, and ceiling. Against the north wall was a fireplace. Against the south wall was a built-in rectangular table with a freestanding porcelain washbasin and a rack with a plate, a mug, and stainless steel knife, fork, and spoon. Beside it was a pantry and an old small refrigerator. Shelves above the washbasin held a kerosene lantern and two military flashlights. A worn porcelain bathtub with lion feet stood beside it. An old square table occupied the center of the room. On it were the two rifles and the stack of flyers.

Mev opened the storage drawer and found the clothes and the lanterns, but not the tear gas grenades her sons had discovered. She took a picture.

She found a carton of milk, two bottles of water, and two Marie Callender's pot pies in the refrigerator, and a box of white rice and two packs of Marlboros in the pantry.

And a green Drone Trekker backpack on the pantry floor. The backpack contained a Phantom 4 Pro kit minus the drone. She took another picture.

Mev turned her attention to the two guns on the card table: a Bushmaster assault rifle and a Winchester hunting rifle. "Both loaded," she said to herself. She took a picture of the table.

As Mev took pictures, Jake entered.

"The Petes are here, and an ambulance is on its way. The ambulance will take Wood's body to Dahlonega for an autopsy. What have you found?"

"A loaded assault rifle and a loaded hunting rifle. Take a look."

"Both high end," Jake said.

"And a fancy drone kit minus the drone."

She showed him the backpack, which included a small monitor.

"So Crockett Wood was operating the drone that Mr. Wilker shot down," Jake said. "I'm taking this kit to John Hicks." John Hicks was the police department's information technology specialist.

"I don't think Crockett Wood lived here. He might have used this cabin only on weekends."

"Probably for hunting. Deer season opens September eighth, this coming weekend."

"What do you suppose he did with the tear gas grenades, between last night and this morning?"

"You told me the boys heard a car. Maybe the driver returned for the grenades."

"It was a truck."

"Whoever the person was, he saw the boys. He could have shot Crockett that morning and returned that night to collect the grenades."

"And not the two guns? That's strange. I think we should investigate Crockett's house in Heron Brook, Jake."

"I'll get a search warrant for his house and his cell phone. We can go to Heron Brook this afternoon."

Jake locked the cabin door with one of the keys from Crockett's wallet.

"I'll check Dawson County tax records to make sure Crockett still owns the house," Mev said.

და

BREAKING NEWS

Crockett Wood Is Dead

Crockett Boone Wood, resident of Heron Brook, Georgia, was found shot to death on his father's property

at 4200 West Bank Road this morning by Chief Jake McCoy and Detective Mev Arroyo. So was his dog.
  Police have no suspects.

Catherine Perry-Soto, Editor

ℰↃℰↃ

Lottie taped a note to Mev's back door and then returned home to hear her nephew's show. Earlier that summer Jorge had persuaded the local radio station to give him fifteen minutes at noon on Tuesdays to interview local Witherstonians involved in local issues.

"And...it's twelve o'clock noon! This is Jorge Arroyo, on WITH-AM, Five-Seventy on your AM dial, welcoming mountain listeners to my Tuesday interview program 'Fifteen Minutes of Fame.' Today we have with us our two candidates for mayor of Witherston, Mrs. Rhonda Rather and Mr. Red Wilker. Hello, Mrs. Rather, Mr. Wilker."

"Thank you for having us, Jorge," Red said.

"I'm honored to be on your show again, Jorge," Rhonda said. "I enjoyed talking with your listeners last month about the Witherston Humane Society, which is still in need of donations."

"If you can plug your pet project, Rhonda, I can plug mine. I urge listeners to join the Witherston Bear Hunting Club, and to buy the best bear rifle on the market at Wilker's Gun Shop."

"Most good people prefer saving bears to slaying them, Red. Bears have thoughts and feelings just like us humans. Would you kill a human?"

"Whoa," Jorge said. "I invited you all here to discuss your platforms, not to advertise. Mrs. Rather, would you tell us what you stand for?"

"I stand for caring for others, including non-human animals, and for creating a sanctuary city for undocumented immigrants, because we all need each other."

"Who's *we*, Rhonda?" Red asked.

"*We* is everybody, Red. White persons, black persons, brown persons, red persons, and everybody in between. Americans, Mexicans, Haitians, Christians, Muslims, Jews, and the poor and the maimed and the lame, the halt and the blind, and others not as lucky as you are."

"And *our* taxes will pay for them all? You can't take care of everybody, Rhonda. If you try, you'll leave nothing for the legitimate residents of Witherston."

"So who are the legitimate residents of Witherston?"

"I'll tell you who are not. Illegal aliens are not, like the Mexicans who will come here to hide from Homeland Security. They will bleed our coffers dry. And they'll marry real Witherstonians and—"

"Real Witherstonians? Holy smokes, Red! Are you a Saxxon! Do you agree with those flyers?"

"Stop, Rhonda. You are way out of line!" Red exclaimed. "I am not a Saxxon!"

"Please, Mr. Wilker. Please, Mrs. Rather," Jorge interjected. "Let's just have a conversation. Mr. Wilker, would you tell us what you stand for in the mayoral race?"

"I stand for preserving Witherston's traditional values and taking pride in our accomplishments. Our ancestors built our prosperous community with hard work. In the nineteenth century, they had to fight off Indians and bears to survive in these mountains. In the twentieth century they had to fight off revenuers." Red laughed. "I like Witherston the way it is. Rhonda wants to change it."

"In the early nineteenth century, Hearty Withers stole the Cherokees' gold in the Georgia Gold Rush, took the Cherokees' land in the Georgia Land Lottery, and then sent the Cherokees westward on the Trail of Tears, leaving only white settlers to call themselves Georgians," Rhonda said. "The Withers built Witherston on top of an abandoned Cherokee village."

"So who are your people, Rhonda? The whites or the Indians? Or the illegal immigrants you've invited to your sanctuary city? You choose."

"I don't have to choose, Red. If I choose one group, I make an enemy of the other. I don't want enemies. Apparently you do."

"Enough," Jorge said.

Rhonda continued. "Choosing sides makes war. If you get elected mayor, which is highly unlikely, you will—"

"Enough, thank you. Time's running out. You each have thirty seconds to remind our listeners why we should vote for you. Mr. Wilker?"

"I will remind you all why you should vote against Rhonda Rather. Rhonda Rather will take away our guns, raise our local taxes, and flout our national laws on immigration."

"Your turn, Mrs. Rather."

"Thank you, Jorge. I will remind you all why you should vote against Red Wilker. He supported Roy Moore last year when that aging child predator was running for the US Senate. Look up Red's letter to the editor of the *Atlanta Journal-Constitution* on the subject. It was in November."

"That's it. We've come to the end of our 'Fifteen Minutes of Fame.'"

"Wait! Don't I get a chance to explain?" Red exclaimed.

"We are out of time, unfortunately. So I thank you, Mrs. Rather and Mr. Wilker, for coming on my show. And thank you, listeners, too, for staying with us. Tune in

next Tuesday to WITH-AM to hear my interview with
Mayor Rich Rather and Juanita Madrugada-Reyes, oppo-
nents for representative to the Georgia General Assembly. They will each have their fifteen minutes of fame.
Good-bye."

Lottie turned off the radio and went to her computer.
She found a letter to the editor from November thirtieth
of 2017.

To the Editor:
I want to speak out against this "Me Too" movement
of women exposing everybody's sexual past. Nothing
good will come of it, for either the men or their accusers.
And their accusers may be lying. Nobody can prove they
are not.
If Roy Moore sexually harassed a few women forty
years ago—if he actually did—he should be forgiven. He
has led an admirable life since then. Shouldn't forty years
of good behavior cancel out whatever bad mistakes he
may have made in his youth?
I say, let the past stay buried. And let us all be
judged by the good we have done in our adult life. I don't
know anybody who didn't make a few bad mistakes that
he regrets. God forgives. So we should too.
Red Wilker
Witherston

"But opposing sanctuary for illegal immigrants is not
doing good," Lottie muttered. "I wonder whether this letter generated any response."

She looked at the next day's letters. "Aha!"

"Aha!" Doolittle said. "Doolittle wanna cuddle!"

Lottie put Doolittle on her lap and caressed her while
she read the response to Red's letter.

To the Editor:

Mr. Red Wilker's condemnation of the "Me Too" movement is based on the millennia-old patriarchal assumption that the man is to be believed and the woman is not. The "Me Too" movement overturns that assumption. In 2017, the woman is believed and the man is not. It's about time!

If a man ruined a woman's life forty years ago, whatever good behavior he may claim thereafter does not cancel out whatever hardships she endured over forty years.

I ask you, Red Wilker, what are you saying about your own past?

Janet Ullmann
Atlanta

"Hellooo, Aunt Lottie! I'm here." Mev let herself in the back door.

Lottie walked into the kitchen with Doolittle perched on her hand.

"Hello, Mev. I'm glad you saw my note before you had lunch. You just missed Jorge's radio program, but you're in time for pimento cheese sandwiches."

"Hi," Doolittle said. "Wanna whistle?" Doolittle commenced his unique version of "On Top of Old Smoky."

"Did you see that Crockett Wood has been murdered, Aunt Lottie? He was shot in his outhouse."

"By that lunatic Alvin Autry?"

"No, Aunt Lottie! I'm serious! Jake and I found his body this morning."

"Oh, Lordy," Lottie said. "I wonder what Mr. Crockett Boone Wood did to deserve this."

Mev describe the crime scene.

"Now tell me about Jorge's show, Aunt Lottie."

"Rhonda and Red went after each other. She brought up his support of Roy Moore in last year's Alabama Senate election. I think Rhonda poked a hole in Red's campaign. Let's eat. I want you to see what I found in the *Witherston Weekly* archives."

Lottie put Doolittle on his perch and brought out the sandwiches and iced tea.

"I've been doing some research for Beau on the 1968 murder. Look at this article from Friday, September sixth, of that year, a time I can actually recall." She turned the computer screen so that Mev could read the article.

Negro Teenager Is Murdered
White Girl is Missing

Witherston entered Georgia's sad racial history last Sunday when a young Negro was murdered, presumably for having a white girl in his car.

Tyrone Lincoln Lewis, age eighteen, a 1968 graduate of Witherston High School and an entering freshman at Atlanta's Morehouse College, was apparently with Allie Marie Camhurst, age eighteen, a 1968 graduate of Witherston High and an entering freshman at Gainesville Junior College, when he was murdered by the Ku Klux Klan.

At 6:45 p.m., Witherston police officers on routine patrol discovered a '57 turquoise Chevy belonging to Tyrone Lewis parked on the shoulder of Orchard Road a quarter of a mile past the bridge over Tayanita Creek. After a brief search they found Tyrone Lewis's body half hidden in the rhododendron bushes that cover the creek's east bank. He had been stabbed multiple times in the chest and throat.

The police found blood on three separate sites: the sandy shoulder of the road where Lewis was likely killed; the path leading into the rhododendron bushes, which showed evidence of a bleeding body being dragged; and a grassy area ten yards away, where a second person might have been killed or wounded.

At 7:30 p.m. Reverend Wade Camhurst of 120 Myrtle Circle called the police to report his daughter missing. He said that when she didn't show up for supper he called her friend Mary Lou Reynolds to see whether Allie was there, but nobody was home.

At the time the police made no connection between Tyrone Lewis's murder and Allie Camhurst's disappearance.

Shortly after 10:00 p.m., Roberta Lewis, Tyrone's mother, of 189 Salt Road, called the police to report a burning cross on her front lawn. The burning cross is the signature of the Ku Klux Klan. The police told her then that her son had been murdered.

Mrs. Lewis told the police that Tyrone and Allie Marie Camhurst had spent the afternoon at her house.

On Monday, after news of the murder had circulated, a resident of Orchard Road called the police to report that he had seen a turquoise Chevy speed by his house toward town about 6:00 p.m. when he was out mowing his lawn. He said that a black man was driving and a white woman was riding in the front seat beside him. A black car was chasing them. He said that four Klansmen wearing hoods were in the black car.

Monday afternoon police combed the Orchard Road Bridge area but did not find Allie's body.

Police located Allie's car parked in front of the Reynolds' home. Mary Lou said she had no idea why Allie would abandon her car. She was distraught.

Reverend Camhurst said that he had never met Tyrone Lewis and that he had not given his daughter permission to go out with Lewis. "What was a Negro man *doing with a white girl?" he asked. "That's the question police should answer."*

Reverend Camhurst, a widower, has invited the Witherston Methodist Church congregation to join him Saturday at 9:00 a.m. at Orchard Road Bridge to search for his daughter's body.

"I wonder who wrote the article. There's no byline."

"Newspapers didn't carry bylines in 1968. Now I'm giving you Tyrone Lewis's obituary."

Tyrone Lincoln Lewis
1950-1968

Tyrone Lincoln Lewis, age eighteen, died on Sunday, September 1, 1968, presumably murdered by the Ku Klux Klan.

Tyrone Lewis was born in Hall County on April 15, 1950, to Lincoln and Roberta Lewis. He is predeceased by his younger brother Rook Lewis.

Tyrone graduated from Witherston High School on Friday, May 24. He was the only Negro in the class of 1968.

The funeral took place at 4:00 p.m. on Tuesday, September 3, at the Frederick Douglass Baptist Church in Witherston.

"Does anything strike you as unusual, from our 2018 perspective, Mev?"

"Tyrone's parents lost both their children. I don't know how they could survive such a tragedy."

"His mother didn't. She died on Christmas day. I wonder whether she committed suicide. What else?"

"There's nothing about who Tyrone was."

"Right. Heart-breaking, isn't it? He was just a local black boy. Now here's an article the *Witherston Weekly* published nine months later on May thirtieth."

Witherston High School Valedictorian Honors Tyrone Lewis

The Ku Klux Klan's murder of Tyrone Lincoln Lewis, age eighteen, remains unsolved after nine months.

On Sunday, September 1, 1968, four Klansmen attacked and killed young Lewis, a Negro, who had Allie Marie Camhurst with him in his car. Allie Camhurst remains missing.

Tyrone's mother, Roberta Lewis, died unexpectedly on December 25. Allie's father, Reverend Wade Camhurst, died unexpectedly on January 31.

At Witherston High School's graduation ceremony last Friday, valedictorian Hal Tucker spoke of Tyrone.

Tucker said, "Last September Witherston High lost a distinguished alum, Tyrone Lincoln Lewis. Tyrone's obituary mentioned that he was a Negro but said nothing about his profound impact on his fellow students. So I will dedicate my valedictorian's speech to him.

"Not only was Tyrone senior class president and a varsity basketball player but he was also an intellectual who made intellectuals out of many of us. Tyrone co-founded the Movie Club with Allie Camhurst and became its first president. Every Sunday at four o'clock in the Bobcat Conference Room Tyrone led an exciting discussion of whatever movie was showing at Black Fox Theater. We learned to analyze plots, directorial styles, screen writing, and cinematography. One Sunday we spent four hours talking about 'In the Heat of the Night' with Sidney Poitier and Rod Steiger. Tyrone was not afraid for us to bring up racial issues.

"And for all four years of high school Tyrone worked nights and summers at the chicken plant.

"So, fellow Bobcats, let us each pledge to do what we can to overcome the racial bigotry that killed Tyrone."

The graduation program concluded with the song selected by the class of 1969, 'This Little Light of Mine.'"

"Their idealism is beautiful," Mev said.

"Yes, dear. And where did it go?" Lottie said. "That was my generation."

"Anything else?"

"One last article, a short one published a year after Tyrone's death on September fifth."

Witherston Marks First Anniversary of KKK Murder

One year ago, on the Sunday before Labor Day, four Klansmen murdered eighteen-year old Tyrone Lincoln Lewis, just days before he was to begin his freshman year at Morehouse College in Atlanta.

Police have not solved the case.

Asked whether the police had any suspects, Chief Conn Kelly said, "No. Our only clue is that the killers drove an old black sedan. These mountains are full of old black sedans. They were used for hauling moonshine. The Klansmen could be from anywhere, from here in the mountains or from out of state. We don't have KKK membership lists, so we don't have a starting place for our search."

Allie Marie Camhurst, who was with Tyrone Lewis that evening and was probably a witness to the killing, disappeared.

"Most probably, the Klansmen killed Allie and either hid her body or took her body with them," Chief Kelly

said. "They could not leave her alive to identify them."
He added, "We've stopped looking."

"So do you want me to open up this cold case, Aunt Lottie?"

"I will work on it with you, dear."

"Where will you start?"

"I will start with this question. If Allie Camhurst was killed that evening, why was her body never found? If she survived, where did she go? She witnessed the murder so she would have had good reason to hide."

"And Tyrone Lewis's murderers would have had good reason to kill her."

"Right."

"Do you remember the case, Aunt Lottie?" Mev asked. "It must have been in the Atlanta papers. How old were you then?"

"Almost the same age as Tyrone and Allie. Seventeen, going on eighteen. I was about to enter my freshman year at the University of Georgia. My new boyfriend Remington Byrd had an African American friend named Alonzo who told us about the murder. Alonzo was upset that the police didn't consider the murder a big deal. We had a segregationist governor then, Lester Maddox, who made white supremacists feel justified in, as he put it, keeping blacks in their place."

"Do you recall much about the Klan in those days?"

"I recall that the Klan threatened the life of my father, who was your father's father. He was my high school's principal, and he promoted integration. So he was a KKK target. By the way, your grandmother desegregated our town's book club later that fall when she invited Alfreda Wright, an African American elementary school teacher, to join. Your grandmother was ahead of her time. The book club read *Black in White America*. So did I."

CHAPTER 6

Tuesday Afternoon:

It looks like Crockett Wood hadn't put his Split Road house on the market," Mev said as Jake turned south onto Witherston Highway. "It's not listed in the Heron Brook real estate ads."

During the hour-long drive from Witherston to Heron Brook Mev browsed the Dawson County Tax Assessor's website, real estate ads, and arrest records. She found much of interest.

"Jake, the owner of the property on Split Road is listed as Harper B. Wood, not Crockett Wood."

"So Crockett lived with his father. When did Harper B. Wood buy it?"

"Nineteen seventy-two. The house is described as a single family residence, fifteen hundred square feet, with two bedrooms and one bath, on twenty and a half acres. Built in nineteen forty-eight. It's now assessed at seventy-five thousand dollars."

"Must be run down. What else can you find?"

"I'm looking at Dawson County arrests for 2010 to 2018. Crockett has run afoul of the law a few times. DUI in 2011 with a Resisting Arrest charge. Another DUI in 2014. Assault Resulting in Bodily Injury in 2017. Let's see. That was in a local bar, Heron's Watering Hole."

"Nice guy."

"Here we are, Mev, at Ten Split Road. Crockett's got a pecan orchard."

As they got out of the vehicle Mev and Jake were greeted by four huge dogs, all barking fiercely, all racing back and forth behind the chain link fence that enclosed a large back yard behind an old farmhouse in need of paint. The porch held two wooden rocking chairs.

"Those dogs look like Bedford," Mev said. Maybe one of them is his mother."

Jake turned the key in the lock, and opened the door.

"This is where Crockett lived," Mev said. "Smells like the dogs lived here too. Leave the door open, Jake."

She took pictures.

They looked around. An old sofa, two old easy chairs, a small television, a coffee table, and a couple of end tables occupied the small living room. A dozen issues of *Recoil Magazine* and one issue of *American Rifleman* lay on the coffee table. Three gun cabinets lined the wall. An oak and glass gun cabinet held rifles and handguns. A steel and glass gun cabinet held an AR-15 semi-automatic rifle and ammunition. A gun locker held three high-powered pistols and ammunition.

"Crockett Wood had enough fire power here for a brigade," Mev said, opening the ammunition drawer." She took more pictures.

"I want to see what he locked up," Jake said, approaching a four-foot-tall safe that stood beside the hearth. "Maybe this key will work. Great. It does."

Jake brought out a file of papers and a manila envelope marked "Cash."

"Let's look at the papers first, Mev."

Mev removed the magazines from the coffee table and spread out the papers.

"I'll take pictures," she said.

In the next few minutes Mev photographed Crockett Boone Wood's certificate of Honorable Discharge from the United States Army for twenty years of service, dated June thirtieth, 1992; Medicare and Social Security documents; a July 2018 statement from a bank in Heron Brook indicating a savings account of approximately thirteen thousand dollars and a checking account of six hundred; a 2017 Georgia kennel license; a Georgia weapons carry license card renewed in 2014, when Wood was clean-shaven; a Georgia lifetime sportsman license; and divorce papers from 1993. And a will.

"Here's his will, Jake. It's homemade, in longhand. Look."

I, Crockett Boone Wood, of Ten Split Road, Heron Brook, Georgia, being of sound mind, write this last will and testament.

I bequeath $4,980 to Ace Melton Barnett (80 Wylie's Road, Heron Brook, Georgia).

I bequeath $1,000 to my twin sister Trudy Lee (Gertrude Lee) Wood (address unknown). If she can't be found in one year's time or if she dies before I die, I bequeath that $1,000 to the Saxxons for America (c/o Ace Melton Barnett, 80 Wylie's Road, Heron Brook, Georgia).

I bequeath $4,000 to my father, Harper B. Wood (Heron Brook Veterans Home, Heron Brook, Georgia). If he dies before I die, I bequeath that $4,000 to the Saxxons for America (c/o Ace Melton Barnett, 80 Wylie's Road, Heron Brook, Georgia).

I bequeath $10 to my ex-wife, Pina Mae Marston Wood (219 Musket Road, Azalea, Georgia). If she dies *before I die, I bequeath that $10 to my cousin, Red Wilker (3950 Black Fox Road, Witherston, Georgia).*

I bequeath the rest of my estate, including whatever property I may own, to the Saxxons for America (c/o Ace Melton Barnett, 80 Wylie's Road, Heron Brook, Georgia).

I want my body to be cremated and my ashes to be scattered on the farm at Ten Split Road, Heron Brook, Georgia. I don't want any funeral.

"He signed his will 'Crockett Boone Wood' and dated it July tenth, 2018. He had two witnesses, Carl Everett Tomson and Lula G. Tomson of six Split Road, Heron Brook. The Tomsons must be his neighbors," Mev said. She took a picture of the will.

"So who's this Ace Melton Barnett? Why don't you google him?"

Mev did. "Here we go, Jake. Ace Melton Barnett does not shun publicity. He wrote letters to the editor of the *Heron Brook Weekly* and the *Atlanta Journal-Constitution.*"

"Why did Crockett will him almost five thousand dollars?"

"Four thousand nine hundred and eighty dollars. That's a strange bequest. Ace Barnett stood to benefit from Crockett's death."

"Let's focus on Crockett for now, Mev. Why do you suppose Crockett moved to Heron Brook after getting out of the army?"

"He got divorced. So he moved in with his father," Mev said.

"Let's see what else he saved for posterity."

The manila envelope marked "Cash" held a US Army Marksman badge and nearly one thousand dollars in fifties.

Jake put the envelope and the file into his briefcase.

"We need to find Trudy Lee Wood, Jake."

"I'll ask the GBI to locate her."

"Let's check out the bedrooms," Mev said.

One bedroom had nothing but a twin bed and mattress. No sheets. The other bedroom had an unmade double bed, a bedside table with a well-thumbed copy of Jared Taylor's book *White Identity*, and a lamp. Mev opened the closet and found plaid shirts, jeans, baseball caps, and a white KKK-style hood and robe. On the robe's red sash was an ironed-on patch of a square white cross with the image of a drop of blood on a circular red background.

Mev pointed to the emblem. "That's a Blood Drop Cross," she said. "It's an insignia of the Klan."

"Somebody's coming," Jake said. "Hear that?"

"It's Catherine," Mev said, looking at the front door.

Catherine Perry-Soto walked in. "Hey, Chief. Hey, Detective Arroyo. I heard you all were here. What's happening?"

"You probably already know, Catherine. You always do," Jake said.

"I'd like to hear your story. Then I'll do some research on my own."

ℰↄℰↄ

After dinner, Lottie brought a pitcher of lemonade over to her niece's porch to get her briefing from Mev. She sat in the rocker, and Mev and Paco sat in the swing. Jaime, Jorge, and Beau sat on the steps tossing tennis balls to the dogs. Mev spoke over the sound of crickets and tree frogs. She told them about Crockett's will.

"Have you ever heard of Ace Melton Barnett, Aunt Lottie?" Mev asked.

"No, I haven't, dear. But I'll investigate."

"Maybe you could check the letters he wrote to the *Heron Brook Weekly* and the *Atlanta Journal-Constitution*. His letters may tell us something about the Saxxons."

"Do you think Crockett Wood was killed because he was a Saxxon, Mom?" Jaime asked.

"We don't know yet. Our first step is to see what's on his cell phone. We'll look at his contacts."

"You and Jake investigate Crockett Wood's murder, Mev. And Beau, Jaime, Jorge, and I will investigate Tyrone Lewis's murder," Lottie said.

"A friend loaned me Witherston High School's yearbook for 1968. It belongs to her grandmother," Beau said. "It has five pictures of Tyrone and seven pictures of Allie. The Movie Club photo shows them together. They were both on the yearbook staff and on the student council."

Beau went inside and came out with the yearbook. He opened it to a photograph of graduating seniors.

"Tyrone was the only black kid in his class," Jaime said.

"Like me," Beau said. He flipped a few pages. "Tyrone was on the varsity basketball team."

"He looks too short to play basketball," Jaime said

"He was my height, five seven," Beau said. "That's what it says here. Maybe he was fast."

"But not fast enough to outrun his killers."

"Allie was yearbook editor. She wrote the preface." Beau put the yearbook on the table for all to read.

Thank you, fellow Bobcats, for choosing me to serve as your 1968 yearbook editor. By the time we look at this book of memories we will be graduating from Witherston High School and going out into the world. What will guide us? Perhaps the wisdom of three recently deceased

Georgia writers will provide a path. I leave you with their thoughts:

> *For fear is a primary source of evil...The xenophobic individual can only reject and destroy, as the xenophobic nation inevitably makes war.*
> ~ *Carson McCullers (1917-1967)*

> *The warped, distorted frame we have put around every Negro child from birth is around every white child also. Each is on a different side of the frame but each is pinioned there. And what cruelly shapes and cripples the personality of one is as cruelly shaping and crippling the personality of the other.*
> ~ *Lillian Smith (1897-1966)*

> *Acceptance of prevailing standards often means we have no standards of our own.*
> ~ *Jean Toomer (1894-1967)*

So farewell, friends. And remember our Bobcat pledge: "To make change for the better."

~ *Allie Marie Camhurst, Class of 1968*

"Wow," Paco exclaimed. "Allie was pushing for civil rights for African Americans."

"She was brave, and she was mature for her age," Lottie said.

"Maybe she was already hanging out with Tyrone."

"In secret. If she was hanging out with Tyrone, she would have had to do it in secret."

"Who gave you the yearbook, Beau?" Jorge asked. "We should interview her grandmother."

"Mona Pattison. Your old girlfriend, Jorge."

"Oh," Jorge said.

"Mrs. Pattison was our second grade teacher, Jorge," Jaime said.

"Oh. Right."

"Mary Lou Pattison is in my book club. I can talk with her," Lottie said. "Shall we go see her together, Beau?"

"Sure. I'm free after school tomorrow."

"I'll call her."

"Okay, Aunt Lottie," Mev said. "You all investigate the 1968 case, and Jake and I'll investigate the 2018 case."

"You said Crockett mentioned a twin sister in his will. What was her name?"

"Trudy Lee. Actually, Gertrude Lee Wood."

"Interesting. She must have been named after her great aunt Gertrude, Obie Wilker's wife and Bullet Wilker's mother. So her father Harper B. Wood and her uncle Bullet Wilker must have stayed close."

"But she and Crockett didn't stay close. Crockett didn't know her address."

"Now isn't that weird! They were twins, and they didn't communicate. I can't imagine Jorge and me not communicating," Jaime said.

"Something must have split them apart," Jorge said. "Maybe their parents favored one over the other."

"Or Crockett did something to Trudy Lee, and she didn't forgive him."

"She's in this yearbook," Beau said. "Here's a picture of her with Crockett at a football game. She was a cheerleader. She was beautiful."

Jorge read over Beau's shoulder. "The caption says, 'The Wood twins.'"

"They both have light eyes."

"Probably blue eyes, and blond or red hair."

"She's tall," Beau said, "almost as tall as her brother."

"But not as skinny."

"We need to find her," Mev said. "But she seems to have disappeared."

"We'll find her, Mev. Everyone leaves tracks," Lottie said.

"Are you going to let Red Wilker know about his cousin's death before he reads Webby Witherston tomorrow?" Paco asked Mev.

"I'll call him right now." Mev went in the house.

ೞೞೞ

Mev reached Red Wilker on his cell phone and told him of his cousin's death.

"I'm sorry to hear that, Mev, truly sorry. Nobody should have to die that way. It's a shame. Truly a shame. But I confess, Crockett and I were not close. Never have been. He's a white supremacist, and I'm not. I've never heard of the Saxxons."

"Have you seen Crockett recently? Or spoken with him?"

"No. I didn't know he was around till I read *Webby Witherston* Sunday morning. And even if I'd have known, I wouldn't have gone to see him."

"Bad blood between you all?"

"That's one way of putting it."

"When did you last see Crockett, Red?"

"Are you interrogating me, Detective Arroyo?"

"No, of course not, Red. If I were interrogating you, I'd come to see you with Chief McCoy. I'm just curious about your last encounter with Crockett."

"That might have been when we graduated from high school."

"From Witherston High? What year did you graduate?"

"1971. I joined the air force that summer and went to Thailand. Crockett married Pina Mae, joined the army, and went to Vietnam. I didn't like Crockett much then, and when he got out of the army, I never went to Dawson County to see him."

"I believe you, Red. Thanks for talking with me."

"I don't know why Crockett was hanging around Witherston. He's got no friends here."

"Good luck with your campaign, Red."

"I bet you're supporting Rhonda," Red replied and disconnected.

☙❧

Mev returned to the porch and reported the phone conversation.

"Do you believe Red, Mev?" Lottie asked "Do you believe that he and his cousin had nothing to do with each other?"

"If they had nothing to do with each other, why did Crockett Wood come here, especially if Mr. Wilker was the only person he knew?" Jorge said.

"And why did Crockett Wood leave ten dollars to Mr. Wilker if he and Mr. Wilker didn't speak?" Beau asked.

"Ten dollars is an insult, Beau," Jorge said.

"Oh."

"Mev, did you tell Red that Crockett mentioned him in his will?"

"I did not. He'll find out in due time."

"What if Mr. Wilker is really a Saxxon too?" Paco said. "No way would he tell us."

"Mr. Wilker is just a right-wing aardvark, Dad," Jorge said, "who likes guns."

"He shot down Mr. Wood's drone," Jaime said.

"Mr. Wilker could have thought he was shooting a big bird, like a hawk or a turkey," Paco said.

"How could Mr. Wilker, the self-acclaimed game hunter, not know it was a drone?" Jorge asked. "Aunt Lottie knew right off."

"Mr. Wilker told me to give the drone to him," Beau said. "Why did he want it?"

"To keep anybody from tracing it to his cousin," Lottie said. "I think he knew more about his cousin than he said."

"Maybe Mr. Wilker killed Mr. Wood because Mr. Wood had something on him," Jorge said.

"Yeah. Maybe Mr. Wilker didn't want Mr. Wood to embarrass him with all that Saxxon stuff," Beau said, "in the middle of his campaign for mayor."

"Beau, can you get us Witherston High School's 1971 yearbook?" Mev asked. "I'd like to see what Crockett Wood did in high school."

"I'll put a classified ad in tomorrow's *Webby Witherston*. I can do it now on my phone."

As Beau pulled his phone out of his pocket, Mev got a call.

"Hi, Catherine," she said. "What's up?"

"Hello, Detective Arroyo. *Webby Witherston* just got an untraceable email. I'll read it to you. 'To the Editor. If Witherston becomes a sanctuary city, Witherstonians will pay for such action, perhaps dearly."

"Jeepers! How was it signed?"

"It was signed, 'A Saxxon.' No name."

"Have you contacted Chief McCoy, Catherine?"

"I've forwarded the email to him. And I also forwarded it to you, Detective Arroyo, but I wanted to call you since you're leading the investigation into Crockett Wood's death."

"Are you going to print the letter?"

"Yes. Of course."

"Thanks for calling me, Catherine." Mev disconnected.

"What did Catherine tell you, Mom?"

Mev opened her email and read Catherine's message aloud.

"Wear your gun, Mevita," Paco said. "You could be in danger."

"So could you, Paco," Mev said. "And so could Beau, and Jaime, and Jorge, and even Lottie."

"Imagine Aunt Lottie with a gun! She'd look like Annie Oakley but more beautiful with silver hair," Jaime said.

"She'd tell the Saxxon, 'Stick 'em up or I'll shoot your brains out,'" Jorge said.

"I'm safe, folks. I'm too long in the tooth," Lottie said.

"Aunt Lottie!"

"What would you do, Mevita, if the Saxxons kidnapped one of the boys? You'd probably do anything they told you to do to get him back."

"That's the point, Paco," Lottie said. "That's the power the kidnapper would have."

CHAPTER 7

WWW. ONLINEWITHERSTON.COM

WITHERSTON ON THE WEB
Wednesday, September 5, 2018

NEWS

Crockett Wood Is Shot Dead in Outhouse

Crockett Boone Wood of Heron Brook, Georgia, was found shot to death at 4200 West Bank Road in Witherston yesterday morning. His body was discovered in his outhouse by Chief Jake McCoy and Detective Mev Arroyo of the Witherston Police. The door had been bolted from the inside.

Chief McCoy said, "The killer stuck a gun through the crescent moon and blew a hole through Wood's heart. Wood didn't have a chance, sitting there with his pants down."

In an initial search of Wood's cabin Detective Arroyo discovered a loaded hunting rifle, a loaded assault rifle, and some fifty four-by-six-inch Saxxons for America flyers.

They also found a DJI Phantom 4 Pro hobby drone kit with the remote control minus the quadcopter.

"Evidently, the missing quadcopter was the one that Red Wilker shot down on Sunday," Detective Arroyo said, "The one that dropped the Saxxon flyers."

Dawson County records show that Crockett Wood resided on a twenty-acre farm owned by his father Harper B. Wood at 10 Split Road in Heron Brook, Georgia, from February of 1993 through the present. His closest neighbor a half-mile up the road, Carl Tomson, said that Crockett Wood bred bullmastiffs for sale. He said that Wood worked in construction and drove a black Dodge Ram. He said that until this past year Wood's father lived with him on the farm.

A black Dodge Ram, registered to Crockett Boone Wood, was found parked behind the Witherston cabin at 4200 West Bank Road in Witherston. A large puppy, possibly a bullmastiff, was found shot to death nearby. On his collar was a tag with the name Bedford.

Wood's arrest record includes several DUIs and two assault charges. In September of 1992 Crockett Wood was arrested in Atlanta for second-degree domestic assault but acquitted when his spouse, Pina Mae Marston Wood, declined to press charges. More recently he was charged with DUI on two separate occasions and assault causing bodily injury on one occasion.

Crockett Wood also had a history of arrests at white pride marches outside Georgia. On July 4, 2012, he was arrested at Saxxons for America protest march against DACA (Deferred Action for Childhood Arrivals policy) in Gainesville, Georgia, for shooting a semi-automatic pistol into the air. On July 18, 2015, he was arrested at a Ku Klux Klan march in Columbia, South Carolina, for as-

saulting a policeman. On August 12, 2017, he was arrested at the "Unite the Right" torch rally in Charlottesville, Virginia, for striking a black woman who carried a "Black Lives Matter" sign.

Catherine Perry-Soto, Editor

Crockett Boone Wood Leaves Bequest to Saxxons

*Crockett Boone Wood, shot to death on Labor Day
on his father's property at 4200 West Bank Road, bequeathed a portion of his estate to the Saxxons for America, c/o Ace Melton Barnett of Heron Brook, Georgia.*

*Wood also made bequests to Ace Melton Barnett of
Heron Brook Georgia ($4,980), his father Harper B.
Wood of Heron Brook ($4,000), and his twin sister Ger-
trude Lee Wood "address unknown" ($1,000). He left
$10 to his ex-wife Pina Mae Marston Wood, should she
survive him. If she predeceased him, he specified that the
$10 should go to his cousin Red Wilker.*

Ace Melton Barnett is treasurer of the Saxxons.

*Chief Jake McCoy and Detective Mev Arroyo dis-
covered Wood's hand-written will in a search of Wood's
Heron Brook home.*

Catherine Perry-Soto, Editor

---

*Witherston Roundtable Endorses Red Wilker for
Mayor*

The Witherston Round Table endorsed Red Wilker for mayor at its monthly luncheon yesterday, according to Roundtable president Trevor Bennington, Jr.

Red Wilker is a member of the Roundtable, as is Mayor Rich Rather. Rhonda Rather, who is Red Wilker's opponent, is not.

The endorsement followed speeches by the two candidates: Rhonda Rather spoke in favor of the sanctuary city, and Red Wilker spoke in opposition to it.

Interviewed afterwards, Wilker said, "Do Witherston's school children want to sit beside illegal aliens who can't speak English, who don't know how to read or write, who will bring crime to our town? Do Witherston's parents want to support illegal aliens who've committed rape and murder? I don't think so. As mayor, I will look out for Witherstonians and nobody else."

When told of Wilker's statement Rhonda Rather said only, "Bless his heart, Red Wilker has no capacity for empathy."

Catherine Perry-Soto, Editor

Saxxons Use Extortion to Stop Sanctuary City

Witherston on the Web received a letter to the editor threatening harm to Witherston if our Town Council does not cancel plans to become a sanctuary city. After consultation with Chief Jake McCoy, I decided to publish it. See Letters to the Editor.

Catherine Perry-Soto, Editor

Crockett Wood Had White Supremacist History

As reported at the time in the Atlanta Constitution, the late Crockett Boone Wood and five other former members of the Ku Klux Klan founded the white supremacist organization Saxxons for America on Labor Day, September 7, 1992, on Stone Mountain, fifteen miles east of downtown Atlanta.

In a salute to the Klan, which had been reconstituted on Stone Mountain in 1915, the Saxxons met on the north face of the granite dome, above the relief sculpture of Jefferson Davis, Robert E. Lee, and Stonewall Jackson.

Wood became the first president of the organization. Upon his election Wood stated, "Saxxons for America will restore the white Anglo-Saxon culture that the Pilgrims established on our continent four hundred years ago. We will spell 'Saxon' with an additional X to symbolize the cross."

The organization is rumored to have as many as two hundred members across Georgia, Tennessee, and North Carolina. With the exception of its leaders, the organization's membership has been kept secret.

Amadahy Henderson, Reporter

NORTH GEORGIA IN HISTORY
By Charlotte Byrd

Gertrude Wilker's diary chronicles the incipient influence of film on American values. On Sunday, September 21, Gertrude Wilker wrote:

Last Thursday we heard horns and shots all

across the valley meaning revenuers were around.
So on Friday Obie loaded our wagon with whis-
key and took me and Boone and Geraldine and
our babies to Dahlonega to celebrate my nine-
teenth birthday and show Buehler and Harper B
to my parents. Obie wanted me to deliver the
whiskey to my father who just bought a model t
with Uncle Rosco so they could run their whiskey
to Atlanta. They are runners now.

On Saturday we left Buehler and Harper B
with my mother and went and saw The Birth of a
Nation at the movie theater. It showed how the Ku
Klux Klan saved white people from dangerous
Negroes. Geraldine and I thought the movie was
scary but Obie and Boone liked it. Lillian Gish
who is the star is beautiful. Boone said the movie
proved we wouldn't be poor if the South had won
the war and the Negroes hadn't took over.

Gertrude Wilker is referring to the way moonshiners
warned each other that IRS agents were in the vicinity.
One agent complained that every time he got close to a
still the mountains suddenly echoed with gunshots, horns,
and cowbells. Not the sound of music. The moonshiners
had each other's back.

D.W. Griffith's "Birth of a Nation," which came out
in February of 1915, inspired William J. Simmons to re-
vive the almost defunct Ku Klux Klan in November of that
year. The movie, a three-hour blockbuster, was based on
"The Clansmen: A Historical Romance of the Ku Klux
Klan," a novel which Thomas Dixon, Jr., published in
1905 and adapted into a play. Dixon has been quoted as
saying,

My object is to teach the north, the young

*north, what it has never known—the awful suf-
fering of the white man during the dreadful reconstruction period. I believe that Almighty God
anointed the white men of the south by their suffering during that time immediately after the
Civil War to demonstrate to the world that the
white man must and shall be supreme.*

*The "first era" Ku Klux Klan, formed in Tennessee
in 1865 to return white supremacy to the South during
Reconstruction, used violence against Negroes and their
sympathizers but did not use the fiery cross or the white
robe and hood. The "second era" KKK, formed in 1915,
adopted the movie's fiery cross as their symbol and the
white robe and hood as their costume.*

OBITUARY

Crockett Harper Wood
1953-2018

*Crockett Boone Wood, age sixty-five, of Heron
Brook, Georgia, died on September 3, 2018, in Witherston on family property at 4200 West Bank Road.*

*Crockett Wood, son of Harper B. Wood and the Ella
Crockett Wood and grandson of Boone Wood and Ger-
aldine Harper Wood, all of Lumpkin County, was born in
Dahlonega on August 8, 1953.*

*Crockett Wood is survived by his father Harper B.
Wood of Heron Brook, Georgia, possibly his twin sister
Gertrude Lee Wood (whereabouts unknown), and his
second cousin Red Wilker of Witherston.*

Crockett Wood graduated from Witherston High School in 1971. He married Pina Mae Marston that June. They had no children and were divorced in 1992.

Crockett Wood joined the United States Army in August of 1971. He retired as a Master Sergeant with an honorable discharge after twenty years. Army records show that Wood served tours of duty in Vietnam, Lebanon, El Salvador, and Kuwait. He possessed a Marksman badge, signifying top-level expertise as an Army sharpshooter.

In his will Wood requested that his body be cremated and that there be no funeral service.

Amadahy Henderson, Reporter

ANNOUNCEMENT

The Witherston Town Council will meet in the mayor's conference room at City Hall at 8:00 p.m. tomorrow night.

Atsadi Moon, Chair of the Witherston Town Council

LETTERS TO THE EDITOR

To the Editor:
If Witherston becomes a sanctuary city, Witherstonians will pay for such action, perhaps dearly.
A Saxxon
Georgia

WEATHER

More sunshine—here, there, and everywhere. More sunshine in Witherston and Atlanta and Washington DC and Mexico City.

High today in Witherston will be eight-two degrees. Low tonight will be sixty-one degrees.

Good morning, sunshine.

Tony Lima, Meteorólogo

CLASSIFIEDS

Wanted to borrow: Witherston High School Year-book of 1971. Contact Beau Lodge, beau-lodge2001@gmail.com

಄಄಄

Lottie called out to Mev as Mev was getting into her car. The sun had just risen.

"Good morning, dear," she said. "You've seen to-day's letter to the editor from the Saxxon? It looks to me like a threat."

"To me too, Aunt Lottie. That's why I'm going to the station early today. Jake and I are thinking that the Saxxon is Ace Melton Barnett, who was mentioned in Crockett's will. We need to locate him."

"Maybe you all are thinking of Ace Melton Barnett because he's the only Saxxon whose name you know. Anyway, I've been thinking. Jaime, Jorge, and Beau may

have invited some trouble for themselves by visiting
Crockett Wood's cabin. I have three key chain siren
alarms which I'd like to give them."

Lottie handed Mev a baggie with three alarms, green
and blue and yellow.

"Thanks so much, Aunt Lottie. But keep one for
yourself."

"I've kept a purple one for myself."

❦❦❦

After Mev had left, Lottie went to her computer. She
googled Ace Melton Barnett and found two letters.

On October 26, 2016, during Donald Trump's campaign for the presidency, Barnett had published a letter to
the editor of the *Atlanta Journal-Constitution*.

To the Editor:
Make America great again. That is why patriots
should vote for Donald J. Trump for president.

Donald J. Trump sides with those of us loyal to the
country true Americans fought to establish in the Ameri-
can Revolutionary War. What kind of country was that? It
was Christian and white. It was "great."

Miscegenation, which is interbreeding among the
races, caused America's decline. When America allowed
in "the tired, the poor, the huddled masses, and the
wretched refuse of other nations," America started turn-
ing brown, and America spiraled downward.

A vote for Donald J. Trump is a vote for a wall to
keep the wretched refuse out of our country.

Take America back.
Ace Barnett
Heron Brook

Barnett's letter elicited the following response on September 28.

To the Editor:

Do white supremacist Ace Barnett and his billionaire hero Donald J. Trump think they were chosen by God to be white and not brown? Do they think they were chosen by God to be born in America and not Mexico? Do they think they were chosen by God to be Christian and not Muslim?

Do they think they were chosen by God to have power over others, power over brown people and black people, power over women, power over the disabled, power over the poor? Do they think God approves of their using their power to cause hardship to others not white, American, Christian, male, and able?

I would like for Ace Barnett and Donald J. Trump to answer these questions.

Janet Ullmann
Atlanta

"Now who could this Janet Ullmann be who writes such good letters to the editor?" Lottie asked herself. She googled Janet Ullmann and found an item in the *Atlanta Constitution* from October 1, 1975.

Weller's Manager Cleared of Rape Charge

Howard ("Howie") Hedge, Manager of Weller's Wine and Oyster Bar at 418 Cotton Farm Circle in Atlanta, has been cleared of the charge that he raped one of his waitresses on the evening of July 4, 1975.

Janet Ullmann, who was twenty-one years of age at the time, reported to police that Hedge, her boss, had raped her in the back of his van after taking her to view the Fourth-of-July fireworks on Stone Mountain.

Hedge said that Ullmann had initiated the sexual encounter and had not resisted him.

In the absence of evidence to substantiate Ullmann's claim, Gwinnett County Superior Court Judge Albert Pate dismissed the case.

Hedge has fired Ullmann for her false accusation.

"Poor girl. That must have been a formative experience," Lottie said aloud.

Lottie clicked on a letter to the editor of the *Atlanta Journal-Constitution* Janet Ullmann had written on September 12, 2016.

To the Editor:

Mrs. Phyllis Schlafly has died at the age of ninety-two.

Mrs. Phyllis Schlafly said, "Men hardly ever ask sexual favors of women from whom the certain answer is No. Virtuous women are seldom accosted by unwelcome sexual propositions or familiarities, obscene talk or profane language."

Mrs. Phyllis Schlafly, a white, healthy, wealthy, well-educated, famous woman with a rich husband and six children, opposed abortion. She must have assumed that "virtuous women" never needed one. I assume that she never needed one.

Mrs. Phyllis Schlafly must never have been raped, must never have been forced to accept sexual advances from a man with power over her life, must never have suffered the humiliation of being disbelieved because she was a woman.

Mrs. Phyllis Schlafly also said, "It's very healthy for a young girl to be deterred from promiscuity by fear of

contracting a painful, incurable disease, or cervical can-
cer, or sterility, or the likelihood of giving birth to a
dead, blind or brain-damage baby."

Did Mrs. Phyllis Schlafly believe that sterility, dis-
ease, and tragic fetal disorders were God's punishment
for women less "virtuous" than she?

If there were a God, Mrs. Phyllis Schlafly would
have died long ago.

Janet Ullmann
Atlanta

"Well done, Janet Ullmann! We are kindred spirits."

Lottie went back to her research for Mev. She found
the letter Ace Barnett wrote to *The Heron Brook Weekly*
on Friday, September 15, 2014.

To the Editor:
Today is the ninetieth birthday of World War II Ma-
rine veteran Lance Corporal Harper B. Wood, not only
the best mechanic Dixie Speedway ever had but also the
greatest patriot still alive in our community. Harper B
proudly killed more than a dozen Japs in the battle of Iwo
Jima in February, 1945. He stayed in the Marines until
1964. Now he lives at the Heron Brook Veterans Home.

Harper B's son Crockett and I invite Harper B's
friends to celebrate Harper B's birthday tonight at five
o'clock in the pasture behind my house at 80 Wylie's
Road. Crockett and I will provide beer.

I will fly the American flag on my mail box, not just
for Harper B but for all the other patriotic vets in Heron
Brook who have fought for America. Sergeant Crockett
Wood also has many kills to his credit, and so do I.

Corporal Ace Barnett
Heron Brook

ဢၹ

Jake called Mev into his office.

"Look here, Mev," Jake said, staring at his computer screen. "Dirk just emailed us Crockett Wood's preliminary autopsy report. And it's very interesting."

Mev read the report over Jake's shoulder.

Dirk Wales, M.D.
Lumpkin County Coroner
Chestatee Regional Hospital
227 Mountain Drive
Dahlonega, GA 30533

September 5, 2018

PRELIMINARY AUTOPSY REPORT
Crockett Boone Wood, age sixty-five

At 9:30 a.m. on Tuesday, September 4, 2018, Chief Jake McCoy and Detective Mev Arroyo of the Witherston Police Department discovered the body of Crockett Boone Wood in a locked outhouse at 4200 West Bank Road in Witherston.

The body was taken by ambulance to the Chestatee Regional Hospital where a routine autopsy was performed by Dr. John Morston, pathologist.

According to Dr. Morston, the deceased, a Caucasian male, six feet, one inch tall and 175 pounds, died of a gunshot wound to the heart on Monday, September third between 6:00 a.m. and 10:00 a.m.

Dr. Morston reported that the deceased was suffering from early stage pancreatic cancer.

Dr. Morston noted three tattoos: On the deceased's right shoulder, the Celtic Cross; on his chest, the number 8122017, and on his back, the words "We must secure the existence of our people and a future for white children. "

Dirk Wales, MD
Coroner

"Pancreatic cancer is usually fatal. Crockett Wood was dying," Jake said. "Maybe that was why he returned to Witherston."

"Out of nostalgia? Crockett doesn't seem the nostalgic type, Jake. What else could have been his motive?"

"To harm his cousin Red when Red's running for mayor?"

"Or to hassle us when we're about to make Witherston a sanctuary city."

"Crockett must have known he was dying. So he had nothing to lose. What do you make of his tattoos?"

"The Celtic Cross is obvious," Mev said. "The white supremacists adopted it to mean white pride. And the words on his back are the 'Fourteen Words' that are the slogan of the white nationalist movement."

"What could the numbers mean? Eight million, one hundred twenty-two thousand, seventeen."

"Let's see. Seven digits. Eight, one, two, two, zero, one, seven."

"Sounds like a phone number, Mev. Eight one two dash two zero one seven."

"Without the area code, we'll never track it down," Mev said.

"Two zero one seven is twenty seventeen. Maybe it's a date."

"Eight dash twelve dash twenty seventeen. That would be August twelfth, 2017. Yes, it's a date, Jake! The date of the "Unite the Right" rally in Charlottesville."

"That date must have meant a lot to Crockett," Jake said.

"How discouraging. Crockett wore the date on his body as a badge of honor. To him, that date must have signified the largest show of white pride in his lifetime. To the rest of us, that date signifies the white supremacist assault on Charlottesville."

"And a white supremacist's murder of Heather Heyer."

"And maybe the moment our country officially recognized the danger white supremacists still pose to our democracy. I guess history is in the eye of the beholder," Mev said. "We need to know more about Crockett's past, Jake. Would you like to drive back to Heron Brook this morning to interview his father? We should inform him of his son's death anyway."

"And you and I need to talk about the Saxxon's letter to the editor."

John Hicks walked into Jake's office with the drone's monitor. "Do you all have time to see the video? It's in two segments."

"Of course."

For the next fifteen minutes, Mev, Jake, and John Hicks watched a movie of Witherston shot from the air. The movie took them from Saloli Stream over Founding Father's Creek to Mev's house, across town to the Lodges' house where Jim Lodge was mowing his lawn until he looked up, and east on Black Fox Road to a large ranch house with a couple of German Shepherds in a chain link enclosure."

"That's Red Wilker's place," Jake commented. "And now the drone's going north up Hiccup Hill."

"There's Tayanita Village," John Hicks said. "See Grass and Weed? There's Amadahy with Franny. She's spotted the drone. Oh, she took a picture! Here comes Atsadi."

Then the video cut off. John Hicks pushed the PLAY button again. "Now you'll see what getting shot down feels like," he said.

In the second segment they got an overview of the parade line-up on the Grays' pasture, a close-up of the KNN float on which Beau and Sally were seated cross-legged on the truck bed holding hands, the Grays' red barn, and the Grays' white farmhouse. Above the farm-house the image suddenly turned into a swirl of colors for a few seconds before they got a long close-up of a ripe zucchini on red soil. Beau's face suddenly appeared on-screen. Then nothing.

"Crockett Wood was looking for something," Mev said. "If he'd just wanted to look at Witherston, he would have videotaped our courthouse and the Witherston Bap-tist Church."

"He was not a tourist," Jake said.

⚜

Mev and Jake rang the bell of apartment thirty-eight at the Heron Brook Veterans Home shortly before lunchtime. They showed their credentials and introduced themselves to the nurse who opened the door.

"We're here to see Mr. Wood," Jake said.

"How do you do? I'm Priscilla," she said. "Nice to meet you, Chief McCoy, Detective Arroyo. Come in."

Priscilla ushered them into the bedroom, where a very elderly man lay sleeping in a hospital bed. On the bedside table was a telephone and a framed photograph of Crockett Wood holding a hunting rifle.

Catherine Perry-Soto stood at Harper B. Wood's bedside.

"Hello, Chief McCoy, Detective Arroyo," Catherine said. "I got here a few minutes ago."

"Hello there, Catherine," Mev said. "Why should we not be surprised that you beat us here?"

"Has Mr. Wood spoken to you yet?" Jake asked her.

"No, not yet."

"And he may not," the nurse said. "I just gave him a sedative after breakfast. He was upset about his son's death. He was screaming. He's not right in his head anymore."

"How did he find out about Crockett's death?"

"Somebody called him a couple of hours ago. He answered the phone, so I don't know who it was. He didn't say anything. He just hung up."

"Who might it have been?" Mev asked her.

"It might have been his ex-daughter-in-law, Pina Mae, who was probably glad Crockett was dead. She hated Crockett, but she did call Mr. Wood every now and then. Or it might have been his race-car buddy Ace Barnett. Or it might have been his daughter, who called him Sunday morning."

"Trudy Lee Wood?"

"Yes. Trudy got Mr. Wood real mad. He screamed, 'You be damned! Go whine to Crockett. He's in Witherston right now!'"

"And Trudy might have been the one to call him today?"

"Possibly."

"What did Trudy look like?" Mev asked.

"Does Mr. Wood have a picture of her?" Catherine asked.

"I never laid eyes on her since she never came here," Priscilla answered. "And Mr. Wood doesn't have a picture of her. But she's been sending him money since he turned ninety, fifty dollars in cash every few months. No return address on the envelopes. Just the name Trudy Wood."

"Did Mr. Wood have any visitors?"

"Crockett came a couple times once a month and called him a couple times a week. And Mr. Barnett came every two or three months. Mr. Wood and Mr. Barnett talked about race cars."

Harper B. Wood opened his eyes. "Who are you?" he screamed at Jake. "What are you doing here?"

"I'm Chief Jake McCoy, of the Witherston Police Department. This is Detective Mev Arroyo. And this is Catherine Perry-Soto, our friend. We've come to offer our condolences for the death of your son Crockett."

"The police? You can't arrest me!" Wood screamed. "I'm ninety-four years old! You're too late!" He laughed loudly. "Where's Crockett?"

"Crockett has died, Mr. Wood," Mev said gently. "That's why we came. We're not here to arrest you, or anybody."

"Crockett is not dead! He came by last week. He brought me whiskey. Where's my whiskey? Nurse!"

"What did you and Crockett talk about?" Catherine asked.

"About his dogs, like we always do. He brings me whiskey, and we talk about his dogs. He raises dogs for protection, guard dogs. They weigh a hundred pounds. He would have been killed a long time ago if he hadn't had his guard dogs. And his guns."

"Why would Crockett have been killed?" Mev asked.

"There are people out there who will kill you and steal everything you have. They would have killed me too if I hadn't had my guns. Nurse! Where's my gun?"

"Why would you have been killed, Mr. Wood?" Catherine asked.

"I ain't talking to you anymore, lady. Not to you either, mister police chief. Not to anybody. You all get out of here. Leave me alone!"

Wood closed his eyes.

"Time for us to go," Jake said. "Thanks, Priscilla."

Priscilla accompanied Mev, Jake, and Catherine out of the apartment.

"Mr. Wood had a trophy on his shelf," Mev said. "Did you all notice it?"

"It's a Dixie Speedway trophy. Mr. Wood won a race there in 1970, just two years after the speedway opened," Priscilla said. "I'm surprised he didn't tell you about it."

"So he was a driver," Jake said. "Is that how he earned his living?"

"No, he earned his living as a pit stop mechanic at the speedway," Priscilla said. "When he got too old for the races he opened a car repair shop here in Heron Brook with his son Crockett."

"How long has he had dementia?" Mev asked.

"For a year, maybe? In the last few months he's been going downhill fast."

"Here's my card, Priscilla," Mev said. "Call me if you remember anything useful to us."

"I wonder why he thought we'd come to arrest him," Mev said to Jake and Catherine as they walked back to their cars.

"Mr. Wood is paranoid," Catherine said.

"He's not right in his head," Jake said.

"What did Crockett Wood's autopsy report say?" Catherine asked Jake. "I understand you got it this morning."

Jake told her.

CHAPTER 8

Wednesday Afternoon and Evening:

As she always did on her way back from her mailbox, Lottie tossed the catalogs, the credit card offers, and the pizza ads into the recycle bin by her back door. Often that was all the mail she had. Today, however, she took into her house a large manila envelope with a handwritten personal address and no return address. She sat down by Doolittle's perch and opened it.

The envelope contained a handwritten letter and eight newspaper clippings. She read the letter first.

Sunday, September 2, 2018
Dear Dr. Byrd,
I am writing you because you and Beau Lodge are investigating the crime that defined my life. I want to help you.

I was Allie Marie Camhurst, the girl who witnessed the murder of Tyrone Lincoln Lewis on Sunday, September 1, 1968. I say "was" because I changed my name.

Even at the age of sixty-eight I remember the event vividly, not only because Klansmen stabbed Tyrone to death in front of my eyes but also because their sons each raped me. I was pregnant. That night, with the help of my best friend Mary Lou Reynolds (now Pattison), I escaped to Atlanta. Tyrone's father helped me "disappear."

I gave birth to Tyrone's son Link in February of 1969. I've never gotten married, but I've become a grandmother. Link and his wife Sadie have two boys.

This morning I learned three things from Wither-ston's online newspaper that prompted me to write you and Beau Lodge. I learned that somebody is occupying a cabin belonging to Harper B. Wood on West Bank Road, and I suspect it's his son Crockett. I learned that Crock-ett's cousin Red Wilker is running for mayor. And I learned that you and Beau Lodge are looking into Ty-rone's murder. So I want to identify Tyrone's killers and my rapists.

Tyrone's killers were Bullet Wilker and Harper B. Wood. My rapists were their sons, Red Wilker and Crockett Wood. I got this information from Crockett's twin sister, who is hiding in Atlanta like me and for simi-lar reasons. (Red Wilker raped her on the night she graduated from high school. She got pregnant and had an illegal abortion that left her unable to bear children.)

If something should happen to me, I want you to take this letter to the police. And something could very well happen to me.

Two weeks ago, I went with four African American friends to Trappersville, Tennessee, where the city gov-ernment was taking down a statue of the Confederate general Nathan Bedford Forrest. My friends knew that some white supremacists known as Saxxons would be there to protest. Sure enough, the Saxxons were there, carrying torches. I carried a sign that said "Nathan Bed-

ford Forrest committed hate crimes." One of the Saxxons grabbed the sign and got in my face. Although he was wearing a hood I recognized him by his blue eyes. And he, Crockett Wood, recognized me. Now Crockett knows I'm alive. Unfortunately, I was wearing my Timber College T-shirt. (A year ago I retired from the Timber College Campus Police.) I fear Crockett will be able to track me down. So now I have to take action.

If Crockett is in Witherston, watch out. Crockett is a dangerous man. I hope he won't find Mary Lou. At least he may not know her married name.

Feel free to use these clippings as you see fit. But please keep this letter confidential until you can use it to convict Crockett and Red.

Red Wilker and Crockett Wood must pay for their crimes.

By the way, I like your column, Dr. Byrd.
Sincerely yours,
Allie Marie Camhurst

"Oh, Lordy," Lottie said to herself. "Red is a rapist!"
"Oh, Lordy," Doolittle said.
"What do I do, Doolittle?"
Lottie laid out the newspaper clippings on her dining room table. The headlines told a story.

Klansmen Murder Teenager in Witherston, Atlanta Constitution, *September 3, 1968;*
Witherston Marks First Anniversary of KKK Murder, Witherston Weekly, *September 5, 1969;*
Georgia Man Jailed for Assault on Black Mechanic at Dixie Speedway, Florida Times-Union, *February 19, 1971,* on which Allie had highlighted the name *Harper B. Wood;*
Crockett Boone Wood Arrested for Domestic Vio-

lence, Atlanta Journal, *September 10, 1992;*

"Saxxons Protest Obama's Election," Gainesville Times, November 8, 2008;

Cheers, Jeers Greet Klan Rally in Nahunta, Florida Times-Union, *February 20, 2010,* to which Allie had affixed a post-it note saying *I went to protest the Klan rally and support Latino immigrants;*

Saxxons for America Resist DACA, Confederate News, *August 5, 2017; and*

White Supremacist Justifies "Unite the Right' Demonstration, USA Today, *August 13, 2017.*

In the *USA Today* article, Allie had highlighted a paragraph:

Interviewed after his arrest, Crockett B. Wood of Heron Brook, Georgia, said, "We must secure the existence of our people and a future for white children." Wood was quoting the infamous "Fourteen Words" coined by white supremacist David Eden Lane, who derived them from Hitler's Mein Kampf.

"Lordy, Lordy," Lottie groaned. "Maybe Allie killed Crockett."

Lottie read through every article. Instinctively, she picked up her phone to call Mev and then realized she didn't want to tell Mev about Allie's letter, at least not yet. Allie was safe from Crockett now, but not from Red. Crockett might have told Red that he'd seen her. Lottie would keep Allie's secret.

Lottie went to the *Trappersville Daily News* website and found the article she was seeking.

Saxxons for America Invade Trappersville

Yesterday, August eighteenth, a group of twenty

white-robed and hooded individuals who identified them-selves as Saxxons for America gathered on the court-house steps to protest the removal of the statue of Gen-eral Nathan Bedford Forrest.

They were met by some fifty supporters of the city's decision.

When Trappersville police attempted to disband the crowd, one of the Saxxons threw a teargas grenade at Mayor Chad Eberly and the members of the Chamber of Commerce, who were on the stage.

Police arrested Crockett Boone Wood from Georgia for illegal use of tear gas and fined him $1,000.

೧೫೧೫೧

At four o'clock, Lottie and Beau seated themselves in rockers on Mary Lou Pattison's screened porch. Mary Lou brought out iced tea and seated herself on the swing. From her house halfway up the slope of Saloli Mountain they had a good view of Witherston.

"Wow, Mrs. Pattison," Beau said, looking through her binoculars, "You can see my house from here. Look, Dr. Byrd. You can see yours." Beau handed Lottie the binoculars.

"You can even see Mr. Wood's cabin on the banks of Saloli Stream," Lottie said. "And his outhouse."

"Did you see Mr. Wood's killer shoot him?" Beau asked Mary Lou.

"No, Beau, I didn't. I spend more time gazing into hawks' nests than into human homes. But I did know Crockett Wood in high school, very slightly. He was a freshman on the basketball team when I was a senior. I remember him as tall for his age.

"What do you remember about Allie Camhurst, Mary Lou?"

"Allie was my best friend. She'd been my best friend since elementary school. We watched movies together, we listened to music together, we both played in the band, we read the same books. I felt lost without her."

"Has she contacted you to say she's alive, Mrs. Pattison?"

"Not in years, Beau. Not in twenty years. I guess I don't know much about her anymore."

"Can you tell us what you do know, Mary Lou?" Lottie asked.

Mary Lou hesitated. "I swore to her that I'd never tell, but she may be dead by now. And she would want me to help you solve the case. I remember that awful night vividly. My parents and I lived on Billy Barton Road less than a mile from Orchard Road Bridge. I was alone in the house because my parents had gone to Savannah for the week. About five-thirty, Allie banged on the back door screaming for me. Her clothes were bloody. She was hysterical. She told me that the KKK had murdered Tyrone and raped her. She said they'd be looking to kill her and she needed to get out of Witherston.

"I gave her a bath, dressed her in my clothes, and cut her hair to make her look different. She took her money from the glove compartment of her car, about two thousand dollars, and put it in her suitcase. She didn't want to take her car. She said if she took her car, she could not disappear. She said she had to disappear. She asked me to take her to Gainesville where she could get a bus and to not tell anybody that she'd seen me, not my parents, not her father, not the police, not anybody. She made me swear to keep her secret. I drove her to Gainesville to catch the eight forty-five bus to Atlanta."

"Did Allie tell you where in Atlanta she was going, Mrs. Pattison?"

"She said she knew somebody in Atlanta who would put her up. On Tuesday, she phoned me. She asked me again not to tell anybody she was alive. I pledged not to tell. 'Let them think I'm dead,' she said. She told me her life was in danger. She wouldn't give me her phone number, but she promised to write me if I got a post office box in Dahlonega and if I would keep her correspondence absolutely confidential. I told her I'd get a post office box the next day and that I wouldn't tell a soul that she and I were in touch. She called me on Friday to give me her post office box number and to get mine. She said when I wrote her, I should address the envelope to 'Boxholder.'"

"Why was her life in danger?" Beau asked.

"She thought Tyrone's murderers would murder her if they found her because she was a witness."

"Did Allie know who they were, Mary Lou?"

"She didn't tell me. Not then, anyway. She was really scared."

"What happened to Allie's car?" Beau asked.

"The police came and searched it. They found Allie's purse in the glove compartment. Since Allie didn't take the purse or her car, the police thought she was probably dead. I lied to the police and told them I hadn't seen Allie. And I cried a lot. I guess I could have gone to jail for deceiving the police."

"So did Allie write you, Mrs. Pattison?"

"Yes, she did, Beau. She wrote me beautiful letters."

"Do you still have them?"

"Yes, I do. I kept every single one."

"May we see them?"

"I don't know, Beau. I just don't know," Mary Lou said. "Fifty years ago, I swore to Allie that I'd never reveal what I knew, and now here I am talking to you. But I don't feel that I'm betraying Allie. She would want that crime to be solved, even though the killers are probably dead."

"Is it more important to keep Allie's secrets or to find Tyrone's killers? We may be able to do that if you show us her letters," Beau said.

"I know. I tell you what. Let's look at the yearbook now, and we can look at Allie's letters another day."

Beau opened the yearbook to its title page: *THE BOB-CATS' ROAR, EDITED BY ALLIE MARIE CAMHURST, CLASS OF 1968.* Allie had inscribed it in green ink.

To my dearest friend Mary Lou. I hope that we will never be apart and that we will keep our confidences forever. I will keep yours and you will keep mine. You are the only one who knows what I have lived through this year. Thank you for all those times when only you understood. Strawberry fields forever. Love, Allie ~ May 1, 1968

P.S. Never forget Amicalola Falls!!!

"What had she lived through, Mrs. Pattison?"

"I guess I can tell you, since he's dead. The truth is that Allie suffered abuse from her father. We didn't call it abuse then, but we'd call it abuse now, pure and simple verbal abuse. Nobody would have believed that Reverend Camhurst, who preached the teachings of Christ on Sunday morning, would go home and berate his daughter on Sunday night. He berated her for just about everything she said or did. He scolded her for wearing mini-skirts. He grounded her for organizing a demonstration against the Vietnam War. He took away her guitar for singing Pete Seeger's song 'Bring 'Em Home' at a school assembly. He got furious when he found her reading James Baldwin's *The Fire Next Time*."

"I read that book," Beau said.

"Allie's father tore up that book," Mary Lou said. "He also took away her Gene McCarthy T-shirt and called Gene McCarthy a communist. He called Martin Luther King a communist and forbade her going to Atlanta for the funeral procession."

"I went," Lottie said. "So did my father."

"Your father must have been the polar opposite of Allie's father. The only reason her father attended her graduation, Allie said, was that she was giving the valedictorian's speech and his parishioners expected him to be there. I'll never forget the last sentence of her speech: 'When you go out into the world, remember that everybody you meet, no matter what race, has the same feelings you have.' Reverend Camhurst scolded her afterward for, as he said, advocating racial egalitarianism."

"Heavens," Lottie said. "I was doing everything Allie was doing then, except that my parents were proud of me. And I was not valedictorian."

"Allie was smart, really smart. She was our class's leader in every way. Allie led us to question authority, all authority. From President Johnson to Governor Maddox to her father. She encouraged us to challenge our parents' views on race, sex, and religion. She was critical of the South from the time we saw *Black Like Me* in Dahlonega when we were freshmen in high school."

"I remember those days, Mary Lou. Our consciousness was raised by the war. We were radicalized."

"I think of that period as the most intellectually exciting time of my entire life," Mary Lou said. "I owe that to Allie."

"What did Allie mean by 'Never forget Amicalola Falls?'" Beau asked.

"Have you ever hiked the trail up to Amicalola Falls, Beau?"

"Yes, Jaime and Jorge and I hiked it in July."

"I had always wanted to hike it, so one Saturday in April, Jim Hopwood, who was my boyfriend then, and Allie and I hiked up. We picnicked on the rocks by the falls and smoked marijuana for the first time. At least it was the first time for Allie and me. What a glorious adventure that was!"

For another half hour Beau, Lottie, and Mary Lou pored over the yearbook, looking for photographs of Allie, Tyrone, and Mary Lou.

"Here's a picture of Allie and me and our friends in the Movie Club. Tyrone is standing by Allie."

"You were Mary Lou Reynolds?"

"Yes, Beau. I was Mary Lou Reynolds then. I met Wally Pattison at the University of Georgia, and we got married right before graduation. We came back to Witherston because Wally was going to Vietnam and I wanted to stay with my parents. They didn't know it then but I was already pregnant with Jack."

"Who is Mona's father," Lottie said.

"Tyrone was popular," Beau observed. "He was elected president of his senior class."

"Right, he was popular. He was everybody's favorite black boy. But since there were no black girls Tyrone couldn't date. In March, I think it was, Allie invited Tyrone to eat with her in the cafeteria. Nobody thought anything about it because they were both on the yearbook staff. Then they started going out with each other secretly. I may have been the only one who knew they were together before graduation. She would never have told her father."

"Allie was pretty. She could have dated anybody, and she chose Tyrone. She must have been really nice. You were pretty too, Mrs. Pattison. How did you and Allie get that long, straight hair?"

"Allie's blonde hair was naturally straight. Mine, as

you can imagine, was dark and naturally wavy, so Allie would iron it for me. I wanted to look like Joan Baez. Allie wanted to look like Mary Travers."

"Who were they?" Beau asked.

Lottie rolled her eyes.

"Beau," Lottie said, "Joan Baez and Mary Travers stopped the Vietnam War, with a little help from their friends."

"Wow," Beau said.

"Before we leave you, Mary Lou, what can you tell us about Crockett Wood?"

Mary Lou turned to the Bobcats Basketball page.

"Here's a picture of the Bobcats' starting line-up. This is my boyfriend Jim, these are the Mason boys, this is Crockett, and this is Tyrone, who was much shorter than Crockett and the other starters. You can see that Crockett was tall for his age, as tall as Jim. Crockett's cousin Red Wilker also made the team, but he didn't start." She pointed to another photo. "Now here's a picture of Red and Crockett shooting baskets."

"Were Red and Crockett close back then?" Lottie asked.

"Close as two peas in a pod. They did everything together. They even got arrested together."

"Arrested? For what?"

"For beating somebody up. I don't remember the details."

Mary Lou turned to the pictures of the class of 1971. "Here's Crockett, with his crew cut. And here's his twin sister Trudy."

"Trudy is better looking than Crockett," Beau said.

At five o'clock Lottie and Beau thanked Mary Lou for her time and got up to leave.

"I've so enjoyed the afternoon with you all," Mary

Lou said. "We'll get together again soon, and I'll show you a few of those letters."

⨯∽⨯

As Lottie drove down the steep mountain road, Beau turned to her. "Dr. Byrd, do you think Allie is alive?"

"I know she's alive, Beau. I got a letter from her which I'll show you when we get to my house. She wants us to keep it confidential. Can you do that?"

"I can do that."

Lottie showed Beau the letter.

"Trudy must have hated Red Wilker for ruining her life," Beau said after reading it carefully."

"Red and Crockett ruined two lives."

"Yes, but Allie has a son and two grandchildren. Trudy has nobody, no children, no family. She must think about that all the time."

"I'm sure she does," Lottie said, "every day of her life."

"Red Wilker killed Trudy's children. That's what he did."

"That might be hard to prove in court, Beau, but you've got a point. Red deprived Trudy of a family, and now she's sixty-five and alone. I'd understand if she were bitter."

"Oh, Dr. Byrd! I didn't mean it that way. You don't have a son, but you have the Arroyos. Jaime and Jorge love you as much as they love their mother."

"I know, Beau. I'm fortunate. By the way, do you know who Nathan Bedford Forrest was?"

"He was a Confederate general who joined the Klan and became the first Grand Wizard."

"Good for you, Beau! You know your Southern history."

"Crockett Wood must have named his dog Bedford after Nathan Bedford Forrest."

"That seems to be so. Now would you like to look at the clippings?"

"Yes, please."

Lottie gave Beau time to read them all.

Beau picked up the *Confederate News* clipping. "I guess I'm a mongrel."

"Why do you say that?"

"This is what Crockett Wood told a reporter at a Saxxons demonstration against DACA. 'The mission of the Saxxons is to prevent the mongrelization of America.' Then he said, 'We consider interracial marriage an abomination.'"

"Crockett Wood was dumb as a rock, Beau. We are all mongrels. There's no such thing as racial purity. There's just variation. Races are social categories, not genetic categories—and that's according to geneticists."

"So white supremacists just don't want people who look different from them to mess with their imaginary category."

"Good way to put it, Beau. Over time, we're all messing with other people's imaginary categories. The white supremacists need to be educated."

 espeso

At five-thirty, Mev and Jake got John Hicks's report.

"Here it is," John Hicks said, finding Mev and Jake in the conference room. "I've emailed you all the complete report, but I wanted to give you the executive summary now. Looks like Crockett Wood has organized a Saxxons rally here for Sunday at three-thirty. You all may want to take action." He set a letter on the table.

Mev and Jake read it silently together.

Witherston, Georgia
Department of Police
September 5, 2018

To: Chief Jake Arroyo, Detective Mev Arroyo

From: John Hicks, IT Specialist

RE: Contents of an iPhone belonging to Crockett Boone Wood (deceased); Video recordings of a hobby drone also belonging to Wood

Executive Summary

On September 4, 2018, I was asked to examine 1) the video recordings of a drone monitor and 2) the contents of an iPhone, both said to belong to Crockett Boone Wood (deceased).

1) DJI Phantom 4 Pro quadcopter

The high-end hobby drone was a DJI Phantom 4 Pro quadcopter that sells for approximately $1,500. It has a range of four miles, a top speed of forty MPH, and a flight time of thirty minutes. Although the drone apparently crashed, two video recordings had been saved on the remote.

Video ~ Sunday, September 2, 2018, 12:53-1:19 p.m.: From corner of Possum Road and Black Fox Road along Black Fox Road to Witherston Highway, up Witherston Highway along Founding Father's Creek to Ninovan Drive, and along Ninovan Drive east to Possum Road and up to Tayanita Village.

*Video ~ Sunday, September 2, 2018, 3:22-3:37 p.m.:
From corner of Possum Road and Black Fox Road up
Possum Road to Emmett and Lydia Gray's farm.*

2) iPhone 8

The iPhone was unlocked. Mr. Wood's text messages, email, telephone log, contacts, and internet search history were accessible without a password.

Mr. Wood sent and received text messages from only one individual, a person named Ace Barnett.

The first of the relevant text conversations was sent by Ace to Crockett on Thursday, August 30, at 11:09 p.m.

Heads up, Crockett. I read in the AJC this morning that in ten days your hometown will be a sanctuary city. Witherston will become a magnet for foreigners. Time to show Saxxon colors don't you think?

Crockett replied:

I read that too. And I read online that my rich, despicable cousin is running for mayor. I do pay attention to my hometown, Ace.

I'll go there this weekend and see what's

up. Maybe drop some flyers. I have a new drone that can do that.

On Saturday, September 1, at 4:44 p.m., Crockett wrote Ace:

Designation for Witherston as a sanctuary city is on Sun, Sep 9 at 4:00 in afternoon unless we stop it.
Ace replied:

Then we stop it. How about we hold a rally at 3:30? I can get fifteen to twenty Saxxons in hoods and robes.

Crockett wrote:

Ok. In front of courthouse on Sun, Sep 9 at 3:30.
I will get back to you.

Ace replied.

Confirmed on date time and place. I will send email blast to Saxxons in GA, NC, and TN.

On Sunday, September 2, at 9:29 a.m., Crockett wrote Ace:

Got an idea. We take somebody hostage before rally to force Witherston to cancel sanctuary city if they want him released.

Ace replied:

> *Taking a hostage is a brilliant idea.*
> *Phone me to give me a name.*
> *We will call the rally Restore America.*

On Sunday, September 2, at 12:09 p.m., Crockett wrote Ace:

> *Have launched a drone for scouting purposes. Will drop Saxxons flyers this afternoon.*
> *On Sunday, September 2, at 4:43 p.m., Crockett wrote Ace:*

> *Can you meet me here tomorrow night at 8:00?*
> *4200 West Bank Road, Witherston*

Ace replied:

> *Yes*
> *And we can conduct some business. Time to settle, ok?*

That's the end of the text conversation. Crockett Wood's email list included very few messages in the past year. The only recent one is the message he sent Beau Lodge on Sunday, September 2, at 4:03 p.m.:

> *Dear Beau Lodge:*
> *I am sixty-five years old and I would like to leave land to your environmentalist club Keep Nature Natural.*
> *I invite you to visit me tomorrow night at*

8:30 after the Labor Day picnic. Come to 4200 West Bank Road.
    Crockett Wood

Beau replied on Sunday, September 2, at 7:22 p.m.:

    Dear Mr. Wood:
    Okay, thanks.
    Beau Lodge

"Holy smokes, Jake! Crockett and Ace meant to kidnap Beau!"
    "Maybe, maybe not."
    "Read on," John Hicks said.

Crockett Wood's phone conversations over the past year were likewise infrequent until Sunday, September 2.
    On Sunday, September 2, Crockett called Ace Barnett at 9:37 a.m. (18 min), 4:05 p.m. (31 min), and 9:50 p.m. (26 min).
    Ace called Crockett at 11:02 p.m. (19 min).
    On Sunday, September 2, Crockett called Red Wilker at 9:01 p.m. (4 min).
    Red called Crockett at 9:21 p.m. (3 min)
    On Monday, September 3, Ace called Crockett at 9:39 a.m. (Zero min, indicating that call was not completed).

Contacts included Ace Barnett (762-848-1213), Priscilla Teller (762-989-1023), Red Wilker (762-341-3845), and Harper B. Wood (762-989-6537).

No voice mail.

The websites Crockett visited fall into four catego-

*ries. In order of frequency they are white supremacy
websites, guns and ammo websites, militia websites, and
right wing political blogs.*

"Red told me that he'd had no contact with Crockett
since high school. He lied, Jake. Why would he lie?"

"Might he have been a Saxxon?"

"If Red had been a Saxxon, he would have interacted
more with Crockett, and Crockett would have bequeathed
him more than ten dollars."

"Which Red would have inherited only if Pina Mae
did not."

"Could Red have killed Crockett?"

"Can't picture it. Red wanted to be mayor. Red
wouldn't have risked getting caught for murder. Anyway,
he fancies himself an upstanding, church-going citizen."

"Let's bring Red in for questioning, Jake."

"I'll give him a call."

"We need to stop this rally, which could get violent,"
Mev said.

"If we can get hold of Ace Barnett's phone, we can
send an email blast canceling the rally," John Hicks said.

"We'll get Ace Barnett's phone, and we'll get Ace
Barnett," Jake said. "He's likely the Saxxon who sent the
letter to the editor. I'll put out an all-points bulletin for
him."

"How about waiting on the APB till after we pay
Barnett a visit, Jake? Are you free to go to Heron Brook
tomorrow morning? With a search warrant? Say, about
nine?"

"Sure, Mev."

"John Hicks, could you please monitor Crockett's
phone and inform us of any messages Crockett receives?"
Mev asked John Hicks.

"Sure, Detective Arroyo. It will be a pleasure," John Hicks said.

"Mev, do you see any reason to keep this kidnapping scheme confidential?"

"No, I don't. But let's not disclose Ace Barnett's name."

"I'll call Catherine," Jake said. "She can put an article into *Webby Witherston* right away."

"My report may motivate some folks to carry weapons," John Hicks said, "I mean, the ones who own weapons. I don't."

"You own a Cherokee bow."

"Oh, sure. I'll just put some arrows in my quiver and carry my bow with me. I'll wear my moccasins too."

"Let's keep your report out of the news until we find Ace Barnett. But we should inform Mayor Rather," Mev said.

"I'll call him."

"Could Red be in danger? Crockett was considerably more interested in Red than Red was in Crockett."

"Red has an arsenal of guns, Mev, and he knows how to use them. I don't think he needs our protection."

"May I alert Tayanita Village?" John Hicks asked.

"I don't see why not," Mev said.

Jake pulled out his cell phone and called Red. "Red, we need to talk a bit about your cousin's death. Can you come down to the station tomorrow, about three o'clock?"

"Sure."

享享享

Before settling down to re-watch one of her favorite movies—*The Bodyguard*—Lottie called Mev and told her Mary Lou's story.

"If Allie is alive, we must find her, Aunt Lottie," Mev said. "She could be Crockett's killer."

"If she killed him, would her action be considered justifiable homicide?"

"Not really. According to the law, homicide is justifiable only when it prevents harm to others. But she might not be sent to prison."

"I think we could make a case that Crockett intended to bring harm to others, Mev."

"Will you be seeing Allie's letters to Mary Lou? If so, Jake and I need to see them too."

"I understand. Mary Lou says she'll show them to Beau and me. But, please, let Allie stay lost. She's suffered enough. We can solve the case without her."

Lottie did not tell Mev that Allie had written her, but she did show her the article from the *Trappersville Daily News*.

"Tear gas seems to be Crockett's weapon of choice," Mev said.

"I wonder who stole his grenades Monday night," Lottie said.

"Whoever killed Crockett is my bet," Mev said.

୧୬୧

"Hi, Dr. Byrd. I got hold of a copy of the 1971 yearbook. May I bring it over tomorrow?"

"Sure, Beau. Come over with Jaime and Jorge after school."

୧୬୧

Chief John Hicks, standing in the center of the Tayanita Council House, called the meeting to order at nine in the evening. Fifteen Villagers and John Hicks's dog Bear

sat on the six-foot-long oak benches that surrounded him.
Solar-powered lanterns illuminated the yurt's interior.

Amadahy had just distributed Saxxons recruitment
flyers.

"Good evening, fellow villagers. Tonight we'll fore-
go Atsadi's Cherokee history lesson in order to discuss a
threat to Witherston. As the Witherston Police Department's IT specialist, I was asked to examine Crockett
Wood's iPhone and drone monitor. I gave Chief McCoy
and Detective Arroyo my report this afternoon. I am free
to give you all a heads-up."

John Hicks summarized his report.

"On Sunday Witherston becomes a sanctuary city,"
Atsadi said. "Do we let the Saxxons stop the ceremony?"

"Why should we get involved?" a villager asked.
"The flyer doesn't mention us. It mentions only blacks
and browns."

"And immigrants and foreigners and gays," Amadahy said. "Do you think the Saxxons just forgot about us
reds? Come on! The Saxxons think whites are the only
real Americans, native-born, straight, Christian, one hundred percent pure, whites."

"And we're not them," Atsadi said.

"We're not them," several villagers echoed.

"Nobody's them," Atsadi said.

John Hicks spoke again. "The whites who took
Cherokees' land and gold two centuries ago destroyed
our civilization not just by their firepower but also by
their ideology of white supremacy. I say we confront
them."

"How, John Hicks? With arrows against their bullets?"

"That's just reenacting the battles of the past," a villager said, "which we lost. Remember?"

"Not with arrows. With photographs," John Hicks said. "We remove their hoods and take their pictures."

"And publish their pictures," Amadahy said.

"With their bios," Atsadi said.

"We'll show the world who they are," John Hicks said.

"Cherokees unite!"

CHAPTER 9

WWW. ONLINEWITHERSTON.COM

WITHERSTON ON THE WEB
Thursday, September 6, 2018

BREAKING NEWS

"A Saxxon" Writes Again

*W*itherston on the Web has received a second letter signed *"A Saxxon." The Saxxon threatens harm to our community if we do not publish it, so we are publishing it.*

Dr. Charlotte Byrd, who proposed the sanctuary city, said, "Witherston will not be held hostage by a group of fascist lunatics who think they can make America all white. America has never been all white and will never be all white."

Chief McCoy advises all citizens of Witherston to be vigilant and to report any unusual activity immediately to the police.

Catherine Perry-Soto, Editor

"Illegal" Immigrants Are Grateful to Witherston

Rhonda Rather has made public the contents of letters she received from the "illegal" immigrants seeking asylum in Witherston and the opportunity to study or work.

According to Rhonda Rather, Sanctuary Coordinator, the three countries of origin of the eleven immigrants are Mexico, El Salvador, and Guatemala. "But our guests have lived in the United States most of their lives," she said to the Witherston Roundtable on Tuesday. "Their stories will break your heart."

Here are two of the stories.

Diego, age sixteen, was brought across the Mexican border into Texas illegally at the age of one by his mother. Growing up there he attended public schools while his mother worked as a maid to support him. When ICE deported his mother six months ago, Diego fled. He rode the Greyhound Bus to Atlanta by himself and found work in construction. When he learned of Witherston's becoming a sanctuary city, he emailed Rhonda a request for asylum. He wrote, "I want to finish school, get American citizenship, and become a pediatrician in some rural community." Diego will stay with the Arroyo family and will arrive on Saturday morning.

Pedro and Julia with their seven-month-old baby Beto will stay with the Lodge family and will arrive on Monday. Julia was born in Guatemala and brought as an infant by her parents to Georgia, where her father found work on a peanut farm. Pedro was born in El Salvador and brought as an infant by his father to Orlando during the Salvadoran civil war. Beto, having been born in Orlando, is an American, but neither Julia nor Pedro is documented. Julia and Pedro earned their undergraduate degrees in community health from a small college in Florida. Upon graduation they got jobs as laboratory technicians. In June of 2018, Pedro was arrested for speeding. After ICE (Immigration and Customs Enforcement) began deporting illegal aliens who had broken the law, Julia emailed Rhonda requesting asylum. In her letter she wrote, "If the United States won't allow us to stay and become citizens, what country will they deport us to? Will they split us up? What will happen to Beto?"

Rhonda said, "I want Mr. Wilker to know that these 'illegal aliens' speak English without an accent, read and write as well as he does, and have neither raped nor murdered."

Diego will speak at the Sanctuary City designation ceremony on Sunday.

Amadahy Henderson, Reporter

NORTH GEORGIA IN HISTORY
By Charlotte Byrd

Maud Olive Withers—"snooty Maud Olive Withers," as Gertrude Harper Wilker called the wealthy heir to Witherston's founders—had joined the prohibition movement not only because of her moral aversion to drinkers but also because of her antipathy towards the Catholic and Jewish immigrants from Europe who, in her opinion, had too great a fondness for alcohol. Like most white Americans of her generation Maud Olive Withers believed in the fundamental superiority of Anglo-Saxon Protestants over members of other races and adherents to other religions.

In a September 12, 1924, letter to the Witherston Weekly, she wrote:

> *To the Editor:*
>
> *Our Anglo-Saxon Protestant nation is being overrun by swarthy, racially and morally inferior immigrants from Europe—Catholics from Germany, Italy, and Greece, and Jews from Eastern Europe—who will soon outnumber us real Americans and dilute our blood. These foreigners, who don't even speak English, drink to excess. They don't abide by our standards of Christian virtue. If the federal government admits these degenerates into our country we must strip the bottle from their lips.*
>
> *Witherston's upstanding citizens must unite against the consumption of alcohol and join me in my efforts to protect north Georgians from the poison that undermines our traditional moral values. I invite all church-going Witherstonians to join the Anti-Saloon League.*
>
> *Please write to me at 1 Withers Hill Road.*
> *Maud Olive Withers*
> *President of Witherston Anti-Saloon League*
> *Member of Women of the Ku Klux Klan*

On September 19, Sheriff Caleb McCoy answered her.

> *To the Editor:*
> *Does Mrs. Withers think she's Anglo-Saxon Protestant? Her father's name was Shane McGillicuddy, which ain't Anglo-Saxon Protestant. It's Irish Catholic.*

Mrs. Withers, proud member of the WKKK whose rich husband HaHa avoided service in the Great War, needs to stop stirring everybody else's pot and stay home and stir her own like a normal wife.

My mother's name is Gola Hicks. She is Cherokee. That's fine with me.

    Caleb McCoy
    Half-breed Sheriff

The Women of the Ku Klux Klan, organized in Little Rock, Arkansas, in 1923, shared the anti-immigrant, anti-Catholic, anti-Jewish, and anti-black values of the Knights of the Ku Klux Klan.

Maud Olive Withers must have been profoundly disappointed on March 22, 1935, when Governor Eugene Talmadge signed the Alcoholic Beverage Control Act and thereby ended prohibition in Georgia. She wrote this letter to the editor of the Witherston Weekly on March 29, 1935, protesting the governor's action:

    To the Editor:
    Although Governor Talmadge protected Georgia's white people against the Negroes, he committed a sin for which his soul will pay in the afterlife. He made debauchery and depravity legal.

    Thank the Lord Mr. Talmadge can't run for re-election in 1936.

    Maud Olive Withers
    Witherston

Maud Olive Withers was correct in saying that Governor Eugene Talmadge "protected Georgia's white people against the Negroes." Eugene Talmadge, a notorious white supremacist associated with the Klan, declared, "We in the South love the Negro in his place – but his place is at the back door."

LETTERS TO THE EDITOR

To the Editor:
Yesterday's letter by "A Saxxon" reminds us why we should all carry guns.
FYI, Mr. "Saxxon": The bullets a woman fires from a pink gun are just as deadly as the bullets a man fires from a black gun.
Ruth Griggs
Witherston

To the Editor:
Wake up, Americans. Your way of life is threatened by the invasion of foreigners, by people who don't look like you or speak like you or think like you or share your values. They will transform the country you know and love.
We Saxxons encourage everybody opposed to cultural genocide to rise up against your immigrant-loving neighbors. Damage their property, scare their children, cut their power. Be a vandal for America.
And show your patriotism: Display the American flag.
A Saxxon
Georgia

စာ

"Good god, Jake!" Mev said, following Jake into the police station. "How can we control this situation? The Saxxon just brought civil war to Witherston. He's making folks fearful that immigrants will destroy their way of life."

"We will proceed crime by crime, Mev. Dahlonega is loaning us a few officers. We will find Barnett. He must be the letter writer."

"But Barnett has committed no crime, at least none that we know of. What can you arrest him for? He's simply encouraged others to commit crimes. Many folks in Witherston are hostile to the sanctuary city anyway. Now he's scared them into thinking they will lose their country."

"And scared people can be dangerous. But how do we fight an idea, particularly a bad idea?"

Mev thought for a moment. "We fight a bad idea with a good idea. I think I'll bring Lottie into this."

"By calling Saxxons 'ignorant fascist lunatics' Lottie just put a bull's eye on the back of her own silk shirt. Wait till tonight to talk to Lottie, Mev. We've got to get on the road now."

დოდა

Lottie was drinking her morning coffee when Mary Lou Pattison called.

"I've decided to share some of Allie's letters with you and Beau," she said. "I don't know where Allie lives or even if she is still alive. If she is alive, she would probably want to help us solve those fifty-year-old crimes. I can bring the letters to your house late this afternoon, if you like."

"I like," Lottie said. "May we include my nephews?"

"Yes. I guess that won't hurt."

"I'll text them. Thanks, Mary Lou! Come at five. You'll get a glass of wine out of this."

eソeソ

After an hour and a half, Jake and Mev reached the outskirts of Heron Brook, Georgia. With the GPS they found Wylie's Road, which was unpaved. It was ten o'clock.

"Here's Ace Barnett's house," Mev said.

Jake turned the Witherston Police jeep into the driveway of a small, white, newly painted ranch-style home with an American flag on the mail box. A ten-year-old white Toyota Corolla with a Christian fish bumper sticker occupied one side of the carport. Behind the fence a large black Doberman paced.

Jake rang the doorbell.

A once attractive blonde woman in her fifties wearing jeans and an oversized white shirt opened the door. She held in her arms a yapping Chihuahua.

"Shush, Pinkie," she said.

"Mrs. Barnett? I am Chief McCoy of the Witherston Police, and this is my partner Detective Arroyo. May we come in?"

"I am Melissa Barnett. Why would the Witherston Police want to see me?"

"We want to see Ace Barnett. Is he your husband?"

"Yes. Why would the Witherston Police want to see him?"

"Is he here?"

"No."

"May we come in?"

Melissa Barnett opened the door. "Come in," she said, setting Pinkie down on a chair. She ushered Mev and Jake into her living room.

"Would you like a Coca-Cola? A beer?"

"A Coca-Cola would be perfect. Thanks," Jake said.

"No, thank you," Mev said. "Nothing for me."

"Have a seat."

While Melissa was in the kitchen, Mev looked around the living room. Above the sofa was a gun rack case with two rifles. On the coffee table was a stack of *American Rifleman* issues. On the end table was a framed eight-by-ten picture of a clean-shaven, handsome young man in Army fatigues standing in front of a tank with helmet in hand.

On the wall over the dining table was a formal wedding picture of that same young man with Melissa. On a hat rack by the door were a black Atlanta Falcons baseball cap and a military field cap.

Mev took pictures.

"We won't keep you long," Mev said when Melissa returned with a bottle of Coca-Cola for Jake. "Do you have any idea where Mr. Barnett could have gone?"

"Not a clue. Is Ace in trouble?" Melissa looked at her watch.

"We understand that Crockett Wood, who was murdered in Witherston on Labor Day, was a friend of Mr. Barnett's. We are investigating," Jake said. "Were you acquainted with Mr. Wood?"

"Crockett was murdered? Where?"

"On his father's property on Saloli Stream right above Witherston."

"That's shitty. On Labor Day, you said?"

"Yes, Labor Day morning. Did you know Crockett?"

"Ace was a long-time friend of Crockett's pappy from the Dixie Speedway. So we knew Crockett."

"Crockett left a will in which he bequeathed four thousand nine hundred and eighty dollars to your husband," Mev said. "He also made bequests to the Saxxons for America, care of your husband. Were you aware of Crockett's will, Mrs. Barnett?"

"I wasn't. I can't speak for Ace."

"Do you have any idea why Crockett would leave your husband four thousand nine hundred and eighty dollars?"

"I do not. I'm sure Crockett owed Ace more than that."

"Have you heard of the Saxxons for America?" Jake asked.

"Is that what you're here for? Yes, I've heard of them. Ace is a Saxxon. So is Crockett. Or so was Crockett."

"What do you know about the Saxxons?"

"The Saxxons are good people. They are Christians. They are family men. They obey God's word. Our country is going to hell because nobody else obeys God's word. Just look at our government. It's full of homosexuals, atheists, Jews, Muslims, blacks, Mexicans, you name it, who are passing laws to make everyone in the country just like them. And Obama, who's from Africa, passed a law allowing immigrants—and I mean Mexicans—to stay here and take our jobs if they came over with their parents. You know what will happen? These immigrants will marry Americans. They'll marry Christian white people and produce mestizos. Christian white people will become a minority."

"I see your perspective," Jake said.

"These immigrants don't even speak English! Stores like Lowe's have to put up signs in Spanish so the Mexicans can buy their shovels."

"Do you know anything about an upcoming Saxxons rally?" Jake asked.

"I know that the Saxxons have a right to hold a rally wherever they like."

"I have a couple of questions," Mev said. "What kind of vehicle does your husband drive?"

"A GMC truck."

"What color?"

"Silver."

"Year?"

"Hell, I don't know. Just old."

"License plate number?"

"No idea."

Jake finished his coke and stood up. "Thank you for your cooperation, Mrs. Barnett. One final request. Do you have a picture of Mr. Barnett we could have?"

Melissa opened the drawer of the end table and extracted a photograph of a bald, slightly overweight man with a red beard staring into the camera.

"You may borrow this," she said. "But I want it back."

"And can you give us Ace's cell phone number?" Mev asked.

"It's seven, six, two, eight, four, eight, one, two, one, three."

As they walked out the door, Jake turned and said, "You're sure you don't know where your husband could have gone, Mrs. Barnett?"

"He could have gone to Rhett's Diner. That's over on Beverly Road, about four miles from here. He spends mornings there."

Thank you, Mrs. Barnett," Mev said. "Here's my card with my cell phone number. Please have Mr. Barnett call me when he comes home."

Jake and Mev plugged Rhett's Diner into the GPS and headed into town.

"Well, she didn't lie about Ace's cell phone number," Mev said. "That's the number Ace used when he called Crockett."

"Good test of her sincerity."

"Should you have produced the search warrant, Jake?"

"Probably, but I didn't want her to clam up. I'll send deputies tomorrow. And I'll put out the APB today."

"I'm calling Ace." Mev punched in his number and waited. "He didn't answer. Let's just go to Rhett's diner, Jake."

At the diner, Rhett Brown told them, "Ace was here, but he left five minutes ago. You'll find him at Hammer 'n Nails over there down on Paxton Street."

At Hammer 'n Nails, the proprietor told them, "Ace picked up a box of screws and left. I think he was going to the creamery down the block. You can walk there."

"Do you believe him, Jake?"

"No, but we might as well go see. We're so close."

Ace was not there.

"We've been played, Jake," Mev said as they got back in the car.

"Melissa sent us on a wild goose chase," Jake said. "I'll have the office get his license plate number and put out an APB."

❧❧❧

BREAKING NEWS

Chief McCoy Issues APB for Ace Barnett

Chief Jake McCoy has issued an all-points bulletin for Ace Melton Barnett of Heron Brook, Georgia, in connection with the murder of Crockett Boone Wood.

Barnett may be driving a silver 2001 GMC Sierra with Georgia license plate #AFP1970.

Barnett was named in Wood's will as a representative beneficiary for a bequest to the Saxxons for America.

Catherine Perry-Soto, Editor

❧❧❧

"Did you mean to announce your APB publicly, Jake?" Mev sat down in Jake's office.

"Catherine called me for an update on the case," Jake said. "I told her of our progress. I thought the citizens of Georgia might help us find Barnett."

"If Barnett reads *Webby Witherston*, he'll skedaddle."

John Hicks walked in holding an iPhone.

"Hi there, Chief McCoy, Detective Arroyo. Our dead friend Crockett Wood just got an email blast from a Saxxon. Do you all want to see it?

From: A Saxxon <u>donotreply@gmail.com</u>

To: Saxxons in Tennessee, North Carolina, and Georgia

RALLY
Thu 09/06/2018 3:11 p.m.

You are called to a "Restore America" rally to protest the establishment of a sanctuary city for non-English-speaking illegal aliens in Witherston, Georgia.

The rally will also honor our fallen leader, Saxxon Crockett Wood, who was murdered there on Labor Day.

The rally will take place on Sunday, September 9, at 11:30 a.m., on Creek Street in front of the Witherston courthouse.

Wear your hoods and robes. Bring signs. Suggestions for signs are "Join the Saxxons to Restore America," "Save America's Heritage," and "Say No to Cultural Genocide."

Bring tiki torches.

I will carry a burning cross, and I will lead the procession.

A Saxxon

Sent from my iPhone

John Hicks paused. "The email is signed 'A Saxxon.' Same as the letters to the editor."

"Can you reply all, John Hicks? And call off the rally?"

"Not possible, Chief McCoy. The 'From' line says 'do not reply at gmail.com.' And the recipients are not disclosed."

"It's too late to stop the rally anyway," Mev said. "So we have to figure out how to use the rally to our advantage."

"Ace Barnett will be there," Jake said. "But he'll be wearing a hood, like everybody else."

"He'll be the one carrying the burning cross," Mev said. "But to take down the Saxxons we need to expose everybody's identity."

"We Tayanita Villagers can solve that problem," John Hicks said. "We'll be mounted. At least some of us will be mounted. We can yank their hoods."

"Mounted! On what?"

"I'll be mounted on Honeybunch, Catherine and Dan's one-eyed horse. Amadahy will be mounted on Penelope. And other villagers will ride our mule Franny, Jonathan and Gregory's donkey Sassyass, and the Zamoras' Clydesdales Felipe and Isabela. Trust us. We'll let the sun shine on the Saxxons' faces."

"And then we can detain Ace Barnett. Great idea, John Hicks," Jake said. "We can use the Saxxons' rally as a trap."

"Might be a good idea to pull Catherine's article about the APB, Jake. We don't want to alert Barnett."

"I'll call Catherine now."

After promising Catherine an interview at the end of the day, Jake disconnected. "Done," he said. "She took the article off Webby Witherston while we spoke."

Mev looked at his watch. "Three-twenty. Wasn't Red supposed to meet us here at three?"

CHAPTER 10

Thursday Afternoon:

Lottie had already poured glasses of chardonnay for Mary Lou and herself when Beau, Jaime, and Jorge came in through her kitchen door.

"Helloooo," Doolittle said from her perch atop her cage. "Doolittle gonna go up?" He stepped up onto Jaime's hand.

After Lottie had introduced Mary Lou to her nephews, the three boys sat down on the floor around the coffee table, where Lottie had set a pitcher of limeade and a plate of pita chips and humus. Doolittle hopped onto the table and helped himself to a chip.

"I've brought copies of a dozen letters to me from Allie. You may take them to Mev," Mary Lou said. "The last time Allie wrote was in 1992. Shortly afterwards I gave up my Dahlonega post office box. Allie called me over the Christmas holidays for four years after that. We talked for the last time in December of 1996, when she told me she'd become a police officer."

"Did you try to contact her?"

"I did, but without success. When I tried to reach her in December of 1999 the post office returned my letter. I haven't heard from her since then. I don't know whether she's still in Atlanta, if she's alive."

Mary Lou opened a manila envelope and brought out a stack of letters. "You can pass these around, Lottie."

After reading each letter carefully, Lottie handed it to Beau and Jaime and Jorge.

Wednesday, September 11, 1968
Dear Mary Lou,

I'm so glad I can still confide in you. I need you. I need Tyrone too, and he's dead. I can't stop crying.

I enclose my house key. Could you please go to my house when Father is gone and get my diary. It's under my mattress. Burn it. Thanks so much, dearest friend!

I was too hysterical Sunday night to tell you all that happened, but now I want you to know everything. It was horrible. After spending the afternoon at Tyrone's mother's house, where we made plans for our courthouse wedding, Tyrone and I headed down Orchard Road toward your house. Suddenly Tyrone noticed a black car following us. I looked back and saw four Klansmen in it, so I told Tyrone to hit the gas pedal. Tyrone drove as fast as he could, thinking we could escape them and hide near the creek. But their car, though it was old, was really, really souped up, and just before the bridge they forced us off the road. Then they pulled us out of our car.

There were four of them, all wearing glory suits. Two seemed to be teenage boys. The other two must have been their fathers. They were all very drunk. Anyway, one boy who had bad breath grabbed me and held me while the driver of the car held Tyrone and the other grown man stabbed Tyrone over and over. Then the two men dragged Tyrone's body down the creek bank into the bushes, and

*the boy with bad breath threw me on the grass and held
me down. The other boy who was really skinny pulled off
my shorts and my panties and raped me. Oh god it was
horrible. I kicked him in the knee as hard as I could. I
hurt him bad, I think. He yelled "Fuck!" I thought I recognized his voice and I screamed his name. Then he held
me down while the other boy, the one with bad breath,
raped me. And made me bleed. Somehow I got loose, and
I jumped up and ran down across the bridge. The boy
with bad breath chased me but he couldn't move very fast
in his glory suit, so I escaped.*

*Thank you for cleaning me up, Mary Lou, and for
driving me to the Gainesville bus station.*

*I am in a safe place. And I have enough money for a
while. I won't tell you the names of the boys who raped
me because I can't prove anything. And if I come out of
hiding, they'll hunt me down and kill me. Someday I will
get my revenge. Now I have to take care of myself.*

*You've been my best friend since elementary school.
I hope we stay best friends till we die. We can't see each
other now, but I know you're with me in spirit. Again
please don't tell anybody that I am alive—not my father,
not your parents, and not the police. We're all safer that
way.*

Love, Allie

Tuesday, October 15, 1968
Dear Mary Lou,

*Thank you for your letter. And thank you for burning
my diary before Father could find it, or the police.*

*Please don't worry. I have a place to live and some-
body to take care of me. I have filed a petition to get a
new name, which I won't be able to tell you.*

*You're right. My father should feel guilty for making
me so unhappy. Does he talk about me at church? I guess*

he wanted me to be the perfect daughter for his congregation to admire. If perfect means marrying a white boy and raising four perfect white children, I'm not. Remember that song we listened to at your house, "Little Boxes" about the houses on the hillside that all look just the same? That life is not for me.

I must tell you. I'm pregnant. Maybe you guessed. I was pregnant before I was raped, and I did not lose the baby. The baby is Tyrone's. If the baby is a girl, I will name her Louisa (for Louise) after you. If the baby is a boy, I will name him Link (for Lincoln) after Tyrone and after his kind father.

I got a job as a receptionist. It's a pretty good job with health insurance. I had to pass a typing test, a spelling test, and a math test. I aced all of them. My boss is kind to me. I told him I was changing my name to escape from somebody in Witherston who wanted to hurt me and to please call me by my new name. I told him that I was going to have a baby in February. He said that I could take February off and come back to work in March. (He has a wife who works, and two children, so he understands.)

Love, Allie
(I'll always be Allie Marie Camhurst to you.)

Friday, February 21, 1969
Dear Mary Lou,
I'm sorry Father had the heart attack, but I don't blame myself for not reconciling with him before his death. He would have been furious with me if he'd known I was pregnant, and with Tyrone's child to boot.

But it's weird. Now I can't stop dreaming of Father. In my dreams he's alive. And kinder.

A week ago, on February 14, my son Link was born. I am happier than I've ever been. I only wish Tyrone were here to see our dear little valentine. Link is dark like Tyrone but with my blue eyes, or rather my mother's blue eyes. My mother would have been happy for me.

Here's what I've been thinking as I nurse my beautiful baby. Hundreds of thousands of years ago, when human beings were few and were split up into tribes—tribes in Africa, tribes in Europe, and in Asia and in the Americas—the tribes found reasons to fight each other. Each one wanted to keep its identity pure. After a few thousand years, some tribes united with other tribes that looked like them and spoke the same language and had similar customs. Over another few thousand years those larger tribes that were geographically separated from one another turned into races. And the races fought each other to keep their identities pure. Then the races formed nations, and the nations fought each other to keep their identities pure. Now here in the South some Caucasian people such the Klansmen, and my father, think that whiteness means social, moral, and intellectual superiority. So they fight to keep their race pure, to preserve whiteness for their descendants.

But now the times they are a changin' as Bob Dylan says, particularly in America. Our generation sees "purity" as a delusion that comes from insecurity and prejudice against people who look or act different. As time goes on, whether they like it or not, our parents' genes will be passed on through generations of people who don't look like them. Their genes will mingle with the genes of their enemies. And in a hundred years there won't be any "purity" left. Do you think we'll have peace then, Mary Lou?

Father wanted to keep the white race pure, and now his genes will be passed down through Negroes as well as whites. Ha! I hope Link has many children.

I go back to work on Monday, March 17. I'm so lucky to have a good job and a good boss. My boss said that I could have his secretary's position when she retires in May and that I would get a raise.

I'm glad you like UGA. Wally must be a good boyfriend for you. You all would be interested in a book called <u>An Education in Georgia</u> by Calvin Trillin. It's about the desegregation of UGA in 1961 by Charlayne Hunter and Hamilton Holmes. After I read it I decided to get involved in the civil rights movement. I met Hosea Williams, who was involved in the Poor People's Campaign last May, and he's going to find me something to do. I want Link to know when he grows up that I did all I could to make a better world for him, and for everybody.

Let me know a good time when you're home alone and I can call you.

Peace.

Love, Allie

Wednesday, September 3, 1969

Dear Mary Lou,

Thank you for your nice letter. And thank you for sending me the clipping from the Witherston Weekly *about the anniversary of Tyrone's death. Looks like I'm safe now, relatively speaking. I don't think the police tried very hard to solve the case. The police might have had connections with the KKK. You know that's possible.*

One day I will expose Tyrone's killers and my rapists, and justice will prevail. Martin Luther King said, "The arc of the moral universe is long, but it bends toward justice." I say, we need to give it a push.

Link is doing fine. Thanks for asking about him. He is a handsome baby. He will go to desegregated schools when he starts first grade as a result of a June twelfth federal court order for DeKalb County public schools. I

remember Father saying, "You can't legislate morality."
I disagree. You can make laws that give people an incen-
tive to behave differently. Integrated elementary schools
will let little white children and little black children play
together. And then when those children grow up they will
make friends of other races without a second thought.

Good for you for majoring in elementary education!
You can help this happen! You'll be a great teacher.

Peace.

Love, Allie

Monday, May 18, 1970
Dear Mary Lou,

A week ago Saturday, Spiro Agnew came down from
Washington to dedicate the Stone Mountain Confederate
Memorial. It's outrageous that the Vice President of the
United States would dedicate a memorial to the Confed-
eracy, which seceded from the Union! Governor Lester
Maddox and Senator Herman Talmage were there too.
What a hellish trio!

This gigantic carving of Jefferson Davis, Robert E.
Lee, and Stonewall Jackson on horseback is an affront to
all black people whose ancestors were enslaved to
whites. Its purpose is to glorify the men who fought the
war to keep slavery—and to express the South's opposi-
tion to integration. It's no coincidence that this monu-
ment was carved on the mountain where the KKK was
resurrected in 1915.

I hope you're doing fine, Mary Lou. Wally sounds
nice. I heard about the May 6 demonstration at UGA af-
ter the four Kent State students were killed by the Nation-
al Guard. The paper said more than 3,000 protested.
Were you and Wally among them?

On a personal note, Link has started talking. A week
ago he spoke his first word, "doggy," and then pointed at

*our cocker spaniel Ringo (who arrived at our house on
Christmas morning). Yesterday Link said, "Mama" and
pointed at me.*

  Love, Allie

  *P.S. The other day I published my first letter (anon-
ymously) to the Atlanta Constitution. I wrote: "Do good
Americans who support equal rights not realize that the
Stone Mountain Confederate memorial reminds black
people of the Ku Klux Klan? The woman who pushed for
the carving in 1914, Caroline Helen Jemison Plane, first
president of Georgia's chapter of the United Daughters
of the Confederacy, actually proposed adding KKK fig-
ures to the group of Confederate heroes. I want to live
long enough to see that carving blasted off Stone Mountain's granite face."*

  "Were you one of those protesters, Mary Lou?"

  "No, Lottie, I regret to say. But I remember it vividly. Wally and I watched from the roof of the journalism
building. Were you?"

  "Yes, I was. So was Remington. We marched across
campus demanding that President Davison condemn the
Ohio National Guard for shooting the students. He re-
fused. Then we sat outside the president's house for
hours. The regents closed down all the colleges in the
university system for two days."

  "Cool," Jorge said.

  "That's what I thought," Lottie said. "Only I said,
'Power to the people.'"

  "I admire Allie," Beau said. "I wish I knew her."

  "You'll feel like you know her after you finish reading her letters, Beau," Mary Lou said.

Sunday, June 4, 1972
Dear Mary Lou,
I wish I could have attended your wedding. Thanks

so much for the pictures. You looked happy. And thanks
for your new address and phone number. I'll call you
sometime.

On the day you got married Link and I were on a bus
to Washington D.C. to participate in the May 21 Emer-
gency March for Peace. You probably saw it on televi-
sion. The papers estimated that we numbered 15,000 de-
monstrators. I carried Link piggy-back. He weighs thirty
pounds, so we mostly sat on a bench in the Washington
Mall. I've sent you and Wally a set of three votive can-
dleholders. I hope you will remember our friendship
when you light the candles. Do you know the song "Lay
Down (Candles in the Rain)"? Melanie Safka wrote it in
1969, right after singing in the Woodstock music festival
in New York.

Peace.
Love, Allie

"Did you know 'Lay Down,' Aunt Lottie?" Jaime
asked.

"Of course," Lottie said. "Everybody in my generation knew it."

"I didn't," Mary Lou said. "At least not in 1972. This
letter told me that Allie and I were traveling down different roads. Wally was headed to Vietnam right after graduation. I was focused on the baby growing inside me who
would be born before Wally could return. I wanted peace
too, but I was not a protester."

"I'd like to play that song," Jaime said.

"Maybe you can play it on Sunday," Jorge said, "for
the sanctuary city ceremony."

"Read on, boys," Lottie said.

Thursday, October 18, 1973
Dear Mary Lou,
Remember the day Tyrone got elected president of

our class? We thought we were making history at Wither-
ston High, and we were. That was in 1967. Well,
Maynard Jackson has been elected mayor of Atlanta, and
he made history. And I know him! Hosea Williams intro-
duced me to him last May, and I worked for his cam-
paign. I made phone calls and addressed envelopes at
night in my kitchen.

Mary Lou, a new world's dawning. When a black
man can get elected mayor of a big city in the South,
black people can hope to have all the privileges that
white people have, like good jobs, good neighborhoods,
good schools, and health care. And respect.

Here I am writing you as if I'm not white. Truthfully,
I don't feel white anymore. Link is not white, and his little
four-year-old friends and their parents, who have become
my friends, are not white. And the people I admire in At-
lanta—Hosea Williams and Maynard Jackson and An-
drew Young—are not white. Anyway, the South is chang-
ing. I dream of the time when black boys can hold hands
with their white girlfriends and white boys can hold
hands with their black girlfriends in public and when they
can kiss each other in public without anybody staring. I
dream of a time when I can take my black son into a res-
taurant without anybody staring. And I dream of a time
when my son can take a white girl to the movies without
getting killed.

The South is changing, and soon the Ku Klux Klan
will disappear. But I promise you that I will never forgive
or forget Tyrone's killers and my rapists. Never. Not ev-
er. They're still out there.

Mary Lou, you and I are probably very different
from each other now. I'm raising my black son in an all-
black neighborhood where I'm the only white person, and
you're raising your white son in an all-white neighbor-
hood where—I assume—blacks can only trespass. I'm a

secretary, and you're a teacher. But if we ever get to-gether again I'm sure we'll talk all night like we used to, about movies, books, music, whatever.

I look forward to talking with you at Christmas.

Love, Allie

"Wow, the time Allie dreamed of is here," Beau said. "I can hold hands with Sally and take her to the movies. Nobody stares. We feel normal."

"You all are normal, Beau," Lottie said, "You all are normal."

"But the Saxxons have come to Witherston, Beau," Jaime said. "They still want to put you down."

"Let's keep reading, boys," Lottie said.

Thursday, January 22, 1976
Dear Mary Lou,

Happy twenty-sixth birthday! I apologize for being such a poor correspondent. But I do love our annual phone calls.

Thanks so much for sending the tribute you wrote about me last September. It made me homesick.

Link is about to turn six. He has been asking about his father, and I've told him that his father was murdered and that I am trying to find his father's murderers. I've told him that he looks like his father, who was handsome and smart and kind. I showed him our yearbook.

I told Link that nobody ever really dies, that every-one lives on in the memories of others, and that his father lives on in my memories of him and in my heart. I also told him that he, my beloved son, was the best thing that ever happened to me and that I would devote my life to making good memories for him.

You know, the opportunity everyone born has, no matter his wealth or education, is to make good memories of himself in the minds of everyone he meets. Just think, the hundred billion humans who have ever been born have all made memories in the minds of their friends and relatives. Those who do something great for their community or their country or the world have made memories in the minds of people they don't even know. So maybe the soul of the planet is simply the wind of memories that blows from the past into the present and from all of us into each other, an eternal wind of memories carried by words blowing through all of our hearts. No god, no gods, just the wind.

What would Father have said if I'd told him that!

Last May I went to a KKK rally in Pensacola looking for Tyrone's killers or my rapists. I didn't find them. I intend to go to KKK rallies from now on, until I find one of them. Then I can't promise what I will or will not do.

By the way, keep your eye on Governor Carter, who's running for president of the United States. He just won the Iowa caucuses. Hosea helped me get a small job working on Carter's campaign staff in Georgia. I like him and his wife Rosalynn a lot.

Love, Allie

P.S. I took Link to see Tubby the Tuba *over Thanksgiving holidays. He loved it. Now Link wants to play the trombone. For Christmas Santa gave him a trombone and I gave him music lessons. That was all I could afford to give him, but he was thrilled.*

"Wow, Allie had an exciting life. Maybe I'll work on somebody's campaign for president."

"Great idea, Beau," Lottie said. "Better to row than to float. You steer your boat in the direction you want."

"Would you all like to see the tribute I wrote that Allie is referring to? The *Witherston Weekly* published it."

Mary Lou produced from the manila envelope a yellowed clipping from the *Witherston Weekly* dated September 5, 1975.

I Will Never Forget My Friend Allie
By Mary Lou (Reynolds) Pattison

On September 1, 1968, the Ku Klux Klan murdered Tyrone Lincoln Lewis and I lost my best friend Allie Marie Camhurst. Whether Allie died that night or fled from the killers we may never know. I think about her every day.

So on this seventh anniversary of her disappearance I am writing a tribute to her.

Allie Camhurst was born on June 14, 1950, in Dahlonega, the only child of Reverend Wade Camhurst and his wife Mary Hanson Camhurst, both now deceased. Mrs. Camhurst died of cancer when Allie was in eighth grade. Reverend Camhurst died of a heart attack five months after Allie disappeared.

Allie graduated from Witherston High School on May 24, 1968, where she was valedictorian, yearbook editor, vice-president of her senior class, representative to the student council, and co-founder of the Movie Club. She was popular, pretty, and truly brilliant.

Allie was passionately interested in the civil rights movement in Georgia. After Martin Luther King was assassinated, on April 4, 1968, she talked a lot about the racial injustices of Georgia's past, particularly the killings of two Negro couples near Monroe, Georgia, in 1946. She hated that the white killers got away.

Allie wanted to see, as she often said, "an even distribution of justice across society." She would quote Medger Evers's motto "You can kill a man but you can't kill an idea," that is, she quoted it until she read Betty

*Friedan's "The Feminine Mystique." Then she changed
it to: "You can kill a woman but you can't kill an idea."
The big idea that motivated her was egalitarianism. Right
before graduation she mimeographed the "Universal
Declaration of Human Rights" which none of us knew
about even though it had been adopted by the United Nations in 1948. Allie's role model was Eleanor Roosevelt,
who chaired the committee that wrote it.*

*Allie's favorite movie was "Lilies of the Field" with
Sydney Poitier. Her favorite book was "Absalom Absalom" by William Faulkner. Her favorite poem was "The
Force that through the Green Fuse Drives the Flower"
by Dylan Thomas. Her favorite singer was Joan Baez.
Her favorite TV show was the "Smothers Brothers Com-
edy Hour." Her favorite Supreme Court Justice was William O. Douglas. Her favorite color was blue.*

*Allie witnessed the murder of Tyrone Lincoln Lewis,
who died because he was a black man who loved a white
woman. That is why Allie is no longer with us.*

"You're a good writer, Mrs. Pattison," Jorge said.

"Not as good as Allie was. But thanks, Jorge."

"I would have liked Allie," Beau said.

"You all would have liked her," Mary Lou said.

"Your tribute to Allie is nothing like the obituary
someone wrote for Tyrone," Lottie said. "Your tribute
told us who Allie was. Tyrone's obituary did not."

"Who wrote Tyrone's obituary, Aunt Lottie?"

"No telling, Jaime. Some unnamed staff writer for
the *Witherston Weekly.*"

"Tyrone's obituary should also have said that Tyrone
won a prestigious four-year scholarship to Morehouse
College, and that he had worked for years at the chicken
plant to earn money for his living expenses," Mary Lou
said. "Tyrone was a star student. He deserved to be re-

membered for more than being a black teenager killed by the Klan."

"Let's finish reading the letters, boys. It's getting late," Lottie said.

Sunday, April 3, 1977
Dear Mary Lou,

Oh my god! Yesterday something <u>incredible</u> happened. At the McDonald's where Link likes to have Saturday lunch I bumped into a woman who recognized me and called me "Allie." I was shocked, but so was she. She said she thought I was dead. She looked vaguely familiar. She asked if we could talk, so I told Link he and Ringo could go outside to the PlayPlace.

This woman turned out to be the sister of one of my rapists. She's in hiding too. She knew the whole story of Tyrone's murder. She knew who the four Klansmen were. She thought one of them had killed me. She said she had to escape Witherston, so when she graduated from high school she took a bus to Atlanta and changed her name legally. She told me to call her Jane.

She works as a waitress in a restaurant about a mile from where Link and I live. I invited her over for Easter dinner. I felt sorry for her since she's all alone. She is divorced, after being married for only a year, with no family. She's had more than her share of difficulties.

I got promoted. I am an office manager now, with responsibility for six other employees.

Love,
Allie

"When Allie wrote that she'd met the sister of one of your rapists, did you figure out who your rapists were, Mrs. Pattison?"

"I had a suspicion, Beau."

Monday, January 19, 1987
Dear Mary Lou,
I thought of you on Saturday, when Link and I joined a "Walk for Brotherhood" and sang "We Shall Overcome." I remembered listening to Pete Seeger sing it on your stereo before I met Tyrone and learned its meaning.

Anyway, Hosea led a group of us (mostly blacks but some whites) through very-white Forsyth County to the courthouse in very-white Cumming to celebrate Martin Luther King's birthday. Link carried a sign that said "Give brotherhood a chance." There were seventy-five of us, and maybe 400 very angry white people resisting us. One man carried a sign that said "Sickle Cell Anemia ~ The Great White Hope." Another man hit Hosea with a rock. I wondered whether one of my rapists was among the Klansmen. I found out later that David Duke, who heads the National Association of White People, was arrested.

How foolish I was to think that integration would transform the hearts of all. Integration has had the opposite effect on some. The KKK is filled with men whose only source of pride is the color of their skin. These men are probably terrified that their sons or daughters might fall in love with a black person and have "mulatto" children. As I did.

Maybe someday I will tell you who my rapists were. It's uncanny. Jane has become my best friend here. She was raped too, and she's suffered from it a lot more than I have. But now she's a Delta stewardess, and she flies to foreign countries.

Hosea says we have to return to Forsyth County next Saturday, so I will go again. So will Jane. Hosea says that there could be 20,000 of us. If we number that many, we'll have the largest civil rights demonstration in Georgia since 1970! Link won't go, thank goodness. He has a *date that night to see <u>Platoon</u>, and I told him he couldn't disappoint his girlfriend.*

I try to keep Link safe, but Link has a passion for social justice. Thank goodness his girlfriend is black. I don't want him to be killed like his father for dating a white girl. I worry about him all the time.

Anyway, Link has done well for himself. He's gotten to be a very good musician. This year he is drum major at his high school. He's going to Morehouse next fall, and he'll play trombone in the Morehouse marching band. He plans to study history and become a lawyer.

I'm glad you and Wally have decided to live in Witherston. Some day, when my rapists are gone, I will return with Link, so you can meet him and I can meet your son Jack.

Love, Allie

P.S. Jane and I saw The Wild Duck *with Liv Ullmann and Jeremy Irons. It showed at an art theater here.*

Sunday, September 1, 1991
Dear Mary Lou,

Today, the Sunday before Labor Day, is the twenty-third anniversary of Tyrone's death. I try to forgive Tyrone's killers and my rapists, as Martin Luther King preached, but I can't. And I won't. I won't ever forgive them. Neither will Jane. That crime left a hole in my heart that is still filled with anger. I want to make those evil people experience as much pain as I have. And as Jane has.

I wish that whatever guilt the Klansmen might have felt over the crime they committed that night could match the pain they inflicted on Tyrone's family and on me. But I don't think white supremacists feel guilt over their actions. They think they are enforcing a moral order that

integration is undermining. They view social equality as
unnatural. So did Father, remember?

Link is starting law school at Mercer Law School
with a full scholarship, and I am going to night school at
Georgia State. I will graduate in 1995 with a BS in Crim-
inal Justice. I want to be a police officer.

I'll call you sometime—probably after 9:00, when I
get home. I'd love to catch up.

Love, Allie

"You're now reading the last letter I got from Allie."

Friday, September 11, 1992
Dear Mary Lou,

Good news. Link is engaged to his long-time girl-
friend. The wedding is next May. I am so happy.

Not good news. Crockett Wood has surfaced. Re-
member him? He was three years behind us in school. I
just saw in the paper that he was arrested for beating up
his wife. He has not changed. He is evil.

I hope you and Wally and Jack are well.

Love, Allie

P.S. Be sure to see the movie <u>Fried Green Tomatoes</u>.
Jane and I loved it.

"Do you think Crockett Wood was one of Allie's
rapists, Mrs. Pattison?" Jaime asked.

"Yes, I do. After writing that he'd been arrested for
beating up his wife, Allie wrote, 'he has not changed.'"

"Then Allie's friend Jane would be Trudy Lee
Wood, Crockett's sister," Jaime said. "If she's alive and
we can find her, we can pretty well prove that Crockett
raped Allie and his father killed Tyrone."

"Right."

"And possibly that Red and Red's father Bullet were the other two Klansmen," Lottie said.

"Was Crockett Wood a white supremacist in high school?" Beau asked.

"Beau, the truth is that Allie and I hardly knew him. He was a freshman when we were seniors. We didn't pay attention to freshmen unless they played football or basketball. Crockett did play basketball, as you see in the yearbook."

"Mary Lou, did Allie ever tell you her new name?" Lottie asked.

"No, she didn't. But I figured it out. I went through the marriage notices in the *Atlanta Constitution* in May of 1993 and found one on May twenty-second for Link Meadows and Sadie Goode. I figured that Link's mother's last name was Meadows."

"Did you tell Allie that you knew?"

"No, I didn't, Beau. I didn't want to invade her privacy. By then Allie and I had drifted apart, and when we talked on the phone we mostly just exchanged pleasantries. Our life experiences had separated us."

"Mary Lou, could Allie have killed Crockett?"

"I don't know. Lottie. I just don't know. The Allie I loved was incapable of murder."

"We don't even know that she's alive, Aunt Lottie."

"She was alive eighteen years ago," Mary Lou said. "I spotted her in Hosea Williams's funeral procession down Auburn Avenue to Ebenezer Baptist Church. It was televised."

"May I show these letters to Detective Arroyo, my niece?"

"Yes. If Allie's alive now she'll be hoping her rapists are found and punished."

"You all want to see Red Wilker's yearbook from 1971? Mrs. Wilker loaned it to me," Beau said. "I found something real interesting."

Beau opened the yearbook to the last page. "Look what's written here."

> *There once was a student named Red*
> *Who tried to get Miss Fink in bed.*
> *When Miss Fink said "No,*
> *You are not my beau,"*
> *Red chased Trudy instead.*
>
> *And Trudy said "No, Red,*
> *Chase my brother instead."*

"Wow," Jorge said. "Who was Miss Fink?"

"She was the social studies teacher," Beau said. "But that's not what's interesting. What's interesting is that the person who wrote the limerick used blue ink and wrote in capital letters like a boy. The person who wrote the next two lines used red ink and wrote in cursive like a girl."

"So a boy wrote the limerick, and a girl wrote the last two lines," Lottie said.

"Trudy Wood wrote the last two lines. Look at Trudy Wood's class picture." Beau turned to the section of seniors in their graduation gowns. "Trudy signed her picture in red ink in that same pretty handwriting. And she wrote only 'Trudy Wood.' Everybody else wrote things like 'best wishes,' 'great knowing you,' 'see you around,' and stuff like that."

"Maybe Trudy didn't like Red much."

"They were cousins, Jaime."

"Why did she write 'Chase my brother instead'?"

"Maybe she didn't like either Red or her brother Crockett," Jorge said.

"Crockett didn't sign Red's yearbook," Beau said. "I checked."

"You want to see Crockett's and Trudy's graduation pictures?" Beau asked.

"Sure."

Beau opened the yearbook to the end of the alphabet, where Crockett and Trudy were shown side by side above their list of their high school activities.

"Crockett has only sports," Jaime said. "Varsity Basketball, 1967-71; Varsity Baseball, 1967-71; Rifle Club, 1967-68."

"Trudy was a good student," Beau said. He read aloud her activities. "Senior Class Secretary, 1970-71; Bobcats Writing Club, 1968-71; Spanish Honor Society, 1969-71; Movie Club, 1968-71."

"She must be smarter than her brother," Jaime said.

"Uh, oh! That's not good for family harmony," Jorge said.

"Here's Red Wilker," Jaime said. "Varsity Basketball, 1967-68; Varsity Baseball, 1967-68; Future Farmers of America, 1968-71; Rifle Club, 1967-71."

"Red dropped out of basketball and baseball after his freshman year," Lottie said," maybe because he and Crockett had gotten cross-ways."

"And Crockett dropped out of Rifle Club after his freshman year," Beau said.

e/೧e/೧

Lottie googled Link Meadows. She found a notice posted on August twenty-fifth, 1995, that Link Meadows had joined the Jameson Parrett Ralston Law Firm in Macon, which specialized in civil rights law.

"Link's not likely to be a murderer," she said to herself.

CHAPTER 11

Thursday Evening:

On the Arroyos' porch after dinner Lottie showed Mev the letters Allie had written to Mary Lou. Jorge was sitting on the steps throwing a tennis ball to Mighty, and Jaime was fiddling with his guitar. The creek, swollen from the rains, was noisy. So were the woods on that late summer night. An owl hooted.

"Allie seems to be sure that Crockett was one of her rapists. Why wouldn't she have talked to the police, I wonder," Mev said.

"If you fire at a bear you'd better kill him. Or the bear will kill you. Allie couldn't prove that Crockett raped her. And Crockett's father had already killed Tyrone. He would not have hesitated to kill her. Besides, she thought the police might have been soft on the KKK. She could have been right. It was the year 1968."

"May I show these letters to Jake? He certainly has no sympathy for the Klan."

"I think Mary Lou would say yes."

"You all know who was governor of Georgia in

1968? Lester Maddox," Jorge said. "In 1964, before he
was elected governor, he organized a rally for the Klan in
Atlanta."

"Right," Jaime said. "So why would Allie have any
confidence in the law in Georgia? Governor Walker had
KKK ties in the twenties, Governor Talmadge had KKK
ties in the forties, and Governor Maddox had KKK ties in
the sixties."

"And probably Witherston's cops had KKK ties in
1968," Jorge said.

"Georgia's past could be written as a hundred-year
resistance to integration," Lottie said. "That's how the
Saxxons would write it, as an heroic resistance. And they
would make Walker, Talmadge, and Maddox the heroes."

"But things are different now," Jaime said. "Dr.
Lodge has more patients than you can shake a stick at,
and they're mostly white women."

"The Saxxons are trying to split Witherston in two,"
Mev said. "How can we go back to the way we were
when no one cared that Jim is married to Lauren and
Greg is married to Jonathan?"

"And that you are married to Paco," Lottie said. "Until now Witherston was diverse but harmonious. We all
got along because our differences seemed less important
than our connections. We were connected."

"We were harmonious," Jaime repeated, with a strum
on his guitar.

"Jaime," Mev said. "Be serious. Aunt Lottie and I
are trying to figure out what's happening to our town."

"Okay, Mom," Jaime said. "Look at it this way.
Witherston was like an orchestra. Everybody playing a
different instrument separately, and we all made music
together. The Saxxons want to stop the music."

"Right," Jorge said. "The Saxxons told everybody
that the strings were better than the horns, and the loud

and crass horns were going to drown them out. So the string players should not play with the horn players."

"The Saxxons told the string players to sabotage the horn players and pour oil into their tubas and trumpets."

"And the players all went home and locked their doors so the other players could not scare their children."

"Good thinking, boys," Lottie said. "I was about to explain how political dualism is the cause of war."

"As you do so well, Aunt Lottie," Mev said. "That's why I came over to ask you to write a letter to *Webby Witherston* countering the Saxxon's letter."

"How could I do better than Jaime and Jorge, Mev? Let them write a letter."

"Woohoo," Jorge said. "We accept your invitation! You all will see it soon."

Jorge and Jorge, followed by Mighty, went inside.

"You all come to my house," Lottie said to Mev and Paco. "I have something to show you."

Lottie brought out the copies of Allie's letters. Mev read them while Lottie uncorked a bottle of Priorat.

"Aunt Lottie, we need to speak to Allie to rule her out if she didn't kill Crockett."

"You said that Allie's new last name was probably 'Meadows,'" Paco said. "So an Officer Meadows is on some police force in Georgia. Or was."

"We can find her."

"Mev, dear, how could Allie have known that Crockett would be in his hunting shack on Labor Day? And how would she have found the place?"

"She might have read *Webby Witherston* last Sunday, Aunt Lottie. Remember loony Alvin Autry's letter to the editor?"

"Our investigations overlap, Mev. Beau and I are investigating a crime of 1968, Tyrone Lewis's murder and

Allie Camhurst's rape. You are investigating a crime of 2018, Crockett Wood's murder."

"It appears that Crockett was one of Allie's rapists."

"Then Crockett's father, Harper B, was one of Tyrone's murderers."

"According to Allie's letters, there were four Klansmen, so who were the two others?"

"Most likely Red Wilker and his father Bullet, who became Witherston's mayor in 1984," Lottie said. "Bullet and Harper B, who were first cousins, grew up together, and their sons were best friends in their freshman year in high school. But something happened that turned them against each other."

"Let me tell you what John Hicks discovered on Crockett's iPhone and drone monitor." Mev opened her phone. She had taken a picture of John Hicks's letter, as she often did with documents. She showed Lottie the document.

"So Crockett originated the kidnapping scheme," Lottie said. "And Ace Barnett planned to carry it out. Ace Barnett may be the Saxxon who wrote the letter to the editor. You need to find Ace Barnett."

"And we need to find Officer Meadows," Mev said. "I'll start with the Atlanta Police Department tomorrow."

Mev's cell phone rang.

"Hi, Jake. What's up?"

"Red's gone missing," he said. "Grace just phoned. She said Red left the house at noon to meet a prospective campaign donor at Rosa's Cantina. She got worried later in the afternoon when their dogs Smith and Wesson came home without him. So she called Ignacio, the bartender, and found out that Red had been at the Cantina having a beer with Mayor Rather when he got a text about twelve-twenty and left. But he didn't take his truck. Grace called

Mayor Rather and several other friends of Red's before
she called me."

"Jeepers, Jake. Do you think Red was the Saxxons'
target?"

"Must have been. But why would the Saxxons
choose someone opposed to the sanctuary city? Red was
on their side."

"Crockett may have wanted to kill two birds with
one stone. He didn't like Red, and Red was a prominent
citizen and well-off financially. He could have known
that Red was running for mayor."

"Crockett's dead, so he didn't kidnap Red," Jake
said. "I'll bet that Ace Barnett kidnapped Red."

"Though he probably didn't do it alone."

"The Town Council meeting starts in thirty minutes,
Mev. I'm going. Can you come with me?"

"I'll see you there."

୧୬୧୬

At eight o'clock, Atsadi Moon convened the town
council. Lottie sat down between Jonathan Finley and
Blanca Zamora on one side of the long conference table,
across from Alvin Autry, Ruth Griggs, and Lydia Gray.
Mayor Rich Rather took his seat at the far end opposite
Atsadi. Mev and Jake stood behind Atsadi. Catherine Perry-Soto with baby Alex in his sling sat on the bench
against the wall next to John Hicks, Rhonda, and Coco
Chanel. Catherine, Rhonda, and John Hicks had come to
observe.

"Hello, everybody," Atsadi said. "I called this emer-
gency meeting to respond to the Saxxon's threat published yesterday in *Witherston on the Web*. This evening
Chief McCoy received a call from Grace Wilker that

makes our deliberations more urgent. I've invited Chief McCoy and Detective Arroyo to join us."

"Welcome, Chief McCoy. Welcome, Mev," Rich said.

"Chief McCoy, would you like to address the town council?" Atsadi asked.

"I would. Thank you, Atsadi." Jake briefed the council on Grace Wilker's phone call. Then he turned to Rich Rather. "Mayor Rather, you saw Red last. Do you know anything more?"

"Well, I guess I did see him last. I had stopped by Rosa's Cantina for a beer and a burger. Red came in and joined me. He said he was expecting someone, but he didn't say who. He was fidgety. About twenty after twelve, he got a text message. He texted something back and told me he was meeting someone nearby. Funny that he left his truck with Smith and Wesson in the back. When I went out, I gave them each a burger."

"Did he say whether the person he was expecting was a man or a woman?"

Rich thought for a moment. "No, he didn't say."

"The police will search the area within a ten-minute radius," Jake said. "Now I'd like to ask Detective Arroyo to tell how our investigation will proceed."

"Thanks, Chief. Let me bring you all up to date on what we have discovered so far. According to John Hicks, who examined Crockett Wood's cell phone, text messages between Crockett and a Saxxon named Ace Barnett show that last Sunday Crockett Wood proposed the kidnapping of a quote, prominent citizen, during the run-up to next Sunday's sanctuary city designation ceremony. Phone records indicate that Crockett and Ace talked several times later that day and that Crockett and Red talked twice that night. Crockett was killed Monday morning. After Red's disappearance, which was a surprise to Jake and me, we assume that Crockett had selected Red Wilker to be the victim."

"Why would Crockett select Red?" Ruth Griggs asked. "Red has publicly opposed the sanctuary city."

"And Red is Crockett's cousin," Blanca Zamora said. "Why would anybody kill a cousin?"

"Crockett and Red didn't like each other. Red never let on that he even had a cousin, and I know him pretty well," Lydia said. "He's a good friend of Emmett's. I didn't find out that Red had a cousin till I read Crockett's obituary."

"Lydia has a point," Mev said. "When I informed Red of Crockett's death, Red said they were not close."

"We have to save Red," Ruth said. "So I will vote to reverse our decision."

"So will I," Alvin said, "but not to save Red's life. I don't give a damn about Red's life. I will vote to save our community from more foreigners who can't speak English who will make us all speak Spanish."

"You two never voted for the proposal," Lottie said to Ruth and Alvin.

"So do we sacrifice the lives of our undocumented visitors over speculation that the Saxxons kidnapped Red? And do we sacrifice all the other people ICE will deport if we don't save them? I will vote to uphold our decision," Blanca said.

"I will vote to uphold our decision because we can't allow our fears to determine the decisions we make on behalf of our constituents," Lottie said. She opened her iPad. "My goodness. Our situation has already made the online edition of the *Atlanta Journal-Constitution*. The headline says, 'White Supremacists hold Witherston hostage.' Let's see what it says."

*A secret, Georgia-based white supremacist organiza-
tion called Saxxons for America has forced the Witherston Town Council to meet tonight to respond to a threat
published as a letter to Witherston on the Web and signed
"A Saxxon." The letter-writer urged those opposed to
"cultural genocide" to inflict damage on supporters of
the sanctuary city project. "Be a vandal for America,"
the Saxxon wrote.*

*As previously reported in the AJC, the council voted
on Wednesday, August 29, to become a sanctuary city
effective at 4:00 p.m. this Sunday.*

*The governor has sent an email message to Wither-
ston's mayor Rich Rather urging the council not to capit-
ulate to the demands of any extortionist. To do so would
give extortionists the power to control our government,
the governor said.*

"Please read it aloud, Lottie," Atsadi said.

Lottie read them the article.

"Is that all?"

"The article goes on to mention our names and how
we voted."

"You didn't tell us about the email, Rich," Jonathan
said. "Were you hoping we'd reverse our decision?"

"Yes, if you really want to know. No good will come
out of Witherston's becoming a sanctuary city."

"We don't have proof that Red's disappearance is
connected to the Saxxons," Jonathan said. "All we know
is that Red disappeared."

"If you all don't overturn the vote and if Red dies,
I'll hold you all responsible."

"*Cállate*, Ruth," Blanca said. "Be quiet."

"Speak English, Blanca," Ruth retorted, "if you can."

"She can't," Alvin said.

"Be civil, Ruth and Alvin," Jonathan said, "if you can."

"Order!" Atsadi said. "Let's be polite."

"May I speak? May I speak for a change?" Alvin said.

"It won't be for a change," Jonathan muttered.

"I will vote a second time against turning Witherston into a community of foreigners," Alvin said. "America is already overrun by Mexicans and Haitians and Vietnamese and Indians. They're planning to conquer us. When I watch CNN, I see newscasters who look foreign and have a foreign accent."

"Like me," Blanca said.

"Let me continue, Mrs. Za-mo-ra. George Washington wouldn't recognize this country. America has lost its identity," Alvin said.

"I'll just ignore that and keep my Cherokee thoughts to myself," Atsadi said.

"*Yo, también*," Blanca said. "I'll ignore it too."

"I won't," Jonathan said. "Do you think all Americans should be like you, Alvin? White with an Appalachian accent, three ex-wives, and a bootlegger father who served time? What do you think is the ideal American type? White, protestant, straight, with only northern European blood in his veins? If there is an ideal American type, we all fall short so we all should feel bad about ourselves. Do you feel bad about yourself?"

"Order!"

"May I change the subject? We must save both Red and the sanctuary city," Blanca said.

"Let's listen to Detective Arroyo, folks," Atsadi said. "Detective Arroyo, what's your plan?"

"We have issued an all-points bulletin for Ace Barnett as a person of interest. We suspect that he wrote the extortion letter and that he, perhaps with assistance from other Saxxons, kidnapped Red."

"We have to find Red too," Blanca said.

"We do, Blanca," Mev said. "We believe that Ace can lead us to Red."

"And that Ace can stop the Saxxons rally on Sunday," Jake added.

"If Ace has already communicated with his fellow Saxxons, we should expect about twenty-five robed white supremacists to descend on the courthouse at three-thirty Sunday waving bamboo tiki torches and yelling obscenities against all the people they hate," Atsadi said.

"And they hate a lot of people," Jonathan said. "Black people, red people, brown people, foreign people, Jewish people, Muslim people, Mexican people, and gay people. And smart people and educated people."

"And journalists," Catherine interjected.

"Who will all come to our ceremony," Rhonda said. "All the more reason not to back down."

"The Witherston police will be there, and so will the Dahlonega police," Jake said, "to prevent violence."

"Then don't let Rhonda talk," Ruth said. "She'll get everybody riled up."

"*Cállate*, Ruth," Blanca said.

"Speak English, Blanca," Ruth said.

"*Tonta*," Blanca said under her breath.

"The police will be there," John Hicks said, "and so will the Tayanita Villagers. Two centuries ago, we Cherokees lost our civilization to white supremacists. Now we'll defeat them."

"So you all will fight them with spears and arrows," Ruth asked. "You Cherokees will look smashing on television."

"No, Ruth, with cameras."

"Who killed Crockett?" Blanca asked.

"Could be Red who killed Crockett," Jonathan said. "Ace wouldn't have killed him. Maybe Red harbored a grudge against his cousin for being a white supremacist."

"Excuse me," Mev said. "I have to take this call." She left the room.

"Red shot down Crockett's drone," Jake said. "Red may have known the flyers came from Crockett."

"Red is a good man," Rich said. "He wouldn't kill anybody. Besides, if he went up to the cabin to kill Crockett, he would have used his own gun."

"Who else bore a grudge against Crockett?"

Lottie thought of Allie but refrained from mentioning her.

"Let's focus on Ace Barnett, for now," Jake said. "We need to stop the Restore America rally."

"I move to proceed with the sanctuary city designation," Blanca said.

"I second the motion," Jonathan said.

"Any discussion?" Atsadi asked.

"If this motion passes, you all may be responsible for Red's death," Ruth said.

"And if it doesn't, we say okay to whatever the Saxxons want from us," Jonathan said.

"Further discussion?" Atsadi paused. "Okay, hearing none we'll proceed with the vote. All in favor say Aye."

"Wait! Don't vote," Mev said, rushing back into the room. "Lauren Lodge just called me. Someone tied a dead raccoon to the handlebars of Beau's bike when Beau and Sally were at the library. The raccoon was still bloody. Beau sounded his siren. Pete Junior heard it and got there immediately."

"When did that happen, Mev?" Jake asked.

"About eight o'clock. Beau and Sally had biked there after dinner to return books."

"That's a hate crime," Jonathan said. "It's a threat to Beau because he's black, or half-black."

"And because he's dating a white girl," Blanca said. "Should the police protect Sally?"

"I will call Colonel Sorensen," Mev said.

"Someone's being a vandal for America."

"How did the perp know it was Beau's bike?"

"Beau and Sally have custom bicycle license plates with their names on them."

"Why a raccoon?" Blanca asked.

"The raccoon is sometimes called a 'coon,'" Lottie said. "And in the early nineteenth century 'coon' was a dehumanizing name for a slave who wouldn't work hard, who defied his master. Racists still use the derogatory epithet for black men they consider insubordinate."

"I think we're voting blind," Atsadi said. "We need to figure out what's happening to Witherston before we make a decision."

"I move to table the vote," Lottie said.

"I second the motion," Jonathan said.

"All in favor say Aye."

"Aye," the members said in unison.

"Let's go see Grace Wilker tomorrow morning," Jake said to Mev as they walked out of city hall.

enen

BREAKING NEWS

Red Wilker Disappears
Town Council Tables Sanctuary Decision

Mayoral candidate Red Wilker has been reported missing.

Grace Wilker called Chief Jake McCoy at 7:15 p.m. this evening to say that her husband went to meet a campaign donor at Rosa's Cantina at noon and disappeared. She found out from Mayor Rather that the two had a beer together there and that Red got a text about 12:20. Red then left. The mayor realized later that Red had gone on foot to his destination and had left his dogs Smith and Wesson in his truck.

"Why would Red leave his dogs? He'd never go anywhere without Smith and Wesson," Mayor Rather said, "unless it would be to meet a lady. And that's in his past. He's way too old to be meeting any young lady."

The Council met at 8:00 p.m. this evening to decide whether to proceed with the sanctuary city designation scheduled for Sunday. Members of the Town Council conjectured that Wilker's disappearance was connected with opposition to the sanctuary city.

Immediately before the vote Detective Arroyo learned that somebody had tied a dead raccoon to Beau Lodge's bicycle about 8:00 tonight when Beau and Sally Sorensen were coming out of the Witherston Public Library.

In view of the disturbing events, the Council tabled the motion to proceed. The Council will reconvene tomorrow at 8:00 p.m.

After the meeting Detective Mev Arroyo said, "We are investigating a possible connection between Red Wilker's disappearance and the Saxxons' recent activities."

Chief McCoy said, "I suspect that the man who delivered the bloody raccoon wanted to be a 'vandal for America.' The police will get him for violating hunting laws. Raccoon season doesn't start until October."

Catherine Perry-Soto, Editor

∾∾∾

Jaime was on the phone with Beau when Mev and Lottie walked in the door.

"Colonel Sorensen won't let Sally go out with Beau now," Jaime said. "He said he had to protect her."

"I will call Colonel Sorensen now. We'll protect both Beau and Sally until the Saxxons have left and the town returns to normal."

"If it ever does," Lottie said. "Who could have predicted that such hatred would show its face in Witherston?"

CHAPTER 12

WWW. ONLINEWITHERSTON.COM

WITHERSTON ON THE WEB
Friday, September 7, 2018

NEWS

Rock is Thrown through Mayor's Window
Rooster Brewster is Shot

*M*ayor Rich Rather called police at 12:15 a.m. this morning to report that a rock had been thrown through a window of his home at 890 Rhododendron Street.

Mayor Rather said, "The rock was probably a warning to my wife Rhonda, who without my knowledge has invited a family of Mexicans to live with us."

At 2:30 a.m., Chief Atsadi Moon called police to report that Brewster, Tayanita Village's sole rooster, had been shot to death inside the chicken coop. Tayanita Vil-

lage is the home of Atsadi Moon, chair of the Town Council and proponent of the sanctuary city proposal.

As previously reported, at 8:00 p.m. yesterday evening, somebody left a dead raccoon on Beau Lodge's bicycle at the Witherston Public Library.

Chief Jake McCoy said only, "We're on it."

Amadahy Henderson, Reporter

Red Wilker Remains Missing
Chief McCoy Issues APB for Ace Barnett

Red Wilker remains missing. Red Wilker, age sixty-five, disappeared some time after 11:45 yesterday between his home at 3950 Black Fox Road and Rosa's Cantina.

Chief Jake McCoy has issued an all-points bulletin for Ace Melton Barnett of Heron Brook, Georgia. He is driving a 2001 silver GMC Sierra, with Georgia license plate # AFP1970. Chief McCoy asks anyone with knowledge of Barnett's whereabouts to contact the Witherston Police Department. Chief McCoy considers Barnett a person of interest in Red Wilker's disappearance, a possible witness to Crockett Boone Wood's murder, and a possible inciter of violence.

"Ace Barnett may be the author of the letter to the editor promoting vandalism as a protest to the sanctuary city designation," Chief McCoy said.

Barnett is five feet, ten inches tall, approximately 200 pounds, bald with a red beard. Barnett was named in Crockett Boone Wood's will as a representative beneficiary for a bequest to the Saxxons for America.

Catherine Perry-Soto, Editor

Ace Barnett Was Pace Car Driver

Ace Barnett, age fifty-eight, is known as "Pace" Barnett to stock car racing fans. He spent thirty years as a pace car driver at the Dixie Speedway in Woodstock, Georgia, before moving to Heron Brook.

Barnett worked with Harper B. Wood at the speedway and met Wood's son Crockett there after Crockett retired from the Army. Barnett, Harper B. Wood, and Crockett Wood shared a belief in the supremacy of the white race. In 1992, Barnett co-founded, with Crockett Wood, the Saxxons for America.

Barnett has been arrested twice: on Saturday, February 20, 2010, at a KKK protest against "the Latino invasion" in Nahunta, Georgia; and on September 4, 2017, at a Saxxons protest against DACA in Atlanta.

Barnett was born on July 4, 1960 in Cumming, Georgia, where he grew up. He enlisted in the US. Army in September of 1978 and was honorably discharged in September of 1980. After his marriage to Melissa Rail he moved to Woodstock, Georgia, where he worked at the Dixie Speedway for thirty years. In 2010, he and Melissa moved to Heron Brook. They have one daughter, Patsy Ann, who is in the US Marine Corps stationed in Guam.

Amadahy Henderson, Reporter.

NORTH GEORGIA IN HISTORY
By Charlotte Byrd

Statewide prohibition in Georgia, which commenced sooner and ended later than nationwide prohibition, indi-

rectly begat stock car racing and NASCAR. Moonshine runners needed fast cars to escape from the revenuers, but they did not want to call attention to themselves. So they used "stock cars," ordinary coupes with engines they modified for speed and power, to transport liquor over backwoods dirt roads. They reinforced the rear suspensions of the cars to keep the back end from sagging under the weight of a hundred gallons of bootleg whiskey.

For entertainment on weekends the runners raced each other to see whose car was fastest. Read Gertrude Wilker's diary entry of September 7, 1936.

> *Yesterday Boone took Harper B and Bullet to watch him race his Ford V8 on Old Bootleggers Trail. Boone got in a fight with a Negro who wanted to race since he runs shine too, but Boone told the Negro he couldn't because racing is for whites. Boone told him Governer Talmadge would back him up. The Negro hit Boone in the face so hard that Boone's left eye swole up. So Harper B raced instead. Harper B learnt how to drive last year when he was 11 and he knows how to drive fast. He beat Buck Smith and Mack Maloney easy because they were driving dodges. Then Harper B and Boone went looking for the Negro and found him and knocked him out. Boone told the Negro that the Klan would get him if he ever showed his black face there again. Bullet told me all about it. Boone and Harper B and Bullet stayed the night in Dawsonville and came home this morning in time for the Labor Day parade.*

Dawsonville, thirty-five miles from Witherston, became renowned for moonshine production and auto rac-

ing, which are celebrated in Dawsonville's annual Octo-
ber Mountain Moonshine Festival.

WEATHER

Warm and sunny weather ahead. High in the low
eighties. Low in the high sixties.
    Saloli Stream, Founding Father's Creek, and Taya-
nita Creek are all about to overflow their banks, due to
the torrential rains in the mountains. Good for fishing if
you like killing happy fish.
    The tide is high but I'm holdin' on.

Tony Lima, Famous Prognosticator

ᏣᎳᏣ

    Mev and Jake looked around the Wilker's cedar-
paneled living room while Grace made coffee.
    "Always accept what your host offers you," Jake had
once told Mev. "Then you can look around while he or
she is in the kitchen."
    Mev could have guessed she was in the Wilkers'
home. Above the brick fireplace an eight-point buck
looked down woefully at her. In the corner, a six-foot tall
black bear stood on his hind legs. The end table held a
big glass bowl full of red squirt guns. The coffee table
held several issues of *Field and Stream,* as well as a pile
of well-worn whodunnits. Mev noticed that the whodunnits were all written by women.
    "Thank you for coming over," Grace said as she
handed each of them a mug of hot coffee. "I am so dis-

tressed. Red hasn't called, and nobody else has. If Red's been kidnapped, wouldn't somebody call me?"

"Did Red ever mention the Saxxons, Mrs. Wilker?" Jake asked gently.

"No, not before Sunday dinner. That was when he told me about the flyers, and about the drone he shot down."

"Did he ever mention his cousin Crockett Wood?" Mev asked.

"Never. When we got married, in 1975, Red said that he had some cousins, but that he never wanted to hear from them again. I gathered that they'd had a falling out in high school. So he didn't invite them to the wedding. He invited only his parents, Bullet and Nelly Wilker. When I asked about his cousins, as I did a couple of times, he said they were none of my business. Once when I said that kinfolk ought to get together, he shouted, 'Let the dead stay buried!' I thought he meant that his cousins were dead."

"When did you find out Red's cousin was Crockett Wood?"

"I asked Bullet, my father-in-law, one night when he'd had too much to drink. Bullet told me that his first cousin was Harper B. Wood, who was the father of Crockett and Trudy. Bullet and Harper B. weren't close either. Harper B. was long gone from Witherston by the time Red and I got married."

"Did Red say anything Sunday morning when he read the news? Red must have realized that it was Crockett who had come to town. Crockett's father is too old."

"Red did get upset. He despised Crockett for some reason. Do you think Crockett's people kidnapped Red to keep Red from becoming mayor? Maybe Crockett didn't want Red to win the election, so he embarrassed Red by dropping those Saxxon flyers."

"What did Red say about the flyers?"

"He said that his sorry cousin had dropped them."

"But why?"

"To ruin his life."

"Was Red afraid of Crockett Wood?"

"Yes."

"What did Red say to you after Crockett called him Sunday night?" Jake asked.

"Did Crockett call him? Red didn't tell me."

"Crockett did call him, about nine o'clock. Red returned the call twenty minutes later."

"Red was upset all evening. He went into his office after dinner and didn't come out until late."

"Where was Red on Labor Day morning, Grace?" Mev asked her.

"Why are you asking me that, Miss Detective Arroyo? What are you suggesting?" Grace sat back in her chair. "Red was with me!"

ↄ⁄ↄↄ⁄ↄ

At noon Lottie received another letter from Allie.

Wednesday, September 5, 2018
Dear Dr. Byrd,
I read about the murder of Crockett Wood on <u>Witherston on the Web</u> this morning. I also saw an article about it in the AJC. Since Allie Marie Camhurst is presumed dead, I won't be a suspect. But I want you to know that I did not kill him.

Nevertheless, I am not sorry that Crockett was killed. He deserved it.

The police ought to question Red Wilker, Crockett's cousin. Crockett's twin sister told me that after Labor Day of 1968 Red and Crockett fell out. Crockett accused

*Red of killing me. Red denied it, but from then on he de-
tested Crockett and feared him. He was afraid that
Crockett would talk, and that they and their fathers would
all be arrested. Crockett might even have been blackmail-
ing him. Red must have been horrified to read that
Crockett had returned to Witherston, right when he was
running for mayor.*

*Again, please share this letter only with those inves-
tigating the case. And keep it out of the papers. If Red
discovers I'm alive, he'll kill me to keep me from talking.
Allie Marie Camhurst needs to stay "dead."*

Sincerely yours,
Allie Marie Camhurst

ↄ⁄ↄ℮⁄ↄ

Mary Lou Pattison opened the envelope with no return address. She sat down to read the hand-written letter.
"Oh, my God!"

Wednesday, September 5, 2018
Dearest Mary Lou,
Yes, I am alive. I apologize profusely *for not writing
you all these years. I can say only that after Link got
married I had to let go of my precious son and get his
father out of my mind. I became a campus cop.*

*But I continued to follow events in Witherston
through <u>Witherston on the Web</u>. I read Wally's obituary
and regretted I had never met him. I read about your retirement party and regretted I couldn't celebrate with
you.*

*Sunday morning I read that Crockett had returned to
Witherston. He's up to no good, I said to Jane. When I
realized that Red Wilker was running for mayor, I*

guessed that Crockett was planning to sabotage Red's campaign.

Then—Hallelujah!—somebody executed Crockett!!!

I think Red did it. The Witherston Police ought to interview him. If Red gets caught for killing Crockett, I'll truly rejoice! And I'll be free to visit you!

In the meantime, would you like to visit me? I live at 1136 Persimmon Avenue, apartment 1015. You can call me at 404-855-3664.

I hope you're well.

Love,

Allie

Mary Lou called Allie. They talked for a half hour. Then she put the letter in her safe.

ᴄ⁓ᴄ⁓

"Mev, can you come here?" Jake called from his office. "We've got a body."

"Whose body?" Mev asked as she hurried across the hall.

"Looks like Red Wilker's. A couple of fishermen found it floating in Founding Father's Creek just south of Black Fox Road. A tree branch snagged it. The Petes are on the scene. Here's the picture Pete Junior just emailed me."

Mev looked at Jake's computer screen. Red Wilker's partially decomposed face stared back at her. "Horrors!" she exclaimed. "Red's body is already rotting."

"Pete Senior says the body may have been in the water for twelve to eighteen hours," Jake said.

"Did he speculate on cause of death?"

"He didn't need to speculate. Red was shot. Shot once in the back of the head from close range. But we'll need confirmation from a coroner."

"So Red was lured to his death yesterday, lured to Rosa's Cantina by someone he thought would contribute to his campaign," Mev said. "And then lured to Founding Father's Creek."

"Where he was shot on the bank and dragged into the water. The Petes found blood in the sand. Something doesn't compute, Mev. If Red went missing yesterday afternoon, was he killed then, before the town council met? Or was he held captive and killed last night, when the council postponed the vote? And if so, how did the killer know what the council decided?"

"Catherine posted an article about it right after the meeting. We need Red's phone, Jake."

"I'll ask the Petes to search for his phone tomorrow. It may be in the creek. Now I've got to tell Grace. I think I'll do it in person. Will you come with me?"

"As soon as I call Catherine. She'll be writing the story. I don't want her to publicize the cause of death until we get confirmation from Dirk."

John Hicks walked into Jake's office holding a cell phone. "Melissa Barnett seems to use her Android mostly for shopping, googling celebrities, and only occasionally calling her husband," he said. "She called Ace at ten fifty, yesterday morning."

"That must have been just after we left her house," Mev said.

"That's what I figured. By the way, this morning the Petes searched the house. They found Ace Barnett's truck in his driveway. But they didn't find Ace. Melissa told them that Ace had gone for a walk. The Petes waited an hour, but Ace didn't return. They confiscated Melissa's cell phone. She's hoppin' mad now."

"I'll have the Heron Brook police watch the house to nab him when he returns," Jake said.

"If he returns."

e/se/s

BREAKING NEWS

Red Wilker's Body is Found

Redford ("Red") Wilker is dead. Two fishermen discovered his body floating in Founding Father's Creek downstream from Black Fox Road.
The body is being sent to Chestatee Regional Hospital in Atlanta for an immediate autopsy.

Catherine Perry-Soto, Editor

e/se/s

Grace Wilker took the news of Red's death not well. And when Jake asked her for Red's cell phone number, she became hysterical.

"Why invade Red's privacy now? Red's dead. Let the past stay buried! Now get out of my house!" she shrieked.

"We need Red's cell phone number to locate his phone," Mev said. "If we find his phone, we may find his killer."

"I don't care who his killer is. Red lived a good life. He was a Christian. Now he's gone. Let him rest in peace."

When they were back in the patrol car, Jake said, "Grace knows something that we need to know. I'll get a search warrant."

"How about giving her time to plan Red's funeral, Jake?"

e/se/s

Lottie attended the town council meeting, where Ruth Griggs wept over the murder of her friend. After much speculation about the role of the Saxxons in Red's death, the council voted four to three to proceed on schedule with the sanctuary city designation.

"Why would the Saxxons kidnap Red, who was on their side anyway, and then kill him before the council had time to reverse its decision?" Rhonda asked after the meeting had been adjourned. "I don't think the Saxxons did it. I think someone who didn't like Red did it."

"And who would that be, Rhonda?" Jonathan asked.

"Could be Rhonda herself," Ruth Griggs said.

"*Cállate*, Ruth," Blanca said.

"I'm a pacifist, Ruth. Remember? You once called me a tree-hugging, animal-loving liberal feminist environmentalist pacifist. Tree-hugging, animal-loving liberal feminist environmentalist pacifists don't do murder."

"Maybe Red knew who killed Crockett," Jonathan said. "And Crockett's killer decided to silence him."

"Maybe Red killed Crockett, and somebody else killed Red in revenge," Blanca said. "Revenge is a powerful motive to kill."

"Maybe the Saxxon who urged us to be vandals for America did it," Lydia Gray said.

"I told you all that this sanctuary idea was un-American," Alvin Autry said. "And illegal."

"What do you think, Lottie?" Atsadi asked.

"I think that the coroner's report will give us a clue," Lottie said, getting up from the table. "I will see you all on Sunday."

CHAPTER 13

Friday Evening:

Lottie went home, phoned Mev, and recounted the council's action. Mev said the coroner would provide the official cause of Red's death.

"It's funny," Lottie said, "the coroner will state the cause of death, say, a gunshot to the head, but that's only the manner of death. The cause of death is more complicated. It may be something that happened fifty years ago."

"Do you mean that Red's death may be related to Tyrone's death, Aunt Lottie?"

"I mean that the causes of a murder, any murder, can be years in the making."

"You're suggesting that Allie killed Crockett and Red?"

"No, Mev. I'm just saying that what happens in the present is motivated by the past."

Lottie disconnected and let Doolittle out of his cage. She poured herself a full glass of chardonnay. Then she pulled up on her screen the exchange of letters to the editor between Red and Rhonda on November thirtieth and December first. She realized that Red's own words supported the story that Allie had told in her letters.

Lottie called Mev back. "Mev, dear, I want to read you a letter to the editor Red wrote last fall against the 'Me Too' movement."

Over the phone, she read Red's letter, which concluded with the plea, "I say, let the past stay buried. And let us all be judged by the good we have done in our adult life. I don't know anybody who didn't make a few bad mistakes that he regrets. God forgives. So we should too."

"'Let the past stay buried,'" Mev repeated. "Red's got something in his own past he wants to stay buried. Red told Grace, 'Let the dead stay buried,' when Grace inquired into Red's relationship with his cousin."

"Crockett called Red on Sunday, right?"

"Right," Mev said. "Let me come over and show you John Hicks's report on the contents of Crockett's iPhone."

"I'll pour you a glass of wine.

Mev arrived with Jaime and Jorge, to Doolittle's delight.

"Hello, Doolittle."

"Hello. Wanna cuddle." Doolittle hopped from his perch onto Jaime's hand.

Mev showed Lottie a copy of John Hicks's report.

"If Allie didn't kill Crockett and Red, here's what might have taken place," Mev said. "On the Thursday night before Labor Day Ace Barnett texted Crockett to tell him about the sanctuary city decision. Crockett already knew about it, and already knew about his rich, despicable cousin's announcement for mayor. Ace and Crockett planned the Saxxons' rally. On the Sunday before Labor Day, Crockett conceived of the kidnapping, and over the phone, he named Red as the victim."

"Perhaps he named Red, or perhaps he named Beau," Lottie interjected. "Crockett asked Ace to meet him at the cabin at eight o'clock Labor Day night, which would have been a half hour before Beau was invited there. Crockett could have targeted Beau because Beau is biracial."

"Maybe Ace Barnett planned to take Beau on his own when he didn't find Crockett, but he wouldn't have been able to handle Beau, Jorge, and me, and our dogs," Jaime said.

"Maybe Ace Barnett took out Crockett," Jorge said. "Crockett owed him money."

"Crockett could have named Beau to Ace, but then why would the Saxxons have taken Red?"

"Maybe the Saxxons didn't," Lottie said. "Go on with your theory, dear."

"Anyway, for some reason or other, Crockett called Red on Sunday night and they talked for four minutes. Red returned the call a few minutes later and they talked for three minutes.

"Now do you want my theory?"

"Go ahead."

"Crockett said something to Red in his phone call that upset Red, so Red called him back. The next morning, Red drove up to Crockett's cabin to talk more, or to have it out with him, or whatever. Red saw Crockett go into the outhouse. He followed the path to the outhouse, stuck his gun through the moon, and fired. Then he left."

"But why would he have killed his cousin?" Lottie asked. Mev's hypothesis made sense to her, in light of Allie's second letter, but she couldn't tell Mev that Allie had written to her.

"All we know is that Red and Crockett, who had grown up together and were inseparable their freshman year in high school, distanced themselves from each other in their sophomore year," Mev said. "We don't know why."

"They might have parted ways after Labor Day of 1968," Lottie said. "If Allie's rapists were Red and Crockett, then Tyrone's killers were Red's father Bullet Wilker and Crockett's father Harper B. Wood, who also parted ways after that Labor Day."

"What could have caused the rift?"

"Something else very consequential happened that Sunday night, Mev. Allie Marie Camhurst disappeared. The police found her blood on the scene and concluded that she had been murdered, like Tyrone. She was never seen thereafter."

"So each of the Klansmen thought that one of the others had done it?"

"Crockett and Red, who were fifteen years old then, knew that Allie could identify them, because she had called out the skinny one's name. Allie said that the other one chased her. Could be that Red chased her and Crockett thought that Red killed her," Lottie said.

"If Crockett accused Red, then Red would have hated him," Jaime said.

"And Red's dad Bullet Wilker would have hated Crockett's dad Harper B Wood," Jorge said.

"Red interpreted Crockett's return to Witherston last weekend as a personal threat to him. Grace Wilker said that it upset him," Mev said.

"Enough to kill Crockett?"

"Could be. Too bad we can't interrogate Red."

"So who killed Red?" Jorge asked.

"If your mother's theory that Red killed Crockett is correct, a Saxxon could have avenged Crockett's death by killing Red," Lottie said.

"Ace Barnett?"

"Conceivably. But that's only if the theory that Red murdered his cousin Crockett is correct."

"Do you think it's correct, Aunt Lottie?"

"I can't say."

"But how would Ace Barnett have known that Red murdered Crockett?" Jaime asked.

Mev's phone beeped, indicating the arrival of an email.

"Another email from John Hicks. Let me check it." Mev paused. "Ace Barnett has sent out a second email blast." She showed it to them.

From: A Saxxon donotreply@gmail.com

To: Saxxons in Tennessee, North Carolina, and Georgia

RALLY UPDATE
Fri 09/07/2018 9:55 p.m.

This is a reminder that Saxxons will protest Witherston's sanctuary city on Sunday afternoon at 3:30. Leave your vehicle in the Kroger parking lot at the corner of Creek St and Immookali Ave. We will assemble there. I will lead the march to the front steps of the courthouse. I will carry a burning cross. Everyone else will carry a tiki torch. Wear your hood and robe. We don't want anyone recognizing us.

A Saxxon

Sent from my phone

"So we know where the Saxxons will assemble,"

Jorge said. "Maybe we can do something there."

"Like what?"

"Like bring leaf-blowers, greet the Saxxons in front of the courthouse, and blow away all their hoods."

"And expose them!"

"We can blow their robes up over their heads!" Jorge added. "I'll send out an email blast to our friends. I'll bet we can get ten leaf-blowers there."

"And the Tayanita Villagers can take everybody's picture," Lottie said.

"Smile! You're on Candid Camera," Jorge said.

"Good thing we're getting help from the Dahlonega police," Mev said. "Those Saxxons will be hopping mad."

"You all might wear masks, Halloween masks, so they can't identify you," Lottie said.

"All the funnier," Jorge said.

"I have another idea," Jaime said. "Tony Lima's band can set up on top of Tayanita Village's hay wagon. We can greet the Saxxons in the parking lot and accompany them to the courthouse, all the time playing our funny songs."

"Right, bro! Like "Purple People Eater' and 'Tiptoe Through the Tulips.'"

"And 'Monster Mash,'" Jaime said.

"How about 'Flushed from the Bathroom of Your Heart'?"

"That one is too sad, Jorge. We don't do love-gone-wrong songs."

"Will you show me the email before you send it, Jorge?" Mev asked. "This will be the first time folks in Witherston will hear about the Saxxons' rally. We need to be careful what we disclose."

"Sure, Mom."

"Send it to Rhonda, Jorge," Lottie said. "For fun!"

"And copy Lottie and me, and Jake too, please. And John Hicks."

"And Catherine Perry-Soto."

Jorge and Jaime asked to be excused, leaving their mother with Lottie.

"Did you find an Atlanta police officer named Meadows?" Lottie asked Mev.

"I put John Hicks on the case. John Hicks said he checked the directory of local and state police employees and found nobody named Meadows. The GBI will track her down."

∽∾∽

Lottie called the Witherston Inn. "Hello, Maisie. This is Charlotte Byrd. I'm trying to reach one of your guests whom I met at the Labor Day Festival. Her first name is Jane, I believe. I don't recall her last name."

"Hello, Dr. Byrd. Let's see. We haven't had any guest named Jane staying with us, but we did have a guest for Sunday night named Janet. Janet Ullmann from Atlanta. Could she be the person you're looking for?"

"Yes, of course. Was Janet here over Labor Day?"

"She was. Looks like she checked in on Sunday evening and checked out Monday morning at ten o'clock."

"Did you happen to take down the number of her license plate? I might be able to reach her that way."

"I did. But even though I trust you, Dr. Byrd, I'm not allowed to give it out to anybody other than the police."

"That's fine, Maisie. I understand. Thanks for talking with me."

Lottie went to her computer and opened the online white pages for Atlanta. She found a Janet Ullmann at 1136 Persimmon Avenue, apartment 1013, telephone number 404-549-6868. On a hunch she went to the Fulton County Tax Assessors website and typed in the name Meadows. There she found an April Camille Meadows in the same apartment complex, at 1136 Persimmon Avenue, apartment 1015, telephone number 404-855-3664. Lottie jotted down the addresses and phone numbers.

"Oh, my. Trudy Lee Wood became Janet Ullmann, and Allie Marie Camhurst became April Camille Meadows. They must have remained close friends over forty years. How nice," Lottie said to herself. "Now what do I do with this information?"

Lottie rang Mary Lou Pattison, but Mary Lou didn't pick up. She left a message for Mary Lou to call her.

Then she checked Mapquest to find the driving time between 1136 Persimmon Avenue and Witherston. One hour and fifty-eight minutes.

Lottie looked at her watch. Ten fifteen. She phoned 404-855-3664.

A woman picked up. "Hello?"

"Hello," Lottie said. "Am I speaking with April Camille Meadows?"

"Yes. This is April Meadows. May I ask who is calling?"

"Charlotte Byrd, from Witherston."

"Oh! How did you find me, Dr. Byrd?"

"I will tell you that later, Allie. But I must tell you now that the GBI is searching for you."

"How do they know I'm alive? Did you tell them?"

"They don't know you're alive. I did not tell them. I shared your letter, the first one, with Beau Lodge, and only Beau. But Detective Arroyo wants to interview you. I think she wants to rule you out as a murder suspect."

"Well, I plan to come out of hiding soon anyway."

"Do you know that Red Wilker is dead?"

"I found out about Red's death the same way I found out about Crockett's death—online. I have been reading *Witherston on the Web* for the last year or so. I would like to come home."

"Then you know that your life is no longer in danger."

"It's not if I can prove I didn't murder Crockett and Red."

"Where were you on Monday morning?"

"Labor Day? Here in my apartment on Persimmon Avenue. I was babysitting my great granddaughter Lila, who is three months old."

"Did you know before Labor Day that Crockett was in Witherston?"

"I found that out on Sunday morning from a letter to the editor. Somebody named Alvin Autry complained about his cabin."

"Had you ever been there?"

"No. Why would I have ever been there? I didn't even know Crockett in high school. He was a freshman when I was a senior."

"Could your friend Trudy Wood have been to the cabin?"

"You mean Jane? Probably. Jane told me her father Harper B. Wood inherited it from his uncle Eddie in 1968. So she might have gone up there when she was in high school."

After a moment's silence, Allie Camhurst asked, "Is Jane a suspect?"

"No, but she may become a suspect. She spent Sunday night at the Witherston Inn, where she registered under the name of Janet Ullmann."

"That's the name she took in 1971, after Red Wilker raped her. Jane didn't want either Red or Crockett to find her."

"Do you think she could have killed Crockett and Red?"

"No. But if she did, she would have had good reason to kill Red. We heard Red's radio interview on Tuesday. I hope everybody in Witherston looked up the letter Mrs. Rather referred to. Did you look it up?"

"I did."

"Imagine! Red figured that forty-seven years of not raping anybody made him a good man, worthy of being mayor, like his father who joined the KKK, murdered Tyrone, and then became mayor. Red had some nerve writing 'God forgives so we should too.' Did you read the response? Jane wrote it."

"I did."

"So maybe Jane did kill Red, and maybe she did kill Crockett. I wouldn't blame her. I would like to have done it myself. Anyway, she's not around."

"Where did Jane go?"

"She works for Delta, so she might have gone anywhere."

"When did she leave?"

"Friday morning."

"I'm speaking at the sanctuary city designation ceremony tomorrow, Allie. Would you like to come? I'm sure that Mary Lou would be thrilled. And you could talk to Detective Arroyo, who is my niece, and clear your name."

"I'll think about it. Mary Lou would be the only one who'd recognize me. Where does Mary Lou live?"

"Forty-Four Hundred Saloli Mountain Road."

"If you see me, Dr. Byrd, please call me 'April.'"

"And you call me 'Lottie.'"

∽∾∽

Jorge sent out the email blast.

From: Jorge Arroyo jorgearroyo01@gmail.com

*To: jaimearroyo01@gmail.com, beau-
lodge2001@gmail.com, pacoarroyo@gmail.com, an-
niejerden@gmail.com, yolandagallo@gmail.com, gbo-
zeman@epa.org, jonathanfinley@comcast.com,
ssorensen@gmail.com, hernandozamora@gmail.com,
ignacioiglesias@gmail.com, atsadimoon@gmail.com,
amadahyhenderson@gmail.com, rhondara-
ther@comcast.com, tonylima@comcast.net*

*C: Mev.WitherstonPolice@WitherstonGeorgia.gov,
Jake.WitherstonPolice@WitherstonGeorgia.gov,
John.Hicks.WitherstonPolice@WitherstonGeorgia.gov,
lottiebyrdwitherston@gmail.com, catherineperryso-
to@webwitherston.com*

HELP TURN AWAY SAXXONS
Fri 09/07/2018 10:49 p.m.

Dear Good Guys:
*The Witherston Police has learned that the Saxxons
for America plan a rally for Sunday at 3:30 p.m. in front
of the courthouse to scare us away from declaring Witherston a sanctuary city. They will leave their jalopies in
the Kroger parking lot, where they will start their march
down Creek Street. They will wear their KKK-style sheets
and pointy white pillow cases and carry tiki torches.
Their leader will carry a burning cross.*
*We can't let the Saxxons intimidate us. So Jaime and
I have devised a three-part plan.*
*1) At 3:00 p.m. behind Kroger Tony Lima's Moun-
tain Band will assemble on Tayanita Village's hay wag-*

on. Atsadi Moon driving the Village's tractor will pull it. The band will play the funniest songs they know, such as "Monster Mash," "The Purple People Eater," and "Tiptoe Through the Tulips." The tractor will follow the Saxxons, real closely! Hehe. (OK, Atsadi?) Tony will bring a mic and amplifier. (OK, Tony?)

2) The rest of us will bring our leaf-blowers. We will meet behind the courthouse at 3:00 and hide in the bushes. When the Saxxons arrive we will pop out with our leaf-blowers powered on High and aim them at the Saxxons. We will blow the Saxxons' sheets off their bodies and their pointy white pillow cases off their heads and get a good look at who they are. Chief Mike Moss will bring the fire engine to shoot water on the burning cross and the tiki torches. (OK, Chief Moss?)

3) Amadahy and other Tayanita Villagers will take pictures. Amadahy will publish them on Webby Witherston. (OK, Amadahy?)

Witherston police and Dahlonega police will be there to protect everybody.

Mom says that the Sanctuary City designation ceremony will take place at 4:00 as planned, with Mayor Rather presiding.

Bring your dogs if you like. Jaime and I will bring Mighty. Beau will bring Sequoyah. We hope John Hicks will bring Bear.

Wear a red T-shirt. And a Halloween mask, if you have one.

Please Reply All to let us know if you are in.

Thanks!

Jorge (and Jaime)

Sent from my phone

By midnight Jorge had received many commitments to participate. Jonathan replied that he and Gregory would wear their Michelle and Barack Obama masks and would bring their leaf blowers. Hernando said that he would wear a Mardi Gras mask and would bring a leaf-blower. Atsadi promised to pull the hay wagon. Amadahy said that she would wear a cat mask and would take pictures of the exposed Saxxons. Chief Moss promised to bring the fire engine. Beau promised to bring Sequoyah and his father and their two leaf blowers. He said he would wear his Lion King mask. Yolanda promised to bring a leaf-blower and said she would wear a red Mexican peasant dress. Ignacio said he would bring a leaf-blower and wear a Darth Vader mask. Rhonda asked to ride on the hay wagon as a singer and said she would bring Coco Chanel.

"I will bring one of our leaf-blowers," Paco wrote. "And I'll wear Jaime's Zorro mask."

Tony Lima said that he would call a band practice for Saturday at ten to learn the new songs.

"Woohoo! The party's on! Seven leaf-blowers plus our two makes nine."

Jorge read the responses to his brother as they put on their pajamas. Mighty was already sound asleep on Jaime's bed.

"Are you going to wear a mask?" Jaime asked.

"I'll wear a black half-mask like the Lone Ranger."

"Why does Beau need to have his father there?"

"Because his father is black, which is not the Saxxons' favorite color."

CHAPTER 14

WWW. ONLINEWITHERSTON.COM

WITHERSTON ON THE WEB
Saturday, September 8, 2018

NEWS

Red Wilker's Body Is Found

*T**he body of Redford ("Red") Wilker was found
Friday in Founding Father's Creek a hundred
yards south of Black Fox Road.*

*Dr. Dirk Wales, Coroner, is expected to disclose the
cause of death later today.*

*According to his wife Grace Wilker, Red disap-
peared shortly after 12:00 noon on Thursday.*

Catherine Perry-Soto, Editor

---

*Town Council Votes Four to Three to
Proceed with Sanctuary City*

The Witherston Town Council voted four to three last night to proceed with the Sanctuary City designation ceremony scheduled for 4:00 tomorrow afternoon. Those in favor were Atsadi Moon, Dr. Charlotte Byrd, Jonathan Finley, and Blanca Zamora. Those opposed were Alvin Autry, Lydia Gray, and Ruth Griggs.

After the meeting Ruth Griggs said, "By our vote we have just invited Vandals for America to do more mischief."

Atsadi Moon, chair, said, "I support holding the ceremony because we cannot allow white supremacists to prevent our doing justice."

Catherine Perry-Soto, Editor

NORTH GEORGIA IN HISTORY
By Charlotte Byrd

Gertrude Wilker wrote the last entry in her diary on Christmas night of 1954. She died of a stroke on December 31 of that year at the age of forty-nine.

Today started off as a pretty good Christmas and ended up as a pretty bad Christmas. This year everybody came to my house for the turkey dinner. Sister Geraldine and Boone, and Harper B and Ella with their twins Crockett and Trudy Lee, who are sixteen months old, arrived before noon. Bullet and Nelly with little Red, who is nineteen months old, arrived an hour or so later. And brother Eddie arrived so late he almost missed the meal. I gave each grandchild a rocking horse that I built myself and painted red. Bullet and Nelly gave me an apron that Nelly had cut out of yellow cloth. Harper B and Ella gave me a blue shawl that Ella had croshayed. Eddie gave me a couple jars of moonshine like he always does.

But after dinner Bullet and Harper B and Eddie got to drinking the moonshine and arguing about politics. Eddie didn't like that Bullet and Harper B joined the KKK last summer and he told them they were ignorant. Bullet and Harper B got mad and called Eddie a darkie lover because Eddie has a Negro friend he visits in Atlanta. Bullet and Harper B said they joined the KKK after the president of the United States said that Negro children and white children had to go to the same schools. Eddie said the law was the law. I said Eddie don't have children so why should he care. Then Boone got into the argument. Boone's been in the KKK a long time. Boone said that Mister Griffin who just got elected governer promised to keep Georgia schools segregated come hell or high water. When the babies heard the yelling and started crying Geraldine said for everybody to go home. So everybody went home. Thank the Lord Christmas is over.

On Monday, May 17, 1954, the United States Supreme Court had ruled in the case of Brown versus the Board of Education that "separate but equal" schools for white students and black students were unconstitutional. Bullet Wilker and Harper B Wood joined the Ku Klux Klan in response to that "Black Monday" Supreme Court decision. So did many other white supremacists in the South. In 1956, some 3,500 Klansmen congregated on top of Stone Mountain to signify their resistance to the federal government.

OBITUARY

Redford Arnold Wilker
1953-2018

Redford Arnold ("Red") Wilker, age sixty-five, died on Thursday, September 6, 2018, in Witherston.

Red Wilker was born in Dahlonega on June 1, 1953, to Bullet and Nelly Redford Wilker. He was their only child.

Wilker is survived by his wife of forty-three years, Grace Eggington Wilker, his dogs Smith and Wesson, and his cat Effie. He was preceded in death by his parents and by his second cousin Crockett Boone Wood who was shot to death on September 3, 2018.

Wilker was the proprietor of Wilker's Gun Shop, which he inherited in 1999 from his father Bullet Wilker.

According to Grace Wilker, Red will be remembered as a sportsman, a collector of stuffed and mounted wildlife including a large black bear which he shot himself, a collector of guns, and a believer in Christ the Lord. She said, "Red had set his heart on becoming mayor of Witherston, like his daddy. He would have been a great mayor."

The funeral service will be held at the Witherston Baptist Church on Sunday at 12:00 noon. Reverend Paul Clement will officiate. The pallbearers will be Mayor Rich Rather, Emmett Gray, Grant Griggs, and Trevor Bennington, Jr. The body will be interred in the church graveyard.

Amadahy Henderson, Reporter

LETTERS TO THE EDITOR

To the Editor:
So-called Mr. Saxxon (author of letters to the editor on September 5 and 6) is trying to kill Witherston's sweet music. Witherstonians won't let him. Witherstonians would rather sing than fight.

Think of us this way. We Witherstonians form a symphony, a unique symphony because we Witherstonians are unique. We are of different colors and different ages. We are different from each other, and some of us are even weird. But we like to play together. We play different instruments—guitar, banjo, harmonica, violin, cymbals, trumpet, French horn, mandolin, maracas, steel pan, dizi, sitar, panpipe, Anasazi flute, African harp, Cherokee drums, and keyboard—and we take turns singing. Our songs come from Spain, Mexico, Kenya, Japan, Tibet, India, Ireland, and the United States. They were sung in the Middle Ages and in the nineteenth century, brought from distant lands, passed down from fiddler to fiddler, from parents to children, in mountains, deserts, prairies, and coasts. They've been translated, sung in fields and on boats and in great halls, played by orchestras and rock bands and choruses, hummed by mothers to their babies.

Now here comes Mr. Saxxon, ridiculous Mr. Saxxon who likes to dress up in a white sheet and a pointy white pillow case with eye holes so he can burn crosses on people's lawns anonymously. Mr. Saxxon writes to Webby Witherston that some of us should inflict damage on others, like the violinists should hurt the African harp player because the African harp player comes from Kenya, or the French horn player should kill the dizi player because the dizi player comes from Tibet. How can we make our music without a harpist or a dizi player?

Do you all really think that a man wearing a sheet and a pointy white pillow case could possibly move our conductor aside, get up in front of us, wave his tiki torch toy, tell us to stop playing together, and then keep us from giggling? We would giggle ourselves off our chairs. The sitarist would yank off Mr. Saxxon's pointy white pillow case, non-violently of course because she's from India, and expose his face. Hehehe. The guitarist would yank off Mr. Saxxon's white sheet and expose his britches, if he's wearing any. Hehehe. The drummer would throw his sticks at him. The trumpeter would blow him a raspberry. And we'd laugh and laugh and laugh.

So if the Saxxons come to Witherston, what do you think we're gonna do?

Jaime Arroyo and Jorge Arroyo
Witherston

WEATHER

I predict that the sun will shine down upon us today and tomorrow, the stars will light up our night skies tonight and tomorrow night, and rain will pour down on us on Monday.

High today will be seventy-nine degrees. Low tonight will be sixty-five degrees. Exactly.

Everything is beautiful in its own way.

Did you all know that the song "Everything is Beautiful" was composed by Ray Stevens, the same Ray Stevens from Clarkdale, Georgia, who wrote "The Streak," "Ahab the Arab," and "I'm My Own Grandpa"? Hard to believe.

Tony Lima, Weather Predictor and Musicologist

❧❧❧

On Saturdays Lottie went next door for a big Southern breakfast with Mev, Jaime, Jorge, and Paco, who cooked it. Today Paco was preparing scrambled eggs, grits, sausage, and biscuits. And orange juice and coffee.

"I've brought blueberries," Lottie said, setting a big bowl on the counter and giving hugs to Mev, Jorge, and Paco.

"Hey there, Jaime," she called into the living room where Jaime was practicing "Lay Down" on his guitar.

"Hey there, Aunt Lottie," Jaime called back. "Our band will play 'Lay Down' at the end of tomorrow's ceremony. I'm going to be the lead singer, since Annie has to do something else."

"What will you all play before the ceremony, *hijo*?" Paco asked.

"As we follow the Saxxons to the courthouse on Atsadi's tractor we'll play Tony's favorite funny songs. You know them, Aunt Lottie. 'Purple People Eater,' 'Monster Mash,' and 'Little Nash Rambler.'"

"'Beep, beep, beep, beep. His horn went beep, beep, beep,'" Jorge sang from the kitchen.

"Then when the Saxxons arrive at the courthouse steps, we'll play 'Tiptoe Through the Tulips,'" Jaime continued.

"And that's when we Good Guys turn on our leaf-blowers and whoosh the Saxxons till their pointy hoods and robes come off," Jorge said. "And Chief Moss will hose them down after they're naked."

"They won't be naked, bro."

"Just imagining best scenario, bro."

As she sat down for breakfast, Lottie opened her iPad. "Have you seen your sons' letter to the editor, Mev?"

Mev read the letter.

"Oh, lord," she said. "You boys have made yourselves targets. Do you think you can ridicule the Saxxons
and the Saxxons won't notice?"

"Ooh-eee! I'm scared," Jorge said.

"We want the Saxxons to notice, Mom," Jaime said.
"That's why we wrote our letter."

"We want folks to laugh at the Saxxons," Jorge said.

"Good strategy, boys," Lottie said. "Laughter may be
more effective than bullets to angry, insecure ignoramus-
es."

Jaime looked at his phone.

"Oh, no!" he said. "Jorge, can you come outside with
me for a moment?"

On the back porch, Jaime showed his brother the
email Annie had forwarded from Ace Barnett.

From: Ace Barnett <paceBarnett@gmail.com>
To: Ann Jerden <anniejerden@gmail.com>

APPLICATION TO JOIN SAXXONS
Sat 09/08/2018 8:09 p.m.

Dear Miss Ann Jerden:
*When I see you on Sunday at 3:15 in the Kroger
parking lot, I will give you a white hood and robe identical to mine. I will also give you a burning cross to carry,
identical to mine. We will lead the procession together.
You will thereby show your allegiance to the Saxxons. If
you are not there on time, we will find you.*
Ace Barnett, Saxxon

Sent from my phone

"Annie's scared, Jorge. What should we do? Ace Barnett is using Annie as protection for himself."

"Tell her to wear her red sneakers, so that the cops will know who she is and won't shoot her."

"They won't know that Annie is even there unless we tell them. So we've got to tell Mom."

"But if we tell Mom, she'll tell Annie's parents, and Annie's parents will ground her. That's what always happens when Annie doesn't follow their ridiculous rules."

"Right. She'll get grounded. But that's better than getting shot."

"Okay. Let's tell Mom now, while Lottie's over here."

As Jorge and Jaime went back into the house Mev's cell phone rang.

"Hey, Jake. Good morning! What's up?"

Mev listened and said, "Are you sending it to Dahlonega? We need to know if the gun fired both bullets."

After another minute she disconnected and turned to her family. "This morning the Hatcher kids found a gun in Founding Father's Creek, right where Black Fox Road dead-ends. They were wading barefoot, and Roddy stepped on it. Mr. Hatcher called Jake, who's over there now. Jake says it's a Beretta M-Nine military pistol, and it still smells of smoke. He's sent it to the lab in Dahlonega to find out whether the gun fired the bullets that killed both Crockett and Red."

"But you don't have the bullet that killed Red, or do you?" Lottie asked.

"The pathologist found the bullet yesterday during the autopsy. Dirk sent the bullet to the lab. Jake said that Dirk has already emailed us Red's autopsy report."

Mev brought her laptop to the table. "Aha! Here it is. Dirk must have written the report late last night."

Dirk Wales, M.D.
Lumpkin County Coroner
Chestatee Regional Hospital
227 Mountain Drive
Dahlonega, GA 30533

September 8, 2018

PRELIMINARY AUTOPSY REPORT
Redford Arnold Wilker, age sixty-five

At 1:30 p.m. on Friday, September 7, 2018, a body identified by Witherston police as Redford Arnold Wilker, was discovered in Founding Father's Creek in Witherston, Georgia.

The body was taken by ambulance to the Chestatee Regional Hospital where Dr. John Morston, pathologist, immediately performed an autopsy.

Dr. Morston determined that the cause of death was a gunshot wound in the head. The 9 mm NATO bullet, of the sort used in military side arms, entered the back of the head and lodged in the cranium.

Dr. Morston estimated that the body of the deceased, a Caucasian male, six feet tall and 200 pounds, had been in the water less than twenty hours after death occurred. Accordingly, Redford Arnold Wilker was shot to death most likely between 12:00 noon and 4:00 p.m. on Thursday, September 6.

Dirk Wales, MD
Coroner

"Both were nine millimeter bullets fired by a pistol," Lottie said. "Could be a coincidence, but I doubt it. The question is whether the gun was fired by the same person in both murders."

"When we learn who the pistol's registered owner is, we'll have a big clue," Mev said. "Jake is checking on it."

"Do you think the killer is Ace Barnett, Mev?"

"Possibly. Ace was in the army, Lottie. He's a Saxxon. He likes guns. But we need to find Allie Camhurst, if only to rule her out as a suspect."

"Mom, Dad, Aunt Lottie, we have something important to tell you," Jaime said. "Annie applied to be a Saxxon and got accepted."

"By Ace Barnett," Jorge added. "Then Ace Barnett sent her an email telling her she has to march with the Saxxons tomorrow and wear the same stylish outfits they are wearing."

"*¡Hijos!*" Paco exclaimed. "I told you not to mess with the Saxxons!"

"And if Annie doesn't show up, they'll find her," Jaime said. "Look at Ace Barnett's email."

Jaime showed them Barnett's email.

"*¡Caramba!* Annie has to carry a cross!"

"But we have a plan," Jorge said. "We tell Annie to wear red shoes, and you tell the police not to shoot at her, Mom."

"I hope the police don't have to shoot at anybody, Jorge."

"The Saxxons may be carrying guns too," Lottie said. "And they'd be within the law in Georgia."

"But we'll be carrying leaf-blowers. And while the Saxxons are trying to hang on to their clothes in the cyclone, Annie can escape."

"I don't know, boys. That would be dangerous," Mev said.

"Can you think of a better plan, dear?" Lottie asked. "If Annie doesn't show up, her life could be in danger."

"If she does show up, her life is at risk," Paco said.

"I'll call Jake," Mev said. "He's coordinating the police effort."

"I'll call Annie," Jaime said. "And I'll tell the band."

"I'll contact my team," Jorge said. "I'm calling us the Good Guys."

☙❧

From: Jorge Arroyo <jorgearroyo01@gmail.com>

To: jaimearroyo01@gmail.com, beaulodge2001@gmail.com, pacoarroyo@gmail.com, anniejerden@gmail.com, yolandagallo@gmail.com, gbozeman@epa.org, jonathanfinley@comcast.com, ssorensen@gmail.com, hernandozamora@gmail.com, ignacioiglesias@gmail.com, atsadimoon@gmail.com, amadahyhenderson@gmail.com, rhondarather@comcast.com, tonylima@comcast.net

C: Mev.WitherstonPolice@WitherstonGeorgia.gov, Jake.WitherstonPolice@WitherstonGeorgia.gov, Johnhicks.WitherstonPolice@WitherstonGeorgia.gov, lottiebyrdwitherston@gmail.com, catherineperrysoto@webwitherston.com

UPDATE FOR SUNDAY
Sat 09/08/2018 9:38 a.m.

Dear Good Guys:
Annie is infiltrating the Saxxons tomorrow to find out who they are. She will have to wear a pointy hood and robe to do this important undercover (!) work. She will also have to carry a burning cross and lead the spooky parade with Saxxon Ace Barnett.

Ace Barnett thinks that nobody will know the differ-ence between him and Annie, but we will. Annie will be wearing red sneakers. So look at everybody's feet.

Let's us Good Guys assemble with our leave blowers behind the courthouse at 3:00. We'll wear funny masks.

When the Saxxons arrive at the courthouse about 3:30, John Hicks will lead his party of five mounted Ta-yanita Villagers onto the platform where they will repre-sent the Cherokees of our community.

Then we Good Guys will jump out of the bushes and whoosh the Saxxons with our leaf-blowers, blow off their hoods, AND rescue Annie.

Then Chief Moss will spray the Saxxons with water from the fire engine to extinguish the burning crosses and the tiki torches.

Amadahy will take pictures and will publish them in Webby Witherston.

We will thereby expose the Saxxons to the world and make Witherston famous.

Wear red.

See you all at 3:00. Ready, set, go!

Jorge (and Jaime)

Sent from my phone

ཀ♡ཀ

Lottie had been home no more than a half hour when Mev called.

"Jake and I just heard from the GBI. On Monday, September 30, 1968, Allie Marie Camhurst filed a peti-tion to change her name to April Camille Meadows. She resides at Eleven Thirty-Six Persimmon Avenue, apart-ment Ten-Fifteen, telephone number four, zero, four, eight, five, five, three, six, six, four. The GBI was unable to reach her, so they've issued an APB."

"I don't think Allie is a murderer, Mev."

"I have other news, Aunt Lottie. The pistol is registered to Crockett Boone Wood."

"That tells us a lot. The shooter must have taken Crockett's pistol, maybe Monday morning when Crockett was in the outhouse, and shot him with it."

"So Red didn't do it. If Red had gone up to the cabin to kill Crockett, he would have used his own gun."

"Ace Barnett could have done it."

"Ace would have used his own gun too, Aunt Lottie. I'm sorry but this information makes Allie Camhurst, AKA April Camille Meadows, our prime suspect. She might have learned Crockett's whereabouts from Webby Witherston and come up here to confront him. She could have entered the cabin, figured Crockett was in the outhouse, taken Crockett's pistol from the table, shot him through the outhouse moon, and then gone after Red. She despised them both."

"For good reason. But if she killed Crockett, which I doubt, I'd hate to see her go to prison for putting into the ground an evil man who raped her. Any prints on the gun?"

"None. The gun had been wiped. Anyway, we have to find Allie if she's alive."

Lottie's phone rang. It was Atsadi Moon.

"Hello, Atsadi. What's up?"

"Hello, Dr. Byrd. I have a request. Will you give a brief speech at the ceremony tomorrow? I have to know now, because Rhonda and I are finalizing the agenda for Catherine to put online.

"Of course, Atsadi! I'd be honored."

"Can you give me a title?"

"Now? Okay. 'The Lion King Got it Right.'"

എൗഌൗഌ

While Jaime was at band practice, Jorge and Paco
waited with Rhonda for the Greyhound Bus to bring Diego Amado to Witherston.

Jorge sent Diego a text message. *Hola, Diego. Soy
Jorge. Bienvenido. ¿Dónde estás?* He included a selfie.
Diego wrote back. *Hola, Jorge. Gracias. We're on a
curvy mountain road. The bus driver says we'll arrive in
Witherston in ten minutes.* He included a selfie.

"A hunk," Rhonda exclaimed. "He looks like Ricky
Martin!"

In ten minutes the bus delivered two passengers, a
white-haired woman in her sixties who disappeared into
the bus station and a slender brown-skinned, black-haired
teenager wearing jeans and a red Atlanta Falcons T-shirt
carrying a well-used brown duffle bag and a guitar case.

"There's Diego," Paco said.

"Diego Amado?" Jorge called out.

"That's me," Diego said, approaching them.

"Hi, Diego. I'm Jorge. My twin brother Jaime plays
the guitar too. Maybe you'd like to join his band." Jorge
shook Diego's hand.

"*Mucho gusto.* I would like to join his band. Yes.
Thanks."

"What's your *repertoire*?" Jorge asked.

"My *repertoire*? You mean the kind of songs I play?

"Right."

"I play Mexican songs. Soft Mexican rock. Do you
know Fernando Lima? I play like him."

"Cool."

Paco gave Diego with a hug. "*Soy Paco.* Welcome to
Witherston."

"*Mucho gusto, Señor Arroyo.*"

"I'm Rhonda Rather. This is Coco Chanel." Rhonda handed her dog to Paco and kissed Diego on both cheeks.

"Pleased to meet you, Mrs. Rather."

After they got into Rhonda's Cadillac, Rhonda turned to Diego. "You're on the program for tomorrow's Sanctuary City designation ceremony. Is that okay?"

"Do I have to make a speech?"

"Just a short one to say hello."

"Oh."

"How about if I interview you, Diego? Would that be better? I know how to do interviews."

"He sure does," Rhonda said.

"Thanks, Jorge! That would be much, much better. *¡Mucho mejor!*"

"I'll correct the agenda," Rhonda said. She called Atsadi.

ↄ∕ↄↄ∕ↄ

At noon Lottie checked *Witherston on the Web.*

BREAKING NEWS

Atsadi Moon Sets Agenda for Sanctuary City Designation

Atsadi Moon, chair of the Witherston Town Council and advocate for the sanctuary city designation, has set the following agenda for tomorrow's ceremony in front of the courthouse.

Program

4:00~ Welcome
By Mayor Rich Rather
4:05 ~ "Weave Me the Sunshine"

By Tony Lima's Mountain Band
4:10 ~ Speech: "The Lion King Got It Right"
By Dr. Charlotte Byrd
4:15 ~Designation of Witherston as a Sanctuary City
By Mayor Rich Rather
4:20 ~ Interview with Diego
By Jorge Arroyo
4:25 ~ "Lay Down (Candles in the Rain)"
By Jaime Arroyo with Tony Lima's Mountain Band
4:30 ~ Benediction
By Pastor Paul Clement
Refreshments
By Witherston Inn

Dr. Charlotte Byrd will give the main address for tomorrow's sanctuary city designation ceremony. Dr. Byrd, professor emerita of history at Hickory Mountain College, is well known in our community not only for her online column "North Georgia In History" but also for her recent book about the Cherokees titled "Invisible Persons." Dr. Byrd submitted the proposal to make Witherston a sanctuary city in response to our president's efforts to export undocumented immigrants.

Catherine Perry-Soto, Editor

"Now I'll have to write it," Lottie said to herself. She set to work.

എഐഎ

When Lottie walked into Mev's kitchen with a bottle of wine, Mev was speaking on the phone; Paco was arranging grilled rainbow trout on a platter with asparagus and new potatoes; and Jaime, Jorge, and Diego were playing dominoes on the kitchen table.

Paco held his finger to his lips. "Mev is talking with the police chief."

Lottie opened the Rioja, poured three glasses, and handed one to Paco and another to Mev.

After a couple of minutes, Mev said, "Thanks, Jake. So Red's killer is probably unarmed now. I wonder if he's still around. Or she. Have a good evening. I'll see you tomorrow at ten." Mev turned to the five of them. "The bullet that killed Crockett Wood and the bullet that killed his cousin Red Wilker were shot by the same weapon, the Beretta M-Nine," she said. "As I see it, somebody went to Crockett's cabin early Labor Day morning, found the cabin empty, took the pistol, shot Crockett through the outhouse moon, and left with the pistol. Then on Thursday, he or she convinced Red to go to Rosa's Cantina, then texted him to meet him or her a quarter mile down Black Fox Road at Founding Father's Creek, shot him there, dumped his body in the water, wiped the pistol clean of fingerprints, and tossed it."

"Clean double murder," Lottie said. "Could be anybody."

"My money is on Allie Camhurst," Mev said.

"Revenge," Paco said. "*Claro*."

"What's this all about?" Diego asked.

"Let's sit down, and we'll tell you the story over dinner," Mev said. "Help yourselves."

"First, a toast to Diego, our guest for as long as he wants to stay in Witherston," Paco said, raising his glass. "*Bienvenido*, Diego."

"*Bienvenido*, Diego," Jorge said. "Welcome."

"Here's to my band's new guitarist," Jaime said.

"How do I tell you guys apart?"

"I part my hair on the left, and Jaime parts his on the right."

"Here's to Diego's new family," Mev said.

"Now let's get Diego up to speed on our sleuthing," Lottie said.

"Okay. I'll give you the simple version of Witherston's recent murderous activity, Diego," Jorge said. "A white supremacist geezer named Crockett Wood got shot in his outhouse the morning after he used his drone to drop Saxxons flyers on us unsuspecting Good Guys. Saxxons for America is a white supremacist hate group. He got shot through the moon with a gun that disappeared. A couple of days later somebody who called himself a Saxxon wrote a letter to the editor threatening harm if Witherston became a sanctuary city."

"Then somebody kidnapped and killed a local firearms dealer named Red Wilker, who was Crockett Wood's cousin. He used the same gun," Jaime said.

"Which he left on the creek bank at the scene of the Mr. Wilker's murder."

"He or she," Mev said.

"That's about it," Jaime said.

"¡Qué horror!" Diego exclaimed.

"Hijos, your version is way too simple," Paco said. "Way, way too simple."

"Let me lay out the facts of the case," Mev said.

While they ate Mev laid out the facts in chronological order. "Here's what we know. On Wednesday, August twenty-ninth, the town council approved Lottie's proposal to make Witherston a sanctuary city. The decision was reported in the *Atlanta Journal-Constitution* and other north Georgia news sources. The mayor's wife had already recruited you, Diego, and a few other immigrants in need of a safe home. On Thursday, August thirtieth, a member of the Saxxons by the name of Ace Barnett

texted the news to Crockett Boone Wood, who had gone
to high school here. Crockett came to Witherston for the
weekend, stayed in his father's hunting cabin, and
dropped the flyers. Crockett and Ace plotted a Saxxons
rally for tomorrow afternoon before our dedication ceremony."

"Is the Saxxons rally still on?" Diego asked.

"Yes," Jaime said. "So is the dedication ceremony."

"Are we immigrants responsible for the Saxxons
coming here?"

"No!" Lottie exclaimed. "You are not, definitely not,
responsible for white supremacists' ignorance."

"White supremacists hate blacks as much as they
hate immigrants," Jaime said.

"And browns like us, and gays, and miscegenists,"
Jorge said.

"What are miscegenists?"

"People who mate with people of a different skin
color and make biracial babies."

"Our friend Beau Lodge is biracial, but he looks
black. So his parents are miscegenists," Jaime said. "And
Beau has a white girlfriend, so white supremacists might
view him as a miscegenist."

"There's more to this story, Diego," Mev said.
"Crockett got the idea to take a hostage, and he named
the target to Ace Barnett in a phone call. We don't know
whom he named. On Sunday Crockett invited Beau to
visit him at his cabin Labor Day night. Jaime and Jorge
went with Beau, and they took their dogs. They found no
one around."

"After we'd entered the cabin we heard a truck come
down the driveway," Jorge said. "The driver must have
seen us, but in the pouring rain all we saw were his taillights disappearing into the woods."

"Beau could have been Crockett's target," Jaime

said. "Beau had announced in our online newspaper Sunday morning that he was investigating a Ku Klux Klan murder that took place in 1968. Two Klansmen killed an eighteen-year-old black dude named Tyrone Lewis for taking a white girl named Allie Camhurst for a ride in his car. Crockett's father was one of the Klansmen."

"Anyway, Tuesday morning Chief McCoy and I went out to investigate and discovered Crockett's body in the outhouse," Mev said.

"He'd been shot inside it with the door locked," Jorge said.

"We think there's a connection between the murder of Tyrone Lewis and rape of Allie Camhurst fifty years ago and the murder of Crockett Wood five days ago," Lottie said. She recounted the events of Labor Day weekend 1968 and summarized the letters Allie Camhurst had written to Mary Lou Pattison.

"According to Allie, two teenagers raped her. Crockett was one of the rapists," Jorge said. "And his cousin Red Wilker was probably the other one."

"If you want to solve a crime, you have to figure out a motive," Mev said. "Tyrone's death could have given someone a motive for killing Crockett and Red. That someone could be Allie, who was planning to marry Tyrone."

"A black and white marriage in 1968 would have been scandalous," Paco said.

"Especially scandalous to the KKK, who were all over Georgia in 1968," Lottie said.

"At the time, the cops couldn't find Allie, so they considered her dead," Jaime said. "But they didn't try very hard."

"We know that Allie went into hiding in Atlanta," Jorge said.

"Mom thinks that Allie offed both Crockett Wood

and Red Wilker because Crockett and Red raped her."

"What's your theory, Mom?"

"Allie Camhurst somehow learned that Crockett would be in Witherston over Labor Day, decided to confront him fifty years after his crime, went to see him on Labor Day morning, found his gun in his cabin, spotted Crockett entering his outhouse, shot him, kept the gun, and shot Red Wilker with it on Thursday."

"How would Allie have known Crockett was at the cabin?"

"She could have read *Webby Witherston*, Dad." Jorge said. "*Webby Witherston* is our online newspaper, Diego. I write a weekly column for it called 'What's Natural.'"

"Okay. But then why would she have waited till Thursday to kill Red? I think your theory may not hold up, dear niece," Lottie said.

"Allie may not even be alive, Mom. She's old," Jorge said.

"She's not old," Lottie said. "She's my age."

"*Hijo*, that's not old," Paco said.

"Aunt Lottie thinks someone else did it."

"I do," Lottie said.

"Here's another theory. Red killed Crockett," Jaime said. "Crockett Wood and Red Wilker were best friends until their sophomore year in high school. They split up on Labor Day of 1968 when their fathers killed Tyrone and they raped Allie. Crockett had something on Red. Red saw on *Webby Witherston* that Crockett was at the cabin. Red might not have wanted Crockett to be back in Witherston just when he's running for mayor."

"What could Crockett have had on Red if they both raped Allie?" Mev asked.

"Well, Crockett could have talked about the rape and accused Red of murdering Allie. He had nothing to lose since he was dying. According to his autopsy report, the geezer had pancreatic cancer."

"Keep going, Jaime."

"So on Labor Day morning Red went up to see Crockett, didn't find him in his cabin, figured he was in his outhouse, took one of Crockett's guns, shot him through the moon, and left with the gun."

"Why would Red need Crockett's gun?" Jorge said. "Red has a bazillion guns."

"And, according to your theory, Jaime, who killed Red?" Mev asked.

"Ace Barnett. Ace killed Red because Red had killed his friend Crockett."

"Or because Crockett had named Red as the person to take hostage and Ace was carrying out Crockett's wishes," Jorge said. "But I have another theory."

"Let's hear it."

"Ace killed Crockett for his money, since Crockett owed him money. Maybe he knew that Crockett had bequested him four thousand, nine hundred and eighty dollars."

"The word is 'bequeathed,' bro. So who killed Red?"

"Maybe Ace killed Red to scare Witherston folks, because big Saxxon Ace Barnett wanted Witherston not to become a sanctuary city," Jorge said.

"What's your theory, Aunt Lottie?" Mev asked.

"I'm still working on it."

"We have to find Allie, if she's alive," Mev said. "We need to talk with her."

"So what happens tomorrow?" Diego asked.

"You'll see the Saxxons," Jaime said.

"And they'll see you," Jorge said. "But don't worry. We've got a plan."

Jorge and Jaime explained the plan.

CHAPTER 15

WWW. ONLINEWITHERSTON.COM

WITHERSTON ON THE WEB
Sunday, September 9, 2018

NEWS

Saxxons Will Protest Sanctuary City

*W*itherston Police have learned that the Saxxons for America will rally this afternoon at 3:30 at the courthouse to protest the Sanctuary City designation ceremony scheduled for 4:00. According to Chief Jake McCoy, the designation ceremony will continue as planned.

"We ask that the Saxxons express their views without violence," Chief McCoy said. "We ask that the Saxxons as well as members of our Witherston community leave their guns at home. But just in case of a disturbance we will have armed officers there to keep order."

John Hicks, chief of Tayanita Village, said that Ta-yanita Villagers would help keep order.

Amadahy Henderson, Reporter

GBI Issues APB for Allie Marie Camhurst

The Georgia Bureau of Investigation has issued an all-points bulletin for Allie Marie Camhurst of Atlanta, age sixty-eight, who goes by the name of April Camille Meadows. The GBI located her car, a white 2014 Toyota Camry Hybrid, Georgia license plate # CBJ8962, at the Forsyth Street bus station in Atlanta.

According to Detective Mev Arroyo, Camhurst is wanted as a person of interest in the recent murders of Crockett Boone Wood and Redford Wilker.

Camhurst was also a witness to the 1968 murder of Tyrone Lincoln Lewis by members of the Ku Klux Klan.

Catherine Perry-Soto, Editor

Red Wilker Was Shot to Death

Chestatee Regional pathologist Dr. John Morston reported yesterday that Redford Wilker had been shot in the back of his head. He died some time between 12:00 noon and 4:00 p.m. on Thursday, September 6.

Wilker's body had been in the water for less than twenty hours before it was discovered in Founding Father's Creek.

Catherine Perry-Soto, Editor

WHAT'S NATURAL
By Jorge Arroyo

Did you know that "race" is not a natural category of humans? NEWSFLASH! Race is a social category invented in Europe in the 1600s.

According to my research, for many centuries Europeans thought that biological species were permanent and created by God. And they believed that the species had been created in a natural rank order something like this: humans at the top just below God and the angels, apes a bit lower than humans, cows a bit lower than apes, and armadillos way lower than cows.

In the 1500s and 1600s, when explorers brought back to Europe drawings of all the strange humans they had seen—some with black skin, others with slanted eyes—the scientists classified the different human groups as different "races" that fell into this rank order: whites highest, yellows in the middle, blacks lowest.

Then in 1859 Charles Darwin published "On the Origin of Species." He explained that there was no natural rank order of things and that species and races evolved. Darwin caused a big stink among people who thought that humans had been divinely created and were absolutely different from beasts.

These days geneticists find more variation within the so-called races than between them. Thus "race" is a human invention, a social category, a way of looking at things. And ranking stuff—species, races—is just a cultural habit. A bad one.

But some people in our society have never gotten this news. Or else they prefer the old model of nature in which their color rules. They are the white supremacists.

NORTH GEORGIA IN HISTORY
By Charlotte Byrd

*I had intended for yesterday's column to conclude
my tales of north Georgia moonshiners, but after learning of Gertrude Wilker's unpublished poetry manuscript I
asked a lovely librarian in the University of Georgia Rare Book Room to scan and email me the eleven poems.
The final poem is titled "A Revenuer Shot My Husband."*

> *The night was starry, the moon was shining.*
> *Obie and Eddie were drinking whiskey.*
> *Out on the porch they sat there whittling.*
> *From the bedroom I heard them talking.*
> *"Who is your sweetie?" Obie asked Eddie.*
> *"None your dam business" Eddie told Obie.*
> *"Why you keeping a secret?" Obie asked Eddie.*
> *"None your dam business" Eddie told Obie.*
> *"You seeing a Negro?" Obie asked Eddie.*
> *"Shut your dam mouth" Eddie told Obie.*
> *"You seeing a man?" Obie asked Eddie.*
> *From the bedroom I heard some shooting.*
> *"I yelled what y'all doing, Obie and Eddie?"*
> *"Obie's dead, Obie's dead!" Eddie was hollering.*
> *I ran out on the porch screaming*
> *"Obie, dear Obie!"*
> *"Obie's been shot," said Eddie to me.*
> *"My husband's shot dead?" I cried to Eddie.*
> *"The revenuers kilt him" said Eddie to me.*
> *"I don't see no revenuer" I said sobbing to Eddie.*
> *"They drove away quick" said Eddie to me.*
> *"So I am a widow" I said to Eddie.*
> *"It's a tragedy, dear sister" said Eddie to me.*

"And Bullet's just six" I said to Eddie.
"Don't worry 'bout nothin" said Eddie to me.
"What will I do?" I said to Eddie.
"I'll care for you" said Eddie to me.
"Where's Sheriff McCoy?" I said to Eddie.
"I gotta leave now" said Eddie to me.
"Good-bye, dear brother" I said to Eddie.
"Say the revenuers shot him" said Eddie to me.
"I will" I said. "You be gone now, Eddie."
The night was starry, the moon was shining.
Out on the porch I sat there weeping.

~ Gertrude Wilker, September 30, 1930

In The Witherston Weekly of Friday, August 22, 1930
I found Obadiah Wilker's obituary as well as an article
about the crime.

Obadiah Wilker
1899-1930

Obadiah ("Obie") Wilker died on Friday,
August 15, 1930, at his home near Witherston,
at the age of thirty-one.
Mr. Wilker was born in Hall County on July
5, 1899, to Arnold and Tabitha Wilker.
Boone Wood, Mr. Wilker's brother-in-law,
attested to the deceased's fine character. Mr.
Wood said, "Obie Wilker was a good man, a
smart man, and honest as the day is long. His
moonshine was the best in the valley."
Mr. Wilker leaves behind his wife Gertrude
Harper Wilker, his six-year-old son Buehler
("Bullet") Wilker, his brother-in-law Eddie
Harper, his sister-in-law Geraldine Harper

Wood, his brother-in-law Boone Wood, and his six-year-old nephew Harper B. Wood.

Pallbearers at his funeral last Monday were Sheriff Caleb McCoy, Mayor Jethro Sullivan, Calvin Autry, and Hiram Slater. Mr. Wilker was interred in the new Witherston Eternal Hills Cemetery.

The article established the official cause of Obie Wilker's death.

Obie Wilker Is Shot By Revenuers

Obie Wilker was gunned down by agents of the Internal Revenue Service on the evening of Friday, August 15, while he was whittling a toy pistol for his son on the front steps of his home on Powder Road. According to his wife, Gertrude Wilker, there were no witnesses.

Mrs. Wilker said she heard shots from her bedroom. By the time she got outside the revenuers were speeding away. She said, "I knew they were revenuers because I'd seen the car before. It was a black Dodge."

Sheriff Caleb McCoy said that so many revenuers drove black Dodges he wouldn't be able to find Obie's killer. He said, "Besides, we don't want to poke the feds."

Obie enjoyed an excellent reputation for his moonshine, which he ran to Atlanta himself in his modified Model T Ford.

Today's column concludes my moonshiner stories, at least for now. Next week "North Georgia in History" will focus on chain-saw carving in the Appalachian Mountains.

LETTERS TO THE EDITOR

To the Editor:
Thursday night somebody tied a dead raccoon to the handlebars of my bike when my girlfriend Sally Sorensen and I were inside the Witherston Public Library.

To that person, the raccoon meant "coon"—not the cute animal with the striped tail who dines at our garbage cans, but rather the black slave who, from the viewpoint of his owner, is lazy and dumb.

The person who left the poor, bloody raccoon was calling me a "coon." I am African-American.

I did some research. I found out that the racial epithet "coon" did not originally come from "raccoon." It was short for the word "barracoon," which meant somebody held in a "barraca," an enclosure for slaves in transit from Africa to America, Brazil, or Cuba.
Beau Lodge
Witherston

WEATHER

High will be in low-seventies. Low will be in mid - sixties. Clouds will come and go.
I got sunshine on a cloudy day. So do you.

Tony Lima, Climatologist, Musician, and Mexican Immigrant

℘℘℘

Lottie, Jorge, and Jaime occupied the back pew of Witherston Baptist Church even though they had arrived early for Red's funeral. Mev and Paco took the pew directly in front of them with Lauren, Jim, and Beau.

When the time came for their favorite hymn, Lottie and Jaime sang out loud and clear.

Jorge just looked around.

"Please be seated," Pastor Paul Clement, Witherston Baptist Church pastor, said from the podium.

"I wonder who all these people are," Jaime whispered to his brother after sitting down.

"Gun lovers and animal killers," Jorge whispered back. "This church is full of them."

"That's Mrs. Pattison up there with the pink hat," Beau said to Jorge and Jaime, turning around to face them.

"Mary Lou is not a gun lover," Lottie said. "Or an animal killer."

"Who's she with?" Jorge asked.

"I don't know. I never saw her before." Lottie gazed at the attractive woman with short, curly white hair and teal-rimmed glasses. She was wearing a maroon leather jacket, black slacks, and heels. The woman turned around and caught Lottie's eye.

"At this sad time, when we lay to rest our beloved fellow citizen, we must remember all the good Red Wilker did in his lifetime," Pastor Clement intoned. "He was an Air Force pilot, a church deacon, a member of the Witherston Roundtable, a sportsman, a businessman, and a candidate for mayor of our town. He was a man worthy of our admiration."

"A deacon," Jorge whispered. "Holy sheep!"

"Shush," Mev said, turning around. "Show respect for the dead."

"Why?"

Pastor Clement continued. "Red Wilker walked up-rightly, and as the Bible says, 'Those who walk uprightly enter into peace; they find rest as they lie in death.' Now let us join together in singing 'How Great Thou Art.'"

Lottie was one of the last to exit the church after the pallbearers rolled the casket out to the awaiting limousine and the mourners nearer the front followed the pallbear-ers. By the time Lottie had caught up with Mary Lou, Mary Lou's friend had vanished.

"Hey there, Mary Lou," Lottie said. "I came to show support for Grace because she's in our book club, but I'm not mourning Red's death."

"I came to see his body, to make sure he's dead," Mary Lou said.

"Who's your friend?"

Mary Lou hesitated. "Please don't tell anybody. That was Allie. She too came to make sure Red's dead."

"Will I be able to see her?"

Mary Lou hesitated. "I don't know. That's up to her."

e/ɔe/ɔ

Jaime jumped off the hay wagon in the alley behind Kroger to give Annie a hug. It was almost three fifteen, when she was supposed to meet Ace Barnett in front of Kroger in the parking lot.

Annie was wearing white jeans, a white T-shirt on which Jorge had inked a black cross, and red sneakers. She had braided her long blond hair.

Jaime, Atsadi Moon, Tony Lima, Dan Soto, Pete Koslowsky III, and Rhonda Rather wore blue jeans and red T-shirts. Except for Rhonda, they had all applied eye black to their cheekbones.

Coco Chanel wore a red ribbon.

"Be careful," Jaime said to Annie. "Wait for Ace Barnett to approach you. Don't show that you know anything about him. And remember, he's dangerous. He could have a gun."

"I'm fine, Jaime. Nothing bad will happen. I've got to go now."

"Do you want pepper spray?" Atsadi called out from his seat on the tractor.

"If she brings pepper spray, Barnett will find it on her," Tony Lima said. "He'll realize she's a spy."

"Right," Annie said. "I'm fine." She disappeared into Kroger through the store's back door.

Jaime rejoined Tony, Dan, and Rhonda on the hay wagon. At three twenty Catherine Perry-Soto arrived with Alex in his baby sling.

"May we come too?" she whispered. "I want to get the story for Webby Witherston."

Her husband Dan grabbed her hand and pulled the two of them into the wagon.

For the next few minutes they waited silently while the Saxxons assembled in the Kroger parking lot. They heard vehicles pull up. At three thirty they smelled kerosene burning.

"The Saxxons have lit the crosses," Jaime whispered.

"And the tiki torches," Dan whispered.

They heard the assembly call of a bugle.

"Showtime," Tony Lima whispered. "Purple People Eater."

Jaime, Tony, and Dan played the song's opening notes.

Atsadi started the tractor. As the tractor pulled the hay wagon around the building, Jaime saw fifteen white-robed and hooded Saxxons with tiki torches marching in rows of three. He spotted the two white-robed and hooded Saxxons with burning crosses at the head of the procession. One wore brown boots. The other wore red sneakers.

Rhonda bellowed the opening bars of "Purple People Eater" into her wireless microphone. She'd changed quite a few words.

> "Well, I saw the things comin' down the road,
> Wearing one pointy hood, one white robe,
> I commenced to shakin' and I said "ooh-eee,"
> They looked like purple people beaters to me."

Jaime and Tony sang the chorus. Dan accompanied them on the harmonica.

> "They were pointy-hooded, white-robed,
> spooky purple people beaters,
> Pointy-hooded, white-robed,
> spooky purple people beaters,
> Pointy-hooded, white-robed,
> spooky purple people beaters,
> Sure looked weird to me."

Rhonda continued.

> "Well they came up here and they made a big fuss,
> I said you purple people beaters can't beat us,
> I heard one say in a voice so gruff,
> 'We couldn't beat y'all 'cause you're too tough.'"

"There's Annie," Jaime whispered to Catherine, "in the red sneakers. The other one with a burning cross is Ace Barnett."

Catherine took a picture.

A Saxxon in the last row turned and shouted at the musicians, "Get out of here! Go back home to your mamas!"

The bugler played the calvary charge.

The brown-booted Saxxon at the front yelled, "March! Hup two three four, hup two three four!"

The fifteen Saxxons chanted, "Hup two three four."

Jaime noted the signs: *JOIN THE SAXXONS TO RESTORE AMERICA! TAKE BACK OUR COUNTRY!* and *SAY NO TO CULTURAL GENOCIDE!*

The two leaders accelerated the pace. "Hup two three four, hup two three four!"

Tony Lima shouted, "Move, Saxxons! Pick up your skirts and move!"

Rhonda giggled into her mic and turned up the volume. Jaime, Tony, and Dan joined in the giggling.

"Now 'Monster Mash,'" Tony Lima said.

Rhonda sang at the top of her lungs.

Jaime, Tony, and Dan stood up on the hay wagon and danced while playing their instruments. Catherine took pictures.

The Saxxons picked up their pace.

Rhonda sang, "The Horn Went Beep, Beep, Beep."

Atsadi honked. Beep, beep. Beep, beep.

Tony sang the next verse.

Atsadi followed the Saxxons at a distance of ten feet as the Saxxons marched up Creek Street.

ଐଔଐ

Lottie sat with Diego on the make-shift stage. She looked out at the people standing on the grass across the street from the courthouse, most of whom she knew to be in favor of the sanctuary city. She spotted Mary Lou and

Allie leaning against a two-hundred-year-old old white oak tree. Mev was heading that way.

Mayor Rather stood at the podium. "Well, well, well. What have we here?" he boomed into the microphone as the Saxxons approached the courthouse steps. "Witherston has visitors."

Jake and eleven other uniformed, armed police officers met the Saxxons on the steps.

"Do you all have a permit?" Jake asked the two leaders.

Before either of them could respond, John Hicks on Honeybunch suddenly emerged from the west side of the courthouse leading a stately procession of mounted Tayanika Villagers. He carried a green SANCTUARY CITY flag. The villagers all wore red CHEROKEES RULE T-shirts. To Mayor Rather's obvious astonishment, Penelope, Franny, Sassyass, and Felipe and Isabela cautiously carried their riders up the courthouse steps onto the stage.

"Oh, my, more visitors!" the mayor exclaimed.

"Your loyal Cherokee militia, Mr. Mayor," John Hicks shouted, dismounting from Honeybunch. "We're here to save Witherston from the racists."

Amadahy got off Penelope and took a picture of the stage party. Then she took a picture of the Saxxons.

"Smile," she said into the mic. "Smile, Saxxons!"

Suddenly Jorge jumped out of the bushes and hollered, "Good Guys, whoosh!" He turned on his leafblower and aimed it at the Saxxons' brown-booted leader. He blew off Ace Barnett's hood.

Paco, Jonathan, Gregory, Beau and Jim Lodge, Yolanda, Hernando, and Ignacio—gleefully masquerading as Zorro, Michelle and Barack Obama, the Lion King, and Darth Vader—emerged from the bushes, ran down the steps, and directed their leaf-blowers at the other Saxxons.

On the hay wagon Dan played "Mr. Tambourine Man."

"Mr. Autry," Beau exclaimed, after he blew off Alvin Autry's hood. "So you're a Saxxon!"

"And who are you, Mr. Lion King?" Alvin Autry asked.

"I'm Beau Lodge," Beau said, ripping off his mask. "Hi."

Paco, Jonathan, Gregory, Jim, Yolanda, and Ignacio blew off the hoods and robes of the rest of the Saxxons.

Chief Mike Moss doused the two burning crosses with his fire hose and turned the water on the tiki torches.

"Good Guys, off," Jorge called out.

Jorge's team turned off the leaf blowers. Chief Moss cut off the water.

"Smile, Saxxons!" Amadahy took a dozen pictures from the stage.

A Saxxon lobbed a tear gas grenade at the stage. Mike Moss turned the water back on, aimed the hose at the stage, and drenched Lottie, Diego, and the mayor.

The mule, the donkey, and the horses backed up in fright. The grenade didn't go off.

Another Saxxon lobbed a tear gas grenade at the fire engine. It didn't go off either.

"Good Guys, whoosh!" Jorge yelled.

His team restarted their blowers.

"Order!" Mayor Rather shouted. "We must have order!"

A third Saxxon flung a dud onto the stage.

Chief Moss aimed the hose at the Saxxons.

Lottie joined the mayor at the podium and grabbed the mic.

"Go home, bigots," Lottie shouted.

The crowd repeated, "Go home, bigots!"

"Ace Barnett, put your arms over your head. You are under arrest," Jake bellowed. "Pete Senior, handcuff him."

Ace Barnett grabbed Annie and held her as a shield. From his pocket he produced a pistol and aimed it at her temple.

"Get away, or I shoot her," Ace said.

"Let her go, Mr. Barnett," Jake hollered. "Let Annie go!"

"No! She stays with me."

Ace Barnett faced the stage, his back to the Saxxons. "Put down the leaf blowers! Turn off the hose!"

"Good Guys, off!" Jorge ordered.

Jorge's team shut down their leaf blowers. Chief Moss cut off the water.

Lottie heard a gunshot. She saw Ace Barnett fall to the ground, pulling Annie down with him.

"Alvin shot him," Lottie shouted.

Jake ran over to Ace Barnett and helped Annie up.

"He's dead. The bullet went through his heart."

Lottie looked at the Saxxons. Except for Alvin Autry and Ace Barnett, they were fleeing down the street to-ward Kroger.

Alvin Autry dropped his gun.

"I shot him," Alvin Autry said. "I shot Ace. I didn't mean to kill him. I just meant to save Miss Jerden. Will I be arrested? I'm eighty-four years old."

"I'm not going to arrest you, Alvin," Jake said. "You saved Annie's life."

"Thanks, Mr. Autry," Jaime said, climbing down off the hay wagon.

❦❦❦

"When we embrace each other we strengthen our community and we all win. When we fight each other we weaken our community and we all lose. And finally, remember that love for another awakens the best in ourselves. The Lion King got it right. We are more than we are because we are one."

Over the applause Lottie continued, "Now let's welcome Diego and our other future residents of Witherston."

"Even though they're not all here yet," Mayor Rather added.

Lottie sat down while her fans cheered.

John Hicks waved his SANCTUARY CITY flag.

"Go Lottie," Rhonda called out from the hay wagon.

Mayor Rather took the mic. "Thank you, Dr. Byrd. Now let me read the official document that Mr. Atsadi Moon, chair of the Town Council, has just given me." He unrolled a scroll tied with a red ribbon. Pete Three gave him a drum roll.

"Whereas Americans live in a time when the federal government endeavors to deport all those undocumented immigrants who work in our factories, clean our houses, and harvest our grapes so that we can have light sparkling wine... What? What are you making me read, Atsadi?"

"Keep reading, Mr. Mayor," Atsadi whispered. "Your wife wrote your speech. And you have two hundred prospective voters listening to you."

"Jesus! Okay."

"Go, Rich," Rhonda shouted.

"And whereas Witherstonians wish to share our bounty with those less fortunate than ourselves, and whereas we wish to promote family values, I, the Honorable Mayor Rich Rather of Witherston, Georgia, declare that henceforth Witherston shall be known as a sanctuary city committed to protecting immigrants, mixed-status families, and refugees from the cruel arm of the U.S. Government Immigration and Customs Enforcement known as ICE."

"What does that mean, Mayor Rather?" Ruth Griggs called out.

"I don't know. Ask Rhonda."

"It means that Witherston will not enforce immigration law, that we will not cooperate with ICE to identify individuals who lack the proper papers to live and work in our country, that we will not allow ICE to break up families, and that we will open our schools and churches and offer our social services to all residents of our community without regard to their immigration status."

"Go Rhonda!"

"Okay, okay. Yes, that's what I am for," the mayor said. "Thank you for clarifying my position for the good citizens of Witherston. Now let me present Jorge Arroyo, who will interview our first visitor," he said.

"*Buenas tardes*, everybody. And *bienvenido*, Diego. Welcome to Witherston, known far and wide for our gold miners, moonshiners, bootleggers, and...well, bear hunters. Oh yes, and for our Town Council, which voted to bring you here to live with us while the government deports your brown friends who don't have the right papers to live where they work. We are happy to have you here, Diego."

"*Muchas gracias*, Jorge." Diego turned to the hundred people remaining on the lawn. "I thank you from the depths of my heart. I promise to study hard and to work hard. I have skills. I can do carpentry work, build houses, and lay tiles."

"And you play the guitar?"

"I do."

"Then you will join Tony Lima's Mountain Band."

Pete Three produced a drum roll.

During the rest of Jorge's interview with Diego Lottie kept her eyes on the old oak. After five minutes she saw Mev shake hands with Mary Lou and Allie and walk away.

ფფფ

"Thank you so much for inviting us to your Sunday dinner party, Lottie."

Lottie handed Mary Lou Pattison and April Meadows each a glass of Rioja.

"I'm so glad you all came. But before the others arrive, could you tell me what Detective Arroyo asked you?"

"We've got company," Doolittle announced.

At that moment the back door opened, and Mev and Paco, Jorge and Yolanda, Jaime and Annie, and Diego walked into the kitchen followed by Mighty. Mev and Paco carried platters of garlic shrimp, batter-fried cauliflower, roasted red peppers, olives, and almonds. Jorge carried a sketchbook. Then the front door opened, and Beau entered with Sally, Lauren and Jim, and Sequoyah. Jim carried a Dutch oven full of meatballs. Lauren carried a Caesar salad.

As was their longstanding custom, Lottie's guests arranged the dishes on the dining room table alongside Lottie's baguettes and bottles of wine.

"Doolittle wanna go up." Doolittle hopped onto Jaime's hand.

"Hi, everybody," Jorge said. "This is Diego. Diego meet, Beau, Dr. Lodge, Judge Lodge, and Sequoyah."

"And Mary Lou Pattison and her friend April Meadows," Lottie added.

"Who was once Allie Marie Camhurst," April said. "I want you all to know who I am. But since I've been April for fifty years please call me April."

"I'm trying to persuade April to move back to Witherston," Mary Lou said.

"So nice to meet you, Mrs. Meadows," Beau said. "I've been wanting to get to know you."

"So you're the young historian who is working with Dr. Byrd to solve the crime of 1968? I read your letter to *Witherston on the Web*."

"Yes, ma'am. We're a team, along with Jaime and Jorge Arroyo."

"Could you tell us what happened to you?" Jaime asked.

April did, over dinner. She told of Tyrone's murder by Harper B. Wood and Bullet Wilker and her rape by Crockett Wood and Red Wilker, and of her tearful bus ride from Witherston to Atlanta that night. She told of giving Tyrone's father the terrible news of his son's death, of staying with him until she found an apartment and a job, of moving back in with him for two weeks after Link's birth, of meeting Hosea Williams with him and accompanying them on marches for justice. She told of raising Link as a single mother.

"Mr. Lincoln Lewis was the father-in-law I wanted," she said. "I would not have joined the civil rights movement without his guidance. Mr. Lewis inspired me, and he inspired Link. He loved his grandson dearly, and his grandson loved him. Link spoke at his funeral the day before his marriage to Sadie."

"As a detective I must ask you, over the years did you ever contemplate killing either Crockett Wood or Red Wilker?"

"Truthfully? No, Detective Arroyo. I wanted them dead, but I never fantasized about killing them myself."

"Tell us about Jane."

"Jane and I met by accident and became best friends. Here's her sad story. Jane, who was Trudy Lee Wood be-

fore she changed her name, found out what had happened
that night on Orchard Road when she witnessed an alter-
cation between Crockett and Red three years afterward.
Crockett and Red got drunk on their graduation night—
that would have been in May of 1971—and got into a
shouting match behind the school. Trudy was there, but
Crockett and Red didn't see her. Trudy heard Crockett
accuse Red of killing me, quote, 'after the rape.' Those
were Crockett's words. Red denied killing me, of course,
and socked Crockett in the face. They fought. Later Red
met up with Trudy and raped her, violently."

"How frightening for Trudy!" Yolanda said.

"Very. Not just the rape but also the discovery that
her father and her uncle were Tyrone Lewis's killers and
her brother and her cousin were Allie Camhurst's rapists.
People had talked about that unsolved crime for three
years, wondering who the Klansmen were."

"What happened to Trudy?"

"Trudy went to Atlanta. All by herself. She couldn't
face her classmates, and she couldn't continue to live
with her father and her brother knowing what they had
done. So she took her savings, rode the Greyhound Bus to
Atlanta, rented a hotel room, and got a job waiting tables."

"What about her mother?" Sally asked.

"Her mother had died in the fall of 1968, when she
was a sophomore. That was a hard time for a teenage girl
to lose her mother."

"That's really, really sad," Beau said.

"Anyway, in Atlanta Trudy found out that Red had
made her pregnant. She told me she'd never felt so alone.
She hadn't heard of anybody giving birth out of wedlock
and she couldn't have afforded a child anyway, so she got
an abortion. Abortion was illegal in 1971, but she had no
choice. She changed her name from Trudy Lee Wood to

Janet Ullmann, married, and after six months found out
that the abortion had damaged her reproductive organs.
Her husband wanted children, so they divorced. She was
already divorced in 1977 when we met."

"Red Wilker killed her future children," Beau said.
"He should have been executed for doing that."

"I agree," April said.

"Where is Trudy now?" Lottie asked.

"Jane, as I call her, eventually got a job as a flight at-
tendant with Delta Air Lines, and she flies all over the
world. I don't know where she is now."

Mev's cell phone rang.

"It's Jake," she said. "I'll take it in the kitchen."

Ten minutes later, Mev returned. "Jake questioned
Alvin Autry about why he shot Ace Barnett. Alvin stated
that he wanted to save Annie's life."

"He did," Annie said. "I'm grateful to him."

"Jake believes him, and has released him. But in the
interview Jake learned that Alvin knew Crockett Wood
from way back. Alvin's father was Calvin Autry, a side-
kick of Boone Wood and Obadiah Wilker, and Alvin
grew up down the road from the Woods. He joined the
Saxxons at Crockett's invitation in the mid-nineties. Alvin said that Ace Barnett shot both Crockett and Red."

"With Crockett's gun?"

"Jake asked him what gun Ace had used. Alvin said
he didn't know."

"Why would Ace kill Crockett and then Red?"

"Alvin didn't give a reason. Jake said that Alvin was
not very coherent."

"Alvin's losing it, Mom. He's really old."

"Really, really old. And paranoid."

"What's Jake going to do, dear?"

"Jake suspects that Alvin's the one who shot both
Crockett and Red, but he's not going to press charges."

"But why would Alvin kill Red?"

"Maybe Red saw Alvin kill Crockett, so Alvin had to kill Red."

"That's weird."

"Alvin's weird, bro."

"Do you think that Alvin took the grenades we saw Monday night?"

"I can't picture Alvin going to Crockett's cabin in the rainstorm."

"Ace Barnett could have gone up there that night and retrieved the grenades for the rally."

"He might have been the one we heard who drove his truck into the woods."

"At any rate, Jake is not disposed to continue the investigation."

"So I'm not a person of interest anymore, Detective Arroyo?"

"You are not, April. And please call me Mev."

"I'll be back soon, Mev," April said, standing up. "But now I must get back to Atlanta."

CHAPTER 16

WWW. ONLINEWITHERSTON.COM

WITHERSTON ON THE WEB
Monday, September 10, 2018

NEWS

*Alvin Autry Fatally Shoots Ace Barnett;
Double Murder Case Is Closed*

*A*t 4:00 yesterday afternoon at a Saxxons for America march to the courthouse, Alvin Autry fatally shot Saxxons leader Ace Barnett.

The Saxxons were protesting the designation of Witherston as a sanctuary city when Jorge Arroyo's makeshift gang of masked leaf-blowers aided by Fire Chief Mike Moss blew away their white hoods and robes and exposed them. A brief battle ensued in which Saxxons threw tear gas grenades onto the stage in an attempt to stop the designation ceremony, but the grenades did not explode.

When Police Chief Jake McCoy moved to arrest Barnett, Barnett seized Annie Jerden and pointed a pistol to her head. Autry, apparently a Saxxon himself, shot Barnett in the back.

The Saxxons fled, leaving their robes and hoods behind.

Chief McCoy said, "According to Mr. Autry, Ace Barnett shot both Crockett Wood and Red Wilker. If Mr. Autry is telling the truth, and I have no evidence to prove otherwise, then I will close the case."

Annie Jerden, a senior at Witherston High School, declined to answer questions about her participation in the march.

Autry, age eighty-four, is a member of the Witherston Town Council, a member of the Witherston Round Table, a former lay leader in the Witherston Methodist Church, and a lifelong Witherstonian. He was not known to have been a Saxxon.

Chief McCoy will hold a press conference on the courthouse steps at noon today.

Catherine Perry-Soto, Editor

ANNOUNCEMENT

Channel 2, which covered yesterday's dedication ceremony, will air a fifteen-minute segment tonight featuring Rhonda Rather, Sanctuary City coordinator, and Jorge Arroyo, organizer of the team of "Good Guys" who interrupted the Saxxons rally. Tune in at 6:00.

Amadahy Henderson reporter.

WEATHER

Baby, the rain must fall. Baby, the wind must blow.
High sixty-five degrees. Low forty-five degrees. Thir-
ty MPH winds out of the west.
No Saxxons on the horizon.

Tony Lima, Rain Detector

ⓔⓢⓔⓢ

Good Guys whoosh Saxxons, by Jorge Arroyo

ⓔⓢⓔⓢ

"Tell me how you did it, Jane."

April and Jane were sitting on April's balcony facing
west toward downtown Atlanta. They were enjoying their
daily gin and tonic, as they had done at six o'clock for the
twenty years they had lived on Persimmon Avenue.

"I credit *Witherston on the Web* for keeping us informed. After we found out that Crockett had gone to my
father's old hunting cabin on West Bank Road I decided
to do something. Remember? That Sunday morning you
said to me, 'Crockett Wood is up to no good.' And I said
to you, 'Crockett Wood has done enough harm. It's time
to stop him.'"

"I remember. We guessed that Crockett might be
planning a Saxxons rally in opposition to the sanctuary
city."

"I didn't tell you I would stop Crockett myself."

"If you had, I might have helped you."

"Actually, I didn't know that I'd do it myself. The
recent white supremacist rallies took me over the edge.
My grandfather, my father, and my brother inflicted a
trainload of misery on people who were not white like
them. They believed they were enforcing the divine order
of things. People say racists are just ignorant and fearful,
and perhaps that's true of most of them. But my kin are
plain malicious."

"How could I not agree?"

"I had decided to confront Crockett. I wanted to tell
him I knew our horrible family secret. Sunday night I
drove up to Witherston and checked into the Witherston
Inn. A desk clerk named Maisie told me that a drone had
dropped Saxxon flyers on the parade floats that day. Maisie showed me one."

"How did you know that Crockett had dropped
them?"

"I didn't know but I suspected. I intended to ask him.
The next morning I went to the cabin, knocked on the

door, and got no answer. The door swung open, so I went in. I found the stack of flyers on the table with two rifles and a handgun. 'Oh, God,' I said to myself. 'Crockett's gonna kill somebody.' I picked up the handgun, saw it was loaded, and took it."

"Then what did you do?"

"I figured Crockett was around somewhere or he would have locked the door. I went back outside and walked behind the cabin where a black truck was parked. A dog ran out of the woods near the outhouse and started barking furiously. He came at me, so I shot him. Then I went up the path to the outhouse. When I got close, I heard the door click shut. I don't know what got into me, but I suddenly wanted to kill Crockett so he'd never hurt another person. I looked through the moon and saw him sitting there. I shot him dead with one bullet."

"Oh, Jane! What did you feel—killing your own brother?"

"I felt scared. Scared of what I'd done. I'd killed my twin. But I also felt relieved that Crockett would never hurt anybody again."

"What did you do then?"

"I put the gun in my bag, drove back to the Witherston Inn, and checked out. I was home in time for our gin and tonic."

"And you didn't say anything to me about it."

"I didn't want to involve you."

"So why did you kill Red?"

"Red Wilker raped us both. He deprived me of ever having children. And he thought he was good enough to be mayor. Unlike my execution of Crocket, I planned my execution of Red. I planned it carefully. On Thursday morning I sent him an email saying that after all these years I had forgiven him, but I wanted to speak to him before I moved back to Witherston. I asked him to meet me at Rosa's Cantina at noon. When he got to Rosa's Cantina, I sent him a text telling him to meet me at the creek. I waited in the bushes on the bank and shot him in the back of his head with Crockett's gun. He never saw me. Then I dragged his body into the creek. The current carried him downstream. I wiped the gun clean of prints and threw it into the creek after him."

"And you were back here by cocktail hour."

"Yes. And the next morning, I flew to Buenos Aires."

"Thank goodness you didn't get caught, or you'd be arrested for fratricide and premeditated murder."

"Thank goodness the case is closed. It won't be reopened, will it?"

The End

About the Author

Photo by Alvaro Santistevan

Dr. Betty Jean Craige is Professor Emerita of Comparative Literature at the University of Georgia. She has published academic books in the fields of literature, poetry translation (from Spanish), history of ideas, and art.

Her non-academic books include *Conversations with Cosmo: At Home with an African Grey Parrot*; four Witherston Murder Mysteries: *Downstream, Fairfield's Auction, Dam Witherston,* and *Saxxons in Witherston*; and the thriller *Aldo*, all published by Black Opal Books.

Fairfield's Auction won first place in the category of Murder and Mayhem in the 2018 Chanticleer International Book Awards. *Dam Witherston* was named Winner of the 2018 New York City Big Book Awards in the Mystery category, Honorable Mention in Mystery in the 2017 Royal Dragonfly Book Awards, and Distinguished Favorite in Mystery in the 2018 Independent Press Awards. *Aldo* was named Distinguished Favorite in the 2018 New York City Big Book Awards in the Mystery category, Second Place in both Mystery and Science Fiction in the Royal Dragonfly Book Awards, and Distinguished Favorite in Crime Fiction in the 2019 Independent Press Awards.

Craige lives in Athens, Georgia, with Cosmo, her very smart, very talkative, very funny African Grey Parrot.

Visit her website:
http://bettyjeancraigebooks.weebly.com/